LOVE
on
MIMOSA LANE

ALSO BY ANNA DESTEFANO

CONTEMPORARY ROMANCE

Three Days on Mimosa Lane (A Seasons of the Heart Novel)
Christmas on Mimosa Lane (A Seasons of the Heart Novel)
A Sweetbrook Family (previously available as *A Family for Daniel*)
All-American Father
The Perfect Daughter (Daughter series)
The Prodigal's Return
The Runaway Daughter (Daughter series)
A Family for Daniel
The Unknown Daughter (Daughter series)

SCIENCE FICTION/FANTASY

Secret Legacy
Dark Legacy

ROMANTIC SUSPENSE

Her Forgotten Betrayal
The Firefighter's Secret Baby (Atlanta Heroes series)
To Save a Family (Atlanta Heroes series)
To Protect the Child (Atlanta Heroes series)
Because of a Boy (Atlanta Heroes series)

NOVELLAS/ANTHOLOGIES

"Weekend Meltdown" in *Winter Heat*
"Baby Steps" in *Mother of the Year*
"A Small-Town Sheriff" (Daughter series)

LOVE
— *on* —
MIMOSA LANE

—A Seasons of the Heart Novel—

Anna DeStefano

Montlake
Romance

Text copyright © 2014 Anna DeStefano

Published by Montlake Romance, Seattle

www.apub.com

ISBN-13: 9781612184548
ISBN-10: 1612184545

Cover design by Kerrie Robertson

Library of Congress Control Number: 2013914351

Printed in the United States of America

Andrew—

*This book, this story, these characters, every page . . . are yours, they're ours,
because you challenge me to dream, never let me give up,
and carry me when I cannot make it on my own.*

*I'm forever where I should be
for as long as you come back to me.*

Chapter One

Before

For a man who'd sworn off risky women, Law Beaumont was fixated. He was mesmerized. On an overly warm Wednesday morning in November, he couldn't keep his eyes off the assistant principal who'd requested a meeting with him at his daughter's elementary school.

His divorce had been finalized a month ago. He was pulling the pieces of his life back together. But this still felt dangerous—openly staring at Kristen Hemmings the way he hadn't let himself since he'd moved his family to Chandlerville, hoping a fresh start in this picturesque place would save them.

Three years later, there was nothing except common sense to keep him and Kristen apart. And clearly neither one of them possessed an ounce of it.

The school secretary had said he could wait in Kristen's office, or he would find her on the playground. Of course he hadn't waited. Of course he was walking toward her and the potential trouble she could mean for his life. Of course the sun was egging him on, shining ridiculously bright for this time of year.

She probably wanted to talk about how the divorce was affecting his daughter. Chloe had been having a hard time all school year. And he'd come for *her*, first and foremost. But Kristen had invited him closer, too, for the very first time. And damn it if he wasn't moving faster with each step it took to reach her side. They'd been circling this moment forever, putting it off each time they'd casually crossed paths in town.

Not that his reaction to her had ever felt casual.

Kristen was what songs were made of. She was poetry. She was tall and curvy and effortlessly confident in her own skin. And her smile was pure tenderness as she knelt in front of his anxious child—whom she'd called over when she'd first spotted Law. Her gentle intensity soaked into Chloe, until Chloe's hesitant grin back sparkled with a hint of her former love for life.

More every day, his daughter mentioned some *nice* thing Ms. Hemmings did for her at school. More every day since January, when Libby had filed for divorce, he'd resisted the urge to call the school and personally thank its second-in-command for the special interest she'd taken in his child.

"Am I in trouble?" his third grader asked, frowning as he reached her side and gutting Law with her worry. She shot him a scared look, reminding him to tread carefully, to be the father she deserved now, no matter how much else he'd already messed up.

"Of course not," Kristen said.

"But my dad is here." Chloe looked down instead of up at Law, making him ache for one of her hugs. "My mom won't like it if—"

"No one's in trouble, sweetie." Kristen stood. Her gaze slid over him, poking holes in his composure.

"Then why am I here?" He didn't sound entirely friendly, and maybe that was for the best.

His daughter was right. There was no telling what new hassle Libby would stir up when she heard about this meeting. School was her turf. And busting his balls for never doing anything right had become her favorite pastime.

They might be divorced, but that didn't mean his ex had learned how to let go of the things she couldn't have, or to value the life that could still be hers, if she'd finally grow up. And he couldn't get a read on Kristen at all. The silent connection he'd sensed between them for years could have been a wishful figment of his imagination. His track record for making sense out of other people had been in the crapper since he was a kid.

Then her bright green eyes narrowed at the directness of his question, a second before the AP reached out her hand. Chloe's attention zinged back and forth between them.

"Dad?" Chloe asked when he kept his hand at his side, his fingers tingling.

"It's okay, darlin'." He'd make everything okay for her again. "I'll be leaving in just a second."

Whatever it took, he'd see Chloe's life settled. Even if it meant walking away from the breathtaking blonde before him, without ever knowing if her skin—just the touch of her hand— was as soft as it looked. He cupped the back of his daughter's head.

"I hope you won't leave, Mr. Beaumont." The AP dropped her arm to her side. She wiped her palm on her suit pants, obviously nervous when she wasn't a nervous sort of woman. But her tone said she intended to dig in those surprisingly dainty heels until they talked about whatever she wanted to talk about. "I know how terribly busy you are. But I have something important to discuss. I need your help. Yours and Chloe's both."

***

Chloe loved her dad, but what was he doing at school? And Chloe liked Ms. Hemmings, not that she'd let her friends see how much. But Ms. Hemmings *talking* with her dad, right there on the playground in front of everybody . . . that meant something bad, no matter what the adults said.

Chloe just knew it, because she knew her mom—at least the way her mom had been lately.

Since the divorce, Chloe stayed only two nights with her dad at his apartment during the school week. The mornings they were together, he always went back to sleep after she left on the bus. He slept a lot of the day, because he worked so late most nights. But when the bus dropped her off in the afternoon, he was always up and trying to make her laugh and taking her out for hamburgers and milk shakes for dinner. Even on days like today, when he'd stayed up later than normal last night, arguing with her mom over the phone.

Her mom and dad fought almost every night still, even though her dad had moved out almost a year ago, when they'd separated. Sometimes she wondered if they'd always been fighting, since long before they had her, only her dad used to try not to let her know. And he'd gotten her mom to try for a while, too, until they both stopped trying for good.

Chloe loved her family. Sort of. But she hated how nothing ever felt right anymore. Not for a long time. She wished it wasn't so hard, making Dad and her friends and everyone believe she was okay with the divorce, when all she wanted was for her par-

4

ents to stop hating each other. And she wished more than anything else that her mom noticed half as much as her dad did—that everything had gotten too crazy, and that Chloe might not be as cool with it as she pretended.

Since January, Mom seemed to care only about herself.

She'd probably been mad last night because Dad had worked the closing shift again at the bar. *What's the point of him asking the judge for more time with my daughter,* she kept saying to everyone, *if he isn't ever home when Chloe's there?* And her mom's friends—Chloe's friends' mothers—would nod and agree.

Now Dad was at school, tired and looking sick. Someone else, her friends or Ms. Hemmings, might think he'd been drinking. Since her dad had moved out, Mom had told people that he was drinking again, especially their divorce judge. But Chloe knew it wasn't true. She'd never seen him take even one drink. But he did look . . . strange, so she hadn't run to him when she'd first seen him on the playground.

At least, that was partly why.

It had been stupid, how she'd thought right off that maybe he'd come to check her out early. They could do something together all day, something fun when no one else was around to see. Maybe they'd go to the zoo in Atlanta, she'd thought. He'd taken her there a lot until the last few months. She loved it, and he loved her, and the Atlanta Zoo had the best milk shakes, so he always took her when she asked. They'd go every week if she wanted, he'd promised—until the animals got sick of them and the zoo threw them out. She hadn't wanted to so much since her parents split. She didn't want to today. She really didn't.

Because if they went, she'd worry about her friends knowing that was what she still liked to do. And they'd make fun of her and call her a baby, the way they had since the divorce, whenever

Chloe forgot to pretend that she didn't care what was happening to her life. Plus, Dad had looked totally weird when he'd stepped outside the school. So she didn't want to talk to either him or Ms. Hemmings, no matter how nice Ms. Hemmings was.

"You need my help?" her dad asked Ms. Hemmings. He dug his hands into his jeans pockets. He did that when he was feeling a lot of things and didn't want it to look like he was feeling anything at all.

"Can I go now?" Chloe asked.

Ms. Hemmings *probably* wanted to talk about the divorce again, which Chloe didn't mind when no one was watching. But not *now*. Not with her dad. *Not* in front of every kid in her class.

All that mattered to third graders at Chandler was who they hung out with at school and on weekends, and who they talked to at night about what had happened that day, on their cell phones or chatting on the Internet. And the most popular girls in third grade talked to Chloe all the time, no matter how much everyone saw her parents still fighting like total losers.

Summer Traver and Brooke Harper had been watching from the swings since the assistant principal called Chloe away. They were talking to each other now and laughing and kept looking over at Chloe like she was the joke.

"Can I go?" she asked again, putting more *pleeaaaase* into her smile up at her dad.

Without checking with Ms. Hemmings, he nodded, giving in, like he had a lot more since January.

She ran before he could change his mind.

A part of her felt bad for being such a brat. But she wasn't going to help the AP or her dad with anything in the middle of recess. She didn't care what Ms. Hemmings wanted, and she hoped her dad didn't either. Maybe that was why he was acting so weird, like he was there but he really didn't want to be.

All she cared about now were her friends and whether her parents stopped messing up, so her life would stop being so totally lame.

***

Calling Law in to school today wasn't the safest play Kristen had ever made, but she'd seen it as a necessary risk. Only, standing there, watching the man watch his daughter rush away from them—his expression clouding with longing and doubt and a fierceness she couldn't describe—she realized she'd underestimated the effect being this close to him would have on her.

Or had she?

She'd kept her distance for as long as she'd known the Beaumont family. For one thing, he'd been married. And she'd been far too attracted to him, regardless. When his troubles with Libby had come to a head, it had made Kristen even more determined to steer clear—no matter how much she hated seeing the fallout from their split backing up on Law and Chloe. But now that his divorce was final, it had become a bit of a private obsession, wondering if something could really happen between the two of them.

Law and Libby's divorce had been one for the record books. Kristen hadn't indulged in the gossip flying around about their floundering attempts to co-parent. Still, the more disturbing of the rumors about Law and Libby—mostly of Law, spread *by* Libby, that he was a heavy drinker and only pretended to care about his child, and had insisted on being awarded time with

Chloe in the custody arrangement only to avoid paying more in child support—had been impossible to tune out.

More than once, Kristen had overheard Chloe's mother, a fixture in the tight-knit group of PTA regulars at Chandler, ranting to the other moms. It didn't seem to matter that her daughter and the other kids could often overhear every word. Libby and her friends actually seemed to prefer it that way.

Small towns like theirs could be enchanting, close-knit worlds, particularly to someone like Kristen. She'd grown up in a *successful* New England family that many had idealized. But her reality had been a much colder, lonelier place than friends and neighbors had known—that is, until everyone had learned every sordid detail of her life in the worst possible way. By then, the words *friend* and *neighbor* had ceased meaning anything to her, and all she'd wanted was to get out.

In contrast, in honest-to-God communities like Chandlerville, there really were loving, caring people who came together, wanting to make life better for one another in small and sometimes vast ways. The often-harsh reality of the outside world magically softened in towns like this, narrowing and hugging you close. Despite recent tragedy, the indomitable spirit still thriving in their suburb northeast of Atlanta had created the kind of home Kristen had dreamed of making hers, since she was Chloe's age.

Chandlerville still had its faults, like everywhere else. It had been through its share of growing pains—most recently a school shooting at Chandler Elementary that Kristen was still reeling from, the same as everyone else. And even in idealistic small towns, there would always be people who looked out for themselves first—sacrificing whatever they needed of others' happiness, in order to achieve their own. Libby Beaumont and her band of beautiful, seemingly well-intentioned, and dedicated mean moms certainly fit that bill.

Despite the rumors Libby had spread about her ex-husband, Kristen had always believed better of Law. Watching him be so deeply affected by his daughter's discomfort at having him at school, she was convinced all over again that she was right.

Law might be a card-carrying bad boy. But he was no deadbeat dad who'd given up on his family without remorse, the way Libby portrayed him. And he was exactly the sort of man Kristen needed—to help her save Chandler's latest lost boy. *That* was why she'd asked him to meet her, despite the fact that they'd never before today spoken one-on-one.

"I have a favor to ask." She stretched her arm out a second time to the tallest, most naturally athletic-looking man she'd set eyes on since college. "I had hoped we could meet in my office this afternoon."

"I'm working lunch at McC's. So if you want me"—Law crossed his arms over his chest, his energy shifting from reserved to hostile, challenging her when she never backed down from a challenge—"this is how you get me."

It was on the tip of her tongue to tell him she'd take him however she could get him. She swallowed the unwise comeback.

Watching Chloe rejoin her friends, Law looked like a father laying bets that his child might one day run from him for good. Then his storm-cloud blue eyes sliced to Kristen, and he sighed, the sound like the air escaping from a deflating balloon.

"I'm assuming this is about my daughter." His hand engulfed hers, the size and warmth of his palm making her feel delicate and feminine—an alien but not altogether unpleasant sensation.

An answering rush of awareness warmed his expression. Kristen jerked her hand away, stunned by how hard it was to let go. She had a job to do here—a difficult one that this man would likely decline to help with.

This town and this school and her staff and students had grown to mean more to her than anywhere else she'd lived— even in college, when, as her success with basketball took off, she should have felt on top of the world. Chandlerville had become her family, not just another job. Doing right by the children entrusted to her care was more than work for her, or a paycheck or a step forward in her career—even if she was taking over the principal's spot next school year. *That* responsibility was what this meeting was about, not her inconvenient physical reaction to Law.

She realized she was staring at him.

She realized she couldn't stop.

"You needed a favor?" he asked in his smoky, bartender's tone.

"I . . . um . . ." She got a grip on the gooey-at-the-knees tremble in her voice. "I hear through the grapevine that you play soccer, Mr. Beaumont—pickup games in the park—and that you're one of the best."

"You've heard?" His measured stare demanded the truth she'd glossed over.

"Okay, I've watched you play myself."

"I know." He nodded and crossed his arms again. "I've noticed you, too. While I scrimmage with the guys, and you run by several times with your girlfriend, and we both try to look like we're not looking at each other."

Evidently she wasn't the only one who didn't back away from a challenge. And wasn't that a sweet little snag in her stick-to-business plan?

"You're hard to miss when you're playing, Mr. Beaumont." She'd marveled at his effortless talent and the pleasure he took in the game. It was a seductive world for her, the love and competitive rush of sport, any sport, any playing field. Basketball might be her preference, but nothing was more magnificent to her than an athlete who could charm his particular discipline into doing his bidding. And every Sunday she'd had the chance, it had become a habit to watch Law do just that, while most of the rest of their town was at church or sleeping in.

He chuckled. "You don't exactly blend into the scenery yourself, Ms. Hemmings, while you keep close to the trees, like I won't know you're there."

His nearly nonexistent smile seemed more for himself than her. It startled her, how much she wanted to see his expression soften into something more genuine.

"I just thought I should get it out of the way," he added, "that I've wondered if you've felt the same . . . *whatever* for me that I have for you. We've kept our distance from each other, and that's fine. We don't have to talk about it—we probably shouldn't, all things considered. But it would just be too . . . weird, right? To finally be here, together, and to pretend this hasn't been going on."

Kristen, the starting center on her NCAA championship basketball team, felt absolutely defenseless. In the face of his brutal honesty, her thoughts, her rationalizations, and her carefully reasoned-through expectations for their meeting were no-shows. She found herself gaping at Law like a schoolgirl with her first crush and no idea how to handle herself.

To finally be here, together, and to pretend this hasn't been going on . . .

She'd had no idea. Or she hadn't wanted to know. It would be so much easier if he'd been oblivious to the pull between them. She'd assumed he'd been too caught up in his own problems to even know she existed. Instead, he'd felt something, too, and he'd shut that something off as firmly as she had. He'd been doing what he had to for his family and himself, while she'd done the same for her job and her own well-being.

Only, now . . .

What the hell was she supposed to do now that she knew, and he didn't seem to care one way or the other?

"What does this have to do with Chloe?" he asked, unaffected by . . . them—or at least giving a better imitation of it than she could.

"This?"

"Soccer? Sundays?"

She shook her head, trying to jar something sensible loose. "Brian Perry," she came up with.

Law's smile was back. "This is about Brian?"

"No, it's about Chloe. Well, not really. At least not just about Chloe . . ."

Damn it. She was flustered, and he seemed to be enjoying it. His smugness should have been a turnoff. Instead, it made her like him even more, how deftly he seemed to recognize and accept the insecure *her* who had made a sudden, mortifying reappearance.

"I hear your daughter's become one of our local soccer allstars," she clarified, "since your family moved here." And word was that no one around was better than Law at teaching kids how to love the sport the same way he did.

"Chloe's a natural talent." His eyes brightened to a nearly aquamarine blue. If it hadn't been her favorite color her whole life, it certainly would be from now on.

"I see." Kristen *was* seeing—and liking far too much.

She preferred her men clean-cut, tailored, and conservative, and so incapable of surprising her that she could practically choreograph their dates before a guy picked her up. How could someone in wrinkled jeans and a ratty metal-band T-shirt, who'd clearly just rolled out of bed, be getting to her this way?

"You see what?" He shot her another unfathomable glance, full of intelligence and wit that she found perversely charming.

"I see that you don't want to take credit for what Chloe's achieved, or that she's being scouted by several of Atlanta's top traveling teams. But Brian's a friend of mine. He's watched you working with your daughter in the park in the afternoons while he coaches his football team. He says you're the best there is."

"At what?"

"Coaching." The reason Kristen was putting them both through this.

She was talking to a man who had *hands-off* stamped all over him, from his rumpled, just-long-enough-to-show-he-didn't-give-a-damn brown hair, down to his biker boots that were authentically scuffed from years of use. She wanted to run her hands all over him. But she was in the market for a coach, not a crush, which made it time to get their conversation back on track.

"I'm asking you to reconsider coaching a local youth soccer team again this winter season," she said. "I've heard you've already told the league coordinator you couldn't."

"You hear a lot."

His voice had hardened. The playfulness went out of his stance. They were back to hostile. She'd struck a nerve, as she'd expected she might.

"I know parents," she said, "who are disappointed you won't be working with their kids."

"Yeah. I'm disappointed, too." He sounded downright furious.

"I think it's absolutely vital that you pull a new team together for kids your daughter's age," she pressed. "And I think it's imperative that we make certain Chloe's on board with the idea."

"You think it's absolutely vital, do you?"

"I think you will, too, once you hear me out."

"And why would I do that?"

Chloe and her friends were heading away from the swings and toward the water fountain by the side door to the school. Law tracked her movements, tuning Kristen out, distant once more as if he no longer cared that she existed.

"Among other reasons," Kristen said, "coaching would give you another season with Chloe. And I understand her mother's got her convinced not to play anymore. I think that's a mistake, for a child her age who's been through as much recent change as Chloe has."

Law's attention whiplashed back; then he returned to watching his daughter and her friends.

"According to my ex," he said, "girls Chloe's age shouldn't be forced to play sports just to make their parents happy. And why else would Chloe keep doing something as filthy and potentially dangerous as soccer, when she's a lock to be on the cheerleading squad with her new friends?"

"Because of you." Kristen should keep out of his never-ending conflict with Libby, but what a load of bull. "The way I see it, spending time with you would be a hell of a reason for any kid to want to keep playing."

He grunted, and then shook his head.

"You really are a crazy optimist," he surprised her by muttering, "just like they say." His eyebrows bunched together as several boys in Chloe's class cut in front of her and her girlfriends when it was their turn at the fountain. "My daughter isn't my biggest fan at the moment, or *any* moment these days when I try to talk with her about soccer or anything much but where she wants to eat dinner. Libby's putting enough pressure on her. Chloe's snobby friends are wanting her to be as mad over boys and makeup and clothes as they are—and *friends* seem to be what's most important to her now. Until things calm down over my divorce, I've pretty much given up on getting my daughter to make up her own mind about anything."

"That's funny," Kristen said, when it wasn't funny at all. "You've never struck me as the giving-up type."

He tensed—all six-foot-five and over two hundred solid pounds of him. She followed his gaze.

The activity unfolding on the other side of the playground was teeming with the potential for adolescent conflict. The boys were splashing water at the girls, one of them in particular refusing to let Chloe have a drink. So far, Kristen wasn't seeing anything that would warrant staff intervention. She was thankful when Law seemed to come to the same conclusion. Chloe wouldn't want a scene just because a kid in her class had once again made her the focus of his unhappiness at being at Chandler.

It wasn't that Fin Robinson was a bully, even though he was grinning as he teased her and laughed along with his buddies and even Chloe's girlfriends now. Kristen didn't like the crowd he'd chosen to emulate a month ago, when he'd landed at Chandler Elementary. She didn't approve of his increasingly disruptive behavior since he'd joined his new foster family. But a sensitive kid emerged from inside Fin every now and then, despite the hardened shell he'd built between himself and the world.

She saw a child still wanting to find his place, desperately hoping to belong. When she looked at Fin, she saw a need for direction, before the path he was toying with stopped being about willful rebellion and morphed into something more problematic and permanent. Not that he was interested in anything Kristen or his foster mom, Marsha Dixon, or his teachers had to say about the better life they could help him claim.

So . . . she'd decided a rough-and-tumble, equally detached man might be a better role model.

A man who obviously loved and cherished his daughter. A man who'd been working himself to death and isolating himself from practically everyone in town since his divorce, trying to secure some peace with his ex-wife. An overwhelmed man she was asking to take on even more responsibility. Fin could learn so much from the discipline and focused intensity and teamwork that playing a game like soccer and working with a coach like Law could give him.

"You said 'reasons'?" Law asked, checking his watch. "What are they?"

"What?"

He slid her another sideways stare. Two seconds later, his attention was back on the playground. She could have sworn she'd felt him in her mind, his thoughts probing and tumbling through her disordered reasoning.

"You said 'among other reasons,'" he repeated.

"Yes . . ." That glance, just that one moment of connection, and every thought in her head except the ones obsessed with him was a complete muddle.

What was wrong with her?

"Whatever they are, they must be pretty important," he said, "for you to get me out of bed and down here to tell me that whatever I do or don't do with my daughter is somehow any of your business."

"The matter I wanted to discuss *is* very important." And Kristen was totally f-ing this up. His mood was taking a definite nosedive toward uncooperative. "And the fact is, Chloe's only one of the kids I think your coaching would help. The other one . . . She's spending a lot of time with one of our newest students, not all of it good, which is too bad, because . . ."

Kristen rambled when she was overstressed or intimidated. She hadn't rambled since she was a teenager. But she liked the feel of Law holding her feet to the fire. She liked him, period, a whole lot more than she could afford to. She'd be happy to stand there all day, verbally sparring with the man, searching for a way beneath his control, the way he'd effortlessly rattled hers. And instead, she needed to do what she'd asked him to school to do, and then get Law the hell away from her again.

She cleared her throat and looked him in the eye—at least, she would have been looking him in the eye, if he weren't ignoring her again.

"The other child," she said, "the one who might benefit the most from your coaching, is why I tried to get Chloe to join us. Convincing him to accept your help isn't the only problem, I'm afraid. I don't think your daughter's going to be terribly fond of the idea."

That got his attention. She nodded toward Fin. Law gave the scene by the water fountain more of his attention, zeroing in on the boy who was giving Chloe the hardest time. Law shook his head.

"You're kidding me," he said. He took a step away from her, looking genuinely ready to bolt this time.

"Yeah. That would be your newest all-star player. *If* you can find a way to make him stop hating the world and everyone in it." Chloe and her friends turned away from the fountain and Fin, who was still laughing at her. Kristen sighed. "Don't ask me why I'm sure it's a good fit, but I am. The boy I'd be asking you to build a team around and give one-on-one attention to, if that's what it takes, is probably the *last* person on earth your daughter would want to be teammates with—assuming you can get her to play for another season. And I really think you should. Please, for both their sakes, help me make that happen."

Chapter Two

Now

"*I didn't mean to make Chloe cry,*" I say to the lady.

She's from Children and Family Services. She gets to decide where I live next, and what I'm supposed to think family means next, once I have to leave Chandlerville. Someone else but me always gets to decide.

So why are we talking about three months ago? Why doesn't she just tell me I have to go, and then pass me off to the next person who will one day pass me off to someone else, too?

"*You must not have liked Chloe very much, Fin,*" the CFS lady says, "*at least not when you first started going to school at Chandler. The school's reports to the county say you two were fighting from almost your first day in her class.*"

The lady's name is Mrs. Sewel, and she's nice enough, I guess. Nicer than a lot of the government people I've had to talk to since my mom stopped being my mom, and there was no one left to care about me but strangers. Mrs. Sewel is smiling while she talks. She does that all the time, even when she's telling me things she doesn't know, about people she doesn't understand.

"*Chloe was always with her mean-girl friends back then,*" I *say. I finally understand why Chloe was like that. But at first, I thought she was a total pain.*

"Mean girls?"

"Brooke and Summer. The ones who laughed at me and her both that day, and the next day and a lot of days after that. They're always laughing at someone, like they're so much better than everybody else. I thought Chloe was like them, so I was mean to her for a while, like at the water fountain that day at recess."

"Maybe Brooke and Summer were treating you like that," Mrs. Sewel says, "because you were new to Chandler."

"They were being girls."

And girls are just mean—a lot meaner than boys. Especially when I'm somewhere new, and everyone knows I don't have any parents and don't belong. Boys will rag on you, but they mostly come around when they see you're cool. But some girls . . . they just want everyone but them to feel bad. And I usually don't care, so I'm just as mean back.

Only, the last three months have changed that. I really do care, even when I tell people like Mrs. Sewel I don't. Especially about Chloe. I care about her most of all—because she was never mean, not really. She's just mixed up, like me, because her mother is totally screwed up, the same as mine was.

"Chloe's still a girl," Mrs. Sewel says. "It sounds like you two have been getting along better."

I nod.

Me and Chloe are the closest to friends I've ever felt. Not that it matters. I've messed up my chance in Chandlerville, like I've messed up everywhere else, and nothing's going to change that. Nothing ever does. But I'd do it all again if I had to. Because that's what friends do for each other, no matter how much helping someone gets you into trouble.

I don't know what else Mrs. Sewel wants me to say, so I don't say anything at all.

She sighs. "I need you to tell me more about that day at recess, Fin. I need you to tell me what you think and feel about everything that's happened since then—especially about last night's Valentine's party. I want to help you, but I can't unless you start talking."

Help me?

She makes it sound so simple, like I'm really going to have a say. She sounds like Ms. Hemmings and Mr. Beaumont, telling me I can make it here. And my foster parents, Mr. and Mrs. Dixon, before they brought me in this morning. She sounds so sure. And when adults sound that way—when they make me want to believe, too—it makes me madder than anything else.

"Why?!" *I yell at Mrs. Sewel.* "What good does talking about things ever do?"

I'm not going to cry.

But my eyes are seeing all fuzzy, and they're probably shiny—and I hate that. I hate all of it, especially how much I want things to really be okay this time, the way Mrs. Sewel is making it sound like it still can be. I want to stay with the Dixons. I want to keep being Chloe's friend. I want to make sure she's okay after Ms. Hemmings took her home this morning. I want to go back to school on Monday and stay in Chandlerville with the Dixons for always and play soccer on Mr. Beaumont's team . . . more than I've ever wanted anything.

"We need to figure this out," *Mrs. Sewel says.*

"Figure out what?" *I ask.* "There's nothing to figure out. There's just me, doing whatever you tell me to do. Kids like me do what people like you say. Nothing's changed. I've been in the system since I was six, and nothing's going to change that. My coked-out mom's gone. There's nobody else. Nobody cares where you send me next."

"The Dixons care."

Yeah. They do. They gave me a real chance the way no other family has. Mr. Beaumont gave me a chance, too, and Ms. Hemmings and Chloe.

"It sounds like the Beaumonts have been good friends. You've spent a lot of that time with them. You and Chloe weren't happy about it to begin with, but look how well that's turned out."

Yeah, things are just great. So great I feel like I'm going to puke up the toast Mrs. Dixon made me eat before coming over. I'm going to lose everyone.

I shrug.

Mrs. Sewel pushes her glasses higher on her nose and looks at her notes, which means she's thinking up another question that I don't want to answer.

"So, Chloe and her mean-girl friends laughed at you the morning Mr. Beaumont came to school. Is that why you wouldn't let Chloe use the water fountain?"

"No, all right! What difference does it make? Chloe never laughed at me. She's always been cool with me, sort of, even the next day at lunch when I ran away from school."

"Even after you and your friends were mean to her, she was cool?"

She'd understood what it felt like not to have anybody she could trust, just like me. That's what made her cool. Of course, I'm not going to say that to Mrs. Sewel. That would be talking about Chloe to somebody else—that would be talking about the things she'd told me, and I'd promised I'd never tell anyone.

But I'd known we were the same, almost from the beginning. And then her mom went and did all the stupid things she's done since November. It had almost felt good, having another kid in Chandlerville who felt as crappy about having a family as I did.

"You didn't know Mr. Beaumont before that day, right?" Mrs. Sewel writes something else, grading me or whatever.

I shake my head.

More notes go into the notebook. "Not until he coached you, because Ms. Hemmings asked him to?"

I rub my eyes, but they keep filling up again. My nose, too.

"Fin?" Mrs. Sewel asks.

I'm not looking at her anymore. She's probably writing something about me not talking. Mostly because I don't know how to say it right—how much meeting Mr. Beaumont and Chloe changed things.

That morning at school turned out to be my best day ever. Even when I have to leave town because of what Chloe and me did last night, wherever I go next, I get to keep the good days that happened after Mr. Beaumont said yes to coaching me.

"What are you remembering?" Mrs. Sewel asks. She hands me a girly box of tissues that I don't take. There are flowers all over it. The tissues are pink. "It's okay to be upset, Fin. You can tell me what you're feeling. I need you to. Tell me all the things about you that I don't have in my notes. That's why I had the Dixons bring you in on a Sunday, instead of waiting until next week or having your foster parents talk with me by themselves. It's time for you to talk about what's really important to you. You can tell me that, can't you?"

I want to tell her to shut up. I want to tell her to take me away from the Dixons already—and Chloe and Mr. Beaumont and the awesome soccer team he's made for us—so I can stop feeling like this and start not caring again, the way I used to not care about anything.

But kids don't tell grown-ups to shut up. And I want another good home like the Dixons', and Mrs. Sewel gets to decide if that

happens. But how do I tell her what happened that day at school,
without saying that even though I'd been living with the Dixons
for a month, I'd hated being there, and I'd hated going to school at
Chandler, and I was already thinking about how to get away from
all of them? That wasn't okay to tell.

"Are you remembering what Mr. Beaumont told you at recess
that day?" Mrs. Sewel asks.

"He didn't tell me nothin'."

"Anything," she corrects me, the same way Mrs. Dixon always
does when I mess up words.

"He asked me." Mr. Beaumont had been cool from the start.
"I'd been mean to Chloe for weeks. He'd seen me be mean to her at
the water fountain. She could have made him stop wanting to
coach me. He could have said I couldn't be part of his team. But
she didn't. He didn't. He asked me . . ."

No one had ever cared about me like that before, especially
not my loser mom. And I hadn't wanted anyone else to even try,
not before Chandlerville. Not since my mom decided getting her
high on was what she loved most, not me. But the Beaumonts had
cared, I'd realized. And the Dixons had cared, too. Even Ms.
Hemmings.

"I know it's hard to talk about it," Mrs. Sewel says.

I stare at her, wishing I could make her stop, because I can feel
the words coming, and more stupid tears coming, and I'm not
going to be able to hold them back. And what's the point of feeling
this way? It's not going to change things.

"Why is it so hard?" she asks.

"It's not hard," I lie.

She sighs. She writes something else.

"It was no big deal!" I say. "None of it."

Mrs. Sewel puts her pen down. She closes her notebook. I wipe at my nose. She folds her hands on top of her desk and watches me.

"Talk to me, Fin. This is too important for you not to."

Too important? That day had been more than important. It was the reason for everything else. It was why I did what I did at the party last night, even though I knew helping Chloe would get me into trouble.

"Mr. Beaumont asked me if I liked to play soccer," I say. "Did I like playing soccer as much as I liked being a badass who had no real friends at all. He asked me if I wanted . . . more."

"More, like being on his team?" *When I nod, Mrs. Sewel keeps talking.* "And you said yes."

Sort of.

I wipe my nose again. "So?"

"So, you'd already told the Dixons no when they wanted to sign you up for the league. What made Mr. Beaumont's asking so different?"

I don't answer. I don't know what to say this time. I really don't.

"Fin, why did you trust Chloe's father to coach you? You didn't know him. Your records say you've refused to play soccer every place you've lived since your mother died, even though it used to be your favorite thing. Tell me why it was different with Mr. Beaumont."

I want to say that she doesn't know that it was different. She doesn't know anything. She doesn't know how I feel. She never will. No one ever will, and I don't care anyway. I didn't care when I lost my mom. I shouldn't care now that I'm losing Chloe and Mr. Beaumont and the Dixons.

Only I do. A lot. And maybe I do want someone to understand, even if I can't stay in Chandlerville, no matter what I say.

"Mr. Beaumont was like me," I say to Mrs. Sewel, crying while I do. "He was standing there on the playground, acting angry and weird after talking with Ms. Hemmings. And he didn't feel like he belonged there any more than me. I can tell when someone feels that way. He didn't like me yet. I could tell that, too. But he was just like me." He was just like Chloe, the way she'd felt to me since my first day at Chandler. "He said he wanted to coach me . . . sort of. And somehow I knew he meant it. And just hearing Mr. Beaumont say that, even though Chloe and me weren't friends yet . . . it made me want to, you know?"

"Want to play soccer again?"

I nod my head.

Then I'm shaking it, because that's not it. I bury my hands in the pockets of my jeans, trying to hold the words back. Mrs. Sewel won't understand. I don't even understand. And I don't want to talk about it anymore. But the feelings from that day and every day after are coming up and out, and there's no stopping them.

"He made me think about staying. He . . . I don't know why. But that day, it was the first time I thought about staying with the Dixons and in Chandlerville and at school. Everything changed after that, just like he said it would, if I let myself start to care about things."

Only now I've gone and ruined it all.

Chapter Three

Before

Kristen watched Law cross the playground toward Fin. She made herself breathe. She'd opened a giant can of crazy for herself, inviting Law to school. But it had been worth it. And besides, this wasn't about her. She could handle any fallout she might have invited into her life.

All that mattered was for Law to come to some understanding with Fin. And then for him to get Chloe on board. So what if the man Kristen had practically been drooling over a minute ago thought she was nuts for asking him to mentor a kid he'd never met?

You're kidding me, he'd said.

Yet there he was, talking to Fin. A little. Hardly at all, actually. But it was a start of something hopeful and positive for the painfully detached boy. She couldn't, she absolutely wouldn't, lose another student to thinking that silently enduring the life he'd been trapped in was the only choice he'd ever have.

Law and Fin had their hands shoved in their pockets. What was it about boys and men that would forever make them the same creatures? Especially when they were uncomfortable or embarrassed, or you challenged them to feel something that they didn't want to.

She could have backed off when Law first balked at her idea. But too much was at stake for Fin *and* Chloe. Law simply had to coach at least one more season.

He had all but sprinted away from her explanation of Fin's precarious situation at the Dixons' group foster home. He'd become so quietly agitated, she'd expected him to head toward the school parking lot and the beat-up truck he drove. But instead, he'd stalked toward an angry little boy who didn't know how to belong to anyplace or anyone, not even himself. Law and Fin were standing with their feet braced shoulder-width apart, thirty-something confronting nine years old as if they'd squared off in a grudge match to see who could pull off *I don't care* the smoothest.

Not that Fin's body language was much different than any other day of the three weeks he'd spent at Chandler. Each time some disruption he'd been involved in had landed him in her office, he'd silently stared at her the way he was looking at Law, daring her to do her worst because nothing could touch him. Watching the two of them together tugged at her heart. It was as if neither of them fit on a happy playground on the outskirts of an affluent, sleepy suburb. And neither of them particularly cared.

"Is everything okay?" asked Daphne Glover, Chloe and Fin's teacher. She had her eye on Chloe. The girl was glaring at her dad's back. She was standing on the other side of the playground from where Law and Fin were talking by the water fountain.

"Of course." Kristen let out a trapped breath, remembering how Marsha Dixon, Fin's foster mother, had sounded at her wits' end yesterday afternoon. No one at the group home she and her husband, Joe, ran had been able to break through Fin's distrust and refusal to settle in.

Kristen pressed her fingers to her mouth and nibbled at the inside of her lip. It was a nervous habit her father had abhorred. But it kept Kristen quiet and still when she needed to be. At the moment, it was helping her keep her distance from what Law was doing.

This was his show now, as Fin stared down at his shoes, back up at the man, and then beyond him to Chloe. The boy said something that Law leaned closer to hear. But even across the playground, Kristen had no problem reading her student's lips.

"Oh, my." Happiness shot through her, filling her up, making her feel light as air, as if she could float out of her skin and hug the perfect moment closer.

How many chances did the universe give you to see trust, or at least hope, take root in someone so determined to face the world alone?

"Did he just . . ." Mallory Phillips started to say. Chandler's more-pregnant-every-day school nurse had joined Kristen and Daphne, stepping to Kristen's other side. Her question fizzled into shocked silence as Law reached out his arm, and Fin squared his shoulders.

And then the small boy and the towering man, both of them mysteries to most everyone in Chandlerville, shook hands.

"Well, I'll be." Kristen exhaled, falling even harder for Law, though he'd probably never let her near him again after today. The man hadn't taken kindly to being roped into this.

"What are they talking about?" Mallory asked. She was wearing puppies on her scrubs today—basset hounds, holding daisies in their mouths.

"Who cares?" This could all fall apart in the next five minutes. But Kristen had learned to savor every victory, especially the small ones. "When have you seen Fin engaging with any adult, except when he's in so much trouble he doesn't have a choice?"

The rest of the boys Fin hung out with, a roving band of mischief he'd immediately gravitated toward his first day at school, gave up on reclaiming his attention. They struck off toward the slides. Chloe and her besties were already there, chattering away, while Chloe kept her dad on radar with an occasional long-suffering glance. The other girls seemed to be ignoring what was happening at the water fountain, but Kristen knew better.

Brooke Harper and Summer Traver ruled the most popular clique in Daphne's class. They reigned supreme over the entire third grade. Their mothers were friends with Libby Beaumont. No way were those girls not tracking every move Chloe's dad made. No way was this not going to make trouble for Chloe—collateral damage that Kristen hadn't counted on.

"Really," Mallory said. "What are they talking about?"

"They're talking about . . ." *I'm sorry*, Fin had said to Law just now, when the boy had refused to acknowledge anyone else's attempts to connect with him. ". . . belonging."

"I didn't think 'sorry' was part of his vocabulary." Mallory gave Kristen a one-armed hug of celebration.

Over the last year, Kristen's once-standoffish clinic nurse had become one of the few people in town Kristen felt she could confide in. She was the only one who'd caught on to Kristen's infatuation with Law.

"If I'm not missing my guess," Kristen said, "Fin's sorry for just about everything he does. Not that he'd let any of us see how much."

Daphne shook her head. "So, what's changed?"

"Simple." Kristen smiled as Fin kicked at the dirt between himself and Law. He cast a glance toward the slides, where his buddies had joined up with the girls.

"What's simple?" Chloe's teacher asked.

Kristen hesitated.

When it came to relationships between people, nothing was ever as simple as you expected it to be. Her family never had been. Neither were the Beaumonts or the Dixons or most of the other families in their "ideal" suburb—not once you took the time to peek under the surface. *Love* was never simple. But even couched in something as everyday as playing soccer and meeting a new coach, the right offer to belong could change who a kid like Fin might become—if Law helped Fin learn to like who he already was.

"Sports." She smoothed her hand into the pocket of her favorite, eggshell-blue pantsuit. She crossed her fingers for luck. "I've never run across a better incentive to straighten up, especially with overactive boys. And ladies, we're looking at two hypercompetitive, gifted athletes, if the stories the Dixons have heard about Fin from Family Services can be believed. We may have finally found someone who speaks Fin's language."

"Libby Beaumont's husband?" Daphne sounded horrified.

"Why not?" Mallory raised a long-suffering eyebrow Kristen's way. "Don't tell me you're buying into what people have been saying about the guy, Daphne. So what if he works in a bar and his bitter ex-wife blames him for everything she's never had in her life? That doesn't automatically make him a bad influence."

Daphne blinked at Kristen, ignoring Mallory. "Doesn't Mr. Beaumont have a prison record? Do you really think he's the right role model for a boy with impulse control and anger issues?"

Kristen inhaled, telling herself to ignore the gossip she knew Daphne and other teachers had helped spread—fed by Libby's never-ending need to be seen as a victim.

"I think Law's a fine man," she said instead.

She bit her lip again. Knowing Daphne, the news of Kristen weighing in on Law's behalf would be all over town by the end of the school day. But staying silent would have felt like a betrayal. Law was talking to Fin because Kristen had asked him to—or at least because Law had wanted to get away from her asking him to.

"I think he works almost every afternoon and half into the night," Kristen added. If she'd dug a hole for herself, she might as well make her swan dive in worth the flak she was about to get. "He works almost every night to support his ex-wife and the child she tried to take from him in their divorce. He's putting up with Libby's antics. He's not retaliating. He's focused on making the most of the time he still has with Chloe. I think that's *exactly* the kind of parent and coach Fin would be lucky to have taking a special interest in him."

Law had mostly kept to himself since moving to Chandlerville. His brother, Dan, lived over on Mimosa Lane. But as far as anyone could tell, they avoided each other, except when they got their kids together to play. No one in town knew Law well, and he hadn't made much of an effort to change that since he'd gotten his own place almost a year ago. So at first, it had been easiest for everyone to believe the things Libby said about him.

But none of her outlandish claims had been substantiated by her lawyers. Otherwise the judge's custody decision wouldn't have awarded Law two nights and three days a week with Chloe. Meanwhile, there had been something cold about Libby when she'd let her guard down in the few private moments Kristen had witnessed the woman spending with Chloe. There was something too lonely about Law's daughter that reminded Kristen of her experience with her own mother. A mother who'd cared more about having a good time on Kristen's father's dime than she had about her only child.

Chloe was too nervous around Libby. Something was off there—more off this school year than ever. *Too* off for Law's ex-wife to be the paragon of parenting she made herself out to be.

"Law is the perfect man for this job," Kristen said, with nothing much to back up her declaration beyond instinct and every moment all these years that she'd secretly watched him from a distance. Or not so secretly, as it turned out.

She cringed at the memory of him calling her on her semi-stalker behavior. Not to mention the thrill she'd gotten from his admission that he'd been covertly watching her, too. Now she was publicly defending him in a way that he'd likely resent.

She should probably stop that.

She should stop everything that made her want to be the one Law was taking a special interest in, instead of Fin. Otherwise, one of her finest teachers, her very observant friend, and every child on the playground would catch her obsessing about an off-limits man her body was still tingling for.

***

"I've got no time to coach a new team," Law said to Fin, remembering the way the boy's smaller hand had shaken his firmly, demanding that Law take him seriously.

Then he'd offered up an apology for harassing Chloe that Law had said he'd need to hear before they talked about anything else. An apology Law hadn't expected to receive—the same as he hadn't expected Kristen's stunned reaction to him a few minutes ago, or his to her, when he'd finally shaken *her* hand. She'd softened a split second before she'd been the one to pull back first.

So far, Fin had surprised him just as much. The kid had said *yes* to Law's angry question about whether or not he knew how to act better on the soccer field than he did on the playground. The boy had made it sound like a four-letter word, but he'd said yes.

"I don't care if you coach me," Fin said now, when playing had to be pretty important to him, or he'd be off laughing it up with his buddies. "It's no big deal."

"Good," Law said, pushing a little harder to see what the boy was made of, the way he'd pushed Kristen to acknowledge the attraction between them. "Because if I do coach, and *if* you even turn up for tryouts, I don't put up with mouthing off or talking back or causing problems with the other players. And you sound like a kid who can't keep quiet and out of trouble for more than five minutes at a time. If it's no big deal to you, then I can cut you the first day and save myself some drama."

Not that Law was going to coach.

Not that he appreciated Kristen's expecting him to care about how his *not* coaching would affect someone else's child, once she'd finished making him worry all over again about Chloe's determination to give up on a sport she'd loved.

He'd beaten a hasty retreat from Kristen's impassioned plea on Fin's behalf. He'd intended to head for his truck and forget everything that spending five minutes with her had made him think and feel and doubt. But Fin had been there. And then Law had been standing next to the kid, damn it. And he was still standing there, still wanting to take the easy way out, but pinned by the boy's angry, detached gaze.

There was something in the air around Fin. He had the edge of a hoodlum who was taking in everything that was said and done, without letting on that he cared about any of it. Even the way the other boys had moved around and away from Fin made it clear they thought he was a punk. Except he wasn't. Law couldn't have said exactly how he knew that, but he did.

"I don't do tryouts," Mr. Tough Guy grumbled.

Law actually laughed at that one. It was impossible not to like a kid who was as cocky as Law had been at the same age. "You'll be at tryouts. And you'll be the first to show up, if you want me to take you seriously after what I've seen of your lousy attitude."

Kristen had said the boy had been orphaned three years ago, and that Chandlerville and the Dixons were the nine-year-old's fourth attempt at settling into a foster home. Marsha and Joe were having trouble integrating him. Everyone in town knew the couple couldn't love and care more for their court-appointed family if the kids had been their biological offspring. Yet their brand of gentleness and kindness hadn't even made a dent.

Which made Law what, exactly, in this plan of Kristen's—some kind of scared-straight boot camp?

He couldn't even talk his own daughter into playing, when soccer had been their thing to do together since she was a toddler, second only to weekly pilgrimages to the zoo. But it wasn't cool to be a jock now, she'd said, not according to her girlfriends or her mother. Not if it meant running around on a soccer field like a boy, sweaty and messy and *gross*, Chloe had dubbed it just that morning, when he'd tried to talk about the upcoming season again over breakfast.

For both their sakes, please help me make that happen . . .

"I don't care how much of a natural Ms. Hemmings tells me you are with a ball," Law heard himself saying. "I care what you can do on the field, with a team. And no one in Chandlerville has seen you do anything but shove people away. You don't want to belong? Then how do you expect to run plays with other kids? You'd have to actually care about someone else to be able to execute at the level my teams play at. I'd need to see how you work on the practice field to consider adding you to my roster. Or you can keep wasting your talent and missing out on the chance to get better, just to prove some stupid point about not needing anyone."

Law was being an ass, something he'd never let himself do in the five years he'd coached Chloe's teams. He knew absolutely nothing about Fin, or the things the boy was dealing with. If Law never saw the kid again, he owed him better than ripping Fin a new one in the middle of recess—because Law still had the shakes from how unexpectedly hard it had been to keep his cool with Chandler's assistant principal.

Kristen had struck a nerve, too many of them. She'd gotten straight to the heart of things, smacking him with too much all at once that no one else in town would have dared to confront him about: Chloe getting worse, not better; Libby's being determined to drag their daughter into the middle of their problems, and him not doing enough to make her stop; Kristen looking and sounding and feeling like the antithesis of his screwed-up life, when all she'd done was ask him to reach out a hand to help a troubled kid. That, and she'd made Law want to be the good man she seemed so determined to believe he was.

And maybe that expectation had been what he'd run from the most.

What had she said about believing Law wasn't the kind of man to give up? He sighed, making himself refocus on the boy.

"I'm betting you care a lot more than you've let people around here know," he said, "about soccer and a bunch of other things. Right?"

Fin shrugged.

"If you care about things," Law tried again, "you should do everything you can to keep them in your life." The way he was doing everything he could to keep Chloe. "If you do get the chance to play, you should play. Don't let being cool to your friends, or not wanting people to know how you're feeling, keep you from doing what you're good at. Don't do that to yourself, or the life you could make work here."

Fin blinked up at him, his eyes suddenly wide and bright and shiny.

A lump rose in Law's throat. Kristen's plan settled deeper. He felt an unwanted connection to her and this parentless boy. He looked over and caught the hopeful, flustered smile on her face, and remembered how good it had felt to know he'd rattled her composure for those few moments.

Damn it.

He was going to regret this.

"I could coach you," he said, reminding himself that there was technically still no team to coach. And if there were, would Fin even want to play after how badly Law had handled this? "Or you could keep picking things up as you go and never learn any more than you can teach yourself. It doesn't matter to me one way or the other."

It really didn't. Unless . . .

Something Kristen said finally registered.

"You'll have to get my daughter to agree to play with us," he said. "Since you two are classmates, that shouldn't be so hard to do. Right? If I coach, team tryouts wouldn't start until after the holidays. But I'd want to work with you in the park before then, to get an idea where your skills are and to catch you up with everyone else. But again, that would depend on Chloe."

Fin smiled. "You'd . . . you'd play with me before the season starts?"

He was suddenly all lit up, this sullen kid—the way Chloe used to look on Christmas morning, opening presents from Santa that Law had spent half the night assembling and wrapping after she'd fallen asleep.

"Really?" Fin asked.

Law nodded, feeling petty and incapable of smiling back.

Fin looked blown away by the idea that anyone would spend time helping him get better at what he loved best. While Law had pretty much been angling to use the boy to keep Chloe from giving up on her soccer. Now he was seeing what Kristen must have from the start: a kid who might be willing to clean up his act if it meant getting the chance to play—assuming he had a coach who didn't have his head stuck up his ass, obsessing about his own problems.

"We'd be practicing at odd times," Law heard himself saying, "whenever I'm not at work. When we do get to the park in the afternoons, you'd be working your butt off until you're ready to hook up with the rest of the team. But I was serious." Law might be more willing now, but that didn't make his one condition for coaching any less of a deal breaker. "You're going to have to talk Chloe into playing, or I'm out. Whatever free time I have, it's hers. And she's telling me she's done with soccer."

Fin's smile faded. "I don't play with girls."

He'd practically spit the words out.

Law grunted. "That's probably a good thing."

He watched the kid do his own quick glance around. Fin and Chloe made eye contact before Fin dragged his gaze back to Law.

Law pointed across the playground. "Wherever we've lived, that *girl* has played on every team I've coached since she was barely out of diapers: boys or girls, whichever team's the best for her age group. And she's always been the MVP. Underestimate her once we get started, and she'll embarrass you every time. Ms. Hemmings wants me to take on one of the park's winter ten-and-under teams. Mostly so you'll have something to do with your time besides blowing your sweet deal with the Dixons. But you're probably right. Why bother? Especially when the only way you get to play is by talking Chloe into showing up you and the other boys, until our team wins the city championships in the spring."

"No way is she a better player than me."

"I guess you'll have to decide how badly you want to prove that."

"I don't got to prove nothin'." Fin sneered up at Law. But he glanced at Chloe again, too, and then he kicked some more at the dirt at his feet.

"No, you don't." Law was being an ass again, pushing the way he was. It was none of his business what this boy did with his life.

Law had made his own share of mistakes—back when having nothing to prove had been his personal mantra. "But you do need to stop giving things up," he said, feeling the coach inside him fully engage. "You don't have to give up everything you really want, Fin, just because it's scaring you to want it."

"What?" Fin's forehead wrinkled.

He peered up at Law as if he were crazy. And maybe Law was, giving advice to anyone about going for what they wanted most, when he was the king of letting dreams go—every one, except for his daughter's happiness. That was the one dream he'd never given up on.

"Never mind." He had to get the hell out of there. He raked a hand through his hair, cursing himself for answering the phone that morning when Kristen had called. "Just apologize to Chloe. See if you can get her on board. If you can, you might want to think about not pushing her around at school in front of her friends. You're just giving her more of a reason to kick you all over the soccer field once we get started." *Once* we get started. "I'll be in touch with the Dixons by the end of the week and let them know if the team's a go. You'll either have gotten your act together by then and decided you want to work with Chloe and me before regular practice starts the first week in February, or you're out."

Law almost hoped the kid did bail. Which pretty much made him the unreliable loser Libby had made him out to be during their divorce. And wasn't he? Hadn't he single-handedly, one by one, made the choices that had led his family to their breaking point?

The bell rang, followed by the unholy uproar of kids sprinting from every direction toward the school's side entrance, dividing into disorderly lines as their teachers appeared from wherever they'd escaped during recess.

He caught another glimpse of Chloe, but his daughter's head was down. She was trailing behind a group of trendily dressed girls who were staring at him and then back at Chloe. Kristen Hemmings was walking toward him with one of the teachers, looking like she wanted to talk again. He nodded at her and took off across the school yard, like the bad-news boy *he'd* once been.

He wasn't giving her another chance to get so close he couldn't think straight. Kristen had him remembering what it was like to want something more, something better than the way his life had bottomed out. Something as good as standing next to her had felt. She'd gotten to him. No one got to him. Not for years.

No matter how much they'd stared at each other in the park and around town, she was so *not* his type. At least, not the type he'd once been drawn to.

Back in the day, Libby had been wild and hell-on-wheels and a little dangerous. She'd been brazenly thrill-seeking and out of control and unpredictable, just like him. Kristen, by comparison, was a pulled-together, professional lady who wore conservative work suits in colors that made him think of mouthwatering ice-cream flavors like peach, pistachio, strawberry, and blueberry. Even when he caught glimpses of her jogging around the park on Sunday mornings, not a single strand of her beautiful golden hair was ever out of place. He'd never seen the first wrinkle in her workout clothes.

Yet she'd all but shivered at his touch. For a moment, he'd felt her melting closer to him, fighting to hide her reaction—at the same time that she'd stared down his initial rudeness and like a champ pitched her plan for Fin. And she'd known enough about shadow lives like his and Fin's to decide Law would be a good match for coaching the boy.

She'd somehow ferreted out how much he still wanted to work with kids. Being on a soccer field, whether he was coaching or playing, made him feel alive. Like he did when he had his daughter with him. Like he'd once felt when he'd held his guitar in his hands.

Kristen . . . with her lethally long legs and curvy figure and brains to back up all the good looks a man needed, to know he'd always need to look more . . . One conversation with her in three years, and she'd ripped him wide open, until he'd been feeling Fin's confusion and isolation, and he'd been offering to help. The strands of music playing in his head took a bluesy turn as he considered the newest contradictions and mysteries he'd discovered about Chandler's soon-to-be principal.

He rounded the building and caught sight of his truck parked out in front. He made himself slow his stride and not sprint away from the school. Barely.

School.

He buried his hands in his pockets and kept walking, stewing over his own disastrous academic experiences.

From the cradle, Lawrence Thacker Beaumont had been bred and raised to follow in his successful litigator father's footsteps. His stubborn refusal to blindly walk that path, the way his older brother had, had disappointed their family at every turn— until his parents had ultimately turned on him. They'd never understood that school hadn't been for him, no matter how smart he was. They'd never tried to understand *him*, the way he was hell-bent on figuring out what his own child needed. He jerked open the creaking door of his ancient Ford and hauled himself inside.

Kristen Hemmings was the kind of trouble he shouldn't be tangling with. The lady had guts, though. He'd give her that.

Regardless of his reputation, she'd somehow known that if he saw Fin firsthand, he wouldn't be able to turn away. She had him thinking how good it would feel, drilling with Fin and

Chloe several nights a week, figuring out what Fin had in him, and how Law and Chloe might bring out even more. He'd just been played by a skilled tactician.

And he'd admire her for it, if he weren't still swamped by the confusing impulses to either shake her for meddling, or kiss her senseless until she was as desperate as he was to find out how they'd fit together. He wanted to know how her mind worked. He wanted to know why she was so committed to helping Fin and Chloe and all the other kids in school. He wanted to know *her*, period.

His cell phone rang, piercing the truck's silence and the ache building at the base of his skull. He checked the display and winced. He wrapped his free hand around the steering wheel so tightly his knuckles turned white. He thumbed the line open.

"Libby?"

"That didn't take long."

"What?" Law sighed, because he already knew. A part of him had been expecting this warped conversation to happen, just not this quickly.

"What are you doing at school, Law?"

"Was it one of the secretaries in the office who called you? Or do you have kids on your payroll now?"

Libby's demand for a divorce last January had started as a threat, he was certain of it. She hadn't wanted him gone as much as she'd wanted whatever he'd said no to. He didn't even remember what they'd been arguing about when she'd made her ultimatum for him to give in, or they were over. He just remembered it being the end—his final line in the sand. They'd put each other and their daughter through enough.

He'd moved out as soon as he'd found an apartment. He'd explained things as best he could to Chloe, and he'd done his damnedest since to soften the blow for her as he and Libby had dismantled what was left of their relationship. Of course, his now ex-wife had done her worst to try to bully him into coming back. And then to make him pay for abandoning her all over again. She'd never forgiven him for going to prison, just like she'd never forgiven him for granting her the uncontested divorce she'd said she wanted.

"The judge gave me primary custody," she said. "That makes school issues my issues, even when you've got our daughter staying at that dump you call an apartment. If I need your help with something at Chandler, I'll ask for it. But we both know how much of a zero you ended up being when it came to your own education."

"You didn't exactly finish your degree either, Lib." They'd been partying too hard. They'd taken too many dreams with them, theirs and others', on their spiral downward.

"We both could have done more," she said, "*had* more, if you hadn't been so hell-bent on screwing up every chance we got."

Law sighed. It was an old argument—the same argument they'd had over the phone last night, and the same grudge that had motivated every bite out of him that she and her lawyers had taken.

"I didn't want *more*," he said. "I wanted our family."

"You wanted Chloe. Not me. It was never about me."

He had no comeback to that. It had been the truth for so long, it felt like forever to him, too. The feelings he'd once had for Libby felt like *never* now. Whatever they'd been, before they'd become this, was so long gone that he *had* been staying in his marriage for his daughter from practically the beginning. He'd tried harder and harder to make things work, but it had never been enough to get Libby to try, too. They'd never had a chance.

"Kristen didn't ask me to come in to talk about Chloe," he finally said, knowing it wasn't the complete truth, but it was enough of one to end this conversation before it got out of control. "She wants me to coach one of the Dixons' foster kids— some new boy she's hoping will find something in soccer to help him want to settle down everywhere else."

"Kristen?"

Law rolled his eyes. "Ms. Hemmings. The assistant principal."

"I know who she is, Law. I just don't recall her being on a first-name basis with parents she's never met before. Assuming that the two of you *haven't* met before. Have you?"

Damn, he was tired. He'd walked right into that one. Now his high-strung, extremely jealous ex was reading too much into things.

"No," he said. "We haven't met before. Knock it off, Libby. I don't have time for this." Dealing with her angst was becoming a never-ending roller-coaster ride. "There's nothing going on with Chloe at school. There's nothing in my life you need to be involved in, period—least of all who I do or don't see personally."

The silence on the other end of the phone catapulted Law's headache from a warning shot to full-on agony.

"Don't think you're going to just bounce right on to some other woman," she said, "and bring her home to your bed while you've got my daughter with you two nights a week."

"I'm not—"

"Don't think you're going to talk my child into playing any more of that filthy sport you waste so much of your time on."

"I spend my time away from Chloe working double shifts at the bar to cover the lease on the house, my rent, and all of our expenses. You made sure of that, when you demanded and got primary custody of our daughter." He felt the anger pumping through his veins. He heard it in his voice. And, as he always had with Libby, he shut it down. She wanted him out of control. He wasn't going to give her the satisfaction, or let himself go down a road that would take him back to behaving like someone he never wanted to be again. "This has got to stop, Lib. I'm doing the best I can. I always have. That wasn't good enough for you. Fine. But it's over. We're over. Let it go. What I do now is none of your business."

"You're my business, as long as we share Chloe." Libby sounded close to tears. "And don't you forget it. Don't push your luck, or you'll find your two nights a week with our daughter a distant memory. I have our divorce judge wrapped around my little finger."

She hung up, leaving Law staring at his phone.

She'd simmer down eventually, he reminded himself. He'd been reminding himself of that for months. He'd hoped they would reach some sort of separate peace, now that the divorce was finalized. He'd hoped they'd find a way to salvage their marriage when he'd moved his family to Chandlerville. He'd hoped for the best when he'd come home from prison, clean and sober, to find Libby fighting to stay clean, too, and seemingly wanting to make things work.

The best he could expect now was that his ex would eventually tire of her tantrums—and that she'd wake up to how much her bad behavior was affecting Chloe.

He started the truck's engine. He imagined Libby getting on the phone with one of her friends and ranting, because he'd once again refused to indulge her. But when he pulled out of the school parking lot, heading home for a few hours of sleep before he got Chloe back with him, he found himself glancing over his shoulder, thinking about the few minutes he'd stood there talking with Kristen.

She hadn't just been concerned about Fin. She'd thought another season of soccer would be the best thing for Chloe, too. Law couldn't get it out of his head now: the look in his daughter's eyes the last month or so—every time she said no when he asked her if she wanted to run a few drills with him. It was like watching a war play out between who his daughter thought she had to be for everyone else, and who she really was.

Kristen had understood what the pressure of making that kind of choice might be doing to Chloe. Why couldn't Libby?

And suddenly, even though he'd just told his ex he wasn't romantically interested in Chandler's AP, he found himself smiling again, the way he had several times while he and Kristen had talked. His instincts had said to get away from the woman, but being next to her had felt too good.

It had been a long time since anything had felt that good.

Chapter Four

"Your dad's a pain," Fin said to Chloe at lunch on Thursday, even though the rest of her class—at least the kids she cared about—had decided she was eating alone today.

It had been an awful morning. Yesterday afternoon, after her dad left school, had been just as bad. Everyone had been talking about her dad, and her dad and Fin. And Fin wouldn't say anything about what her dad had wanted. By the time the school bus dropped her at her dad's apartment, she'd been so mad she hadn't talked to him at all.

They hadn't gone for milk shakes or anything before the sitter came over and he left for work. She'd just sat in her room all night, getting snarky texts from her friends, who'd still wanted to know what was up. And then her mom had called, saying all over again that Chloe should be a cheerleader and not join whatever soccer team her dad was thinking about coaching—evidently with Fin or something. And then once her dad got home late, her mom had called again, on the house phone, and she and Dad had fought for like an hour.

Now everyone had been teasing her at school all morning.

Summer and Brooke especially. Word had gotten around about the soccer team and Fin possibly being on it. Not that Chloe had let her dad talk to her about it yet, so she didn't know what was happening. But her friends were already making fun of her about it—as if she'd *really* go back to playing, when her mom would make it a total hassle if she did.

It had made Chloe so mad, she'd finally yelled at Summer and Brooke on the playground, telling them to shut up about it. After that, they'd totally ditched her for the rest of recess. And then there hadn't been any room left for Chloe at their lunch table—the table they always sat at together.

Thomas Kilpatrick and Sam Nash were sitting with Summer and Brooke today, even though they usually acted like buttheads toward all the girls. Like yesterday, when they and Fin had laughed at her and Brooke and Summer, when Fin wouldn't let Chloe have a drink at the water fountain. Now Chloe's friends were hanging out with Fin's friends like *they'd* been friends forever. All because her dad had come to school yesterday and made her already lousy life even lousier.

She'd been reading a book all lunchtime, pretending that she didn't care if Summer and Brooke ever saved her a place at their table again. Just like she pretended she didn't care when her mom talked mean about her dad to people. Chloe was good at looking like she didn't care about a lot of things. She'd just taken her tray of spaghetti she wasn't going to eat to her own table and opened the book she wasn't really reading, as if that was what she'd wanted to do all along.

But she'd almost started crying on her way to the other side of their class's section in the lunchroom. Somehow she hadn't. Except now Fin was standing in front of her, making her feel like she was going to lose it again. Because everyone was staring back and forth between Brooke and Summer's table, and Chloe and Fin.

"Your dad's a pain," he said again.

She glared up from her book. "I know."

"So are your friends."

She slammed her book closed. "At least I have friends."

"You mean the ones who are sitting with Thomas and Sam, instead of you?"

"You mean the guys who aren't sitting with *you* today, who always call Brooke and Summer and me stuck up and snobby and know-it-alls?"

"Well, you are. You don't like anybody but yourselves."

"No, we don't like you and Thomas and Sam—because you're gross. All the time. You fart and even when you don't, you smell like you never shower, even though Sam's and Thomas's families have more money than God. And you pick on everyone, especially me and Brooke and Summer. And you're always in trouble . . . Of course my friends don't like you."

Except her friends were laughing *with* Thomas and Sam right now. She could hear them. Maybe Summer and Brooke thought *she* was gross, and that was why they'd acted the way they had since yesterday—the way they did anytime Chloe didn't do things the way they thought she should. Maybe they'd always felt that way about her, like her mother felt about pretty much everything now.

Her mom had been cool once, a long time ago. Chloe could barely remember now. But when she'd been really little, her mom had seemed . . . normal and maybe even happy. Now it was like nothing Chloe or her dad did would ever make her happy again.

Chloe's family had gotten so messed up. Her parents seemed to want everyone in Chandlerville to know they were freaks. Why *would* anyone really like Chloe?

Except the more she'd sat alone at lunch, pretending to read, the more she'd started to wonder . . .

Where did her friends get off treating her like this, just because her mom and dad were nuts? Summer's mom drank like Chloe's did, even though none of their parents knew that their kids knew. Brooke's dad was gone all the time, and her mom never said anything about it. Brooke thought it was because her mom was with another man a lot of the times she got a sitter for Brooke and said it was because of some fund-raising thing at school. Except none of the other kids' moms who hung out with Brooke's mom would have a school thing those nights. So where else was Brooke's mom going?

Summer's and Brooke's moms kept it together in public, the way Chloe's mom hardly ever did now. Not about Dad. But why did Chloe's friends get to make fun of *her*, when their own parents were freaks, too? Maybe Fin was right. Maybe Brooke and Summer weren't her friends. Like Thomas and Sam hadn't been acting like Fin's friends, after he'd talked with her dad yesterday and started acting so weird.

He'd been sitting by himself today, not eating, just like her. And now he was talking to her, which he never did.

"I'm sorry, okay?" he said, so fast it sounded like all one word.

Chloe just stared at him. He looked pissed off, not sorry.

What had her dad said to him? This couldn't be just about soccer.

"For being gross?" She smiled at him and tried to look mean, the way Summer and Brooke would have. "Is that what you're sorry about?"

Only it made her feel a little sick, acting like her friends. In fact, she'd started not liking Fin because Summer and Brooke hadn't liked him first. And suddenly she couldn't smile, thinking about how she hadn't said good-bye to her dad that morning or hugged him on the playground yesterday, because she was worried what her girlfriends would say. She didn't like it that Fin looked almost like he was going to cry now, and she didn't even know why, except she knew it had something to do with her.

"When isn't he gross?" Summer asked.

She and Brooke had walked over to stand behind Chloe, like they hadn't ignored her for half an hour. They were both smiling. Being mean to Fin, or anybody, was one of their favorite things. Chloe had never liked that about them, but her mom had said to get over it. Popular girls were special. They got to act differently. They got everything they wanted—everything her mom hadn't gotten when she was in school, and she and *her* mom had been living in a trailer with even less than she and Dad and Chloe had now. If Chloe wanted to be like her friends, Mom said, she had to stop worrying so much about how everyone else was feeling, and start doing things the way Summer and Brooke did.

But all Chloe really wanted—the only reason she went along with so much of what her mom wanted—was to calm Mom down and get her parents to cool it, and get her mom to remember all the things about their family that used to make her happy. Chloe just wanted something about her life to feel normal again.

"When aren't you a stuck-up brat?" Fin said back to Summer, making Sam snicker.

Sam and Thomas had walked over to stand next to him.

"Maybe my nose is in the air," Summer said, "because you keep stinking things up."

"Maybe it's your crappy perfume that smells so bad," Sam said, like he hadn't just been hanging out with her, liking the way she smelled.

Sam liked Summer. All the girls knew that was why he acted like he hated her. And most of them wished he'd act that way with them. Chloe didn't, though. It reminded her too much of how her mom treated her dad, all mean and nasty, when she was worried about everything Dad did still, even though they weren't married anymore.

"At least she doesn't stink like she forgot how to wipe her butt," Brooke said.

"If I smell like crap," Sam said, "your rotten-flower perfume smells like a funeral."

He and Thomas laughed together this time, even though everyone knew Thomas liked Brooke more than he liked any other girl their age.

Sam nudged Fin's shoulder, because Fin was just standing there and not laughing any more than Chloe was.

He usually liked it when his friends were being this way—at least, he usually acted like he did, the way he acted like he didn't care what anyone thought about him. Only Chloe had always thought that maybe he did. She'd always wondered if Fin wasn't a lot like her, because he seemed to be just going along with everyone else a lot of the time, the same as she did. She'd never dared to ask him, because he'd only have made fun of her. And even if he hadn't, their friends would have.

Now he was looking at Chloe instead of Thomas and Sam,

and everyone was staring at him. Then her. And then him again. She looked down at her book. But Chloe hadn't looked away from Fin fast enough. Not before she'd seen it.

He *was* sorry. He was . . . upset. He was really upset about something.

"Hey, Fin, if you like Chloe so much," Thomas teased, totally not getting it, "why don't you just get it over with and kiss her?"

Sam made kissing noises, and then everyone was laughing.

Fin's hands were bunched into fists.

"Leave him alone!" Chloe shouted at their friends.

She could feel her face getting red while she tried not to cry. For herself. And for Fin. He looked ready to punch someone out, and he had to know that he couldn't, not at Chandler most of all. After what had happened last winter between Troy Wilmington and Bubba Dickerson, the teachers didn't put up with anyone acting out at anyone else.

"Leave him alone," she said again, ashamed of how Summer and Brooke were laughing even harder at her, and how it was making her want to do almost anything to stop them. "I'd rather kiss a muddy soccer ball than kiss Fin. I hate him. I'll always hate him. So just leave us both alone, okay?"

And that was when she really did start to cry.

Because Fin did, too.

Right there in front of everybody, he wiped at his eyes, as if she'd hurt his feelings or something. She shouldn't care. Like her mom had said, she should only care about being with her friends—and Summer and Brooke were laughing about what she'd said now, instead of laughing at her. Chloe couldn't apologize to Fin the way she wanted to, not and be one of the cool girls in class everyone wanted to be like.

But she wanted to say sorry. She really, really wanted to. She didn't like being mean like this. She never had.

"You six knock it off and get in line," Mrs. Glover said from behind them. "You're holding everyone up. We'll be late for math."

The rest of their class was lining up at the lunchroom doors. Chloe's friends left first, then Fin's. Thomas and Sam were saying stuff to Brooke and Summer that made them laugh again. Fin looked like he wanted to scream at Chloe, but he didn't. He didn't say anything. He just kept staring.

"What's the use?" he finally asked, only she didn't know what he meant, and he didn't really seem to be talking to anyone but himself.

She should say something to him. But Summer and Brooke were looking at her again, like they wanted to be friends and they wouldn't gossip about her to everyone else the first chance they got. And Fin was watching them and Sam and Thomas and balling up his fists even tighter, like he really was going to yell and make everything even worse.

"Fin and Chloe?" Mrs. Glover said over the sound of their class talking and laughing—everyone, it felt like, talking and laughing about her and Fin.

And then, no matter how much Chloe didn't really want to, she ran toward her friends who weren't really her friends.

"Fin!" Mrs. Glover shouted.

Chloe stopped and looked back.

Fin was running too—past her and everyone else and out of the lunchroom. And he kept running, down the hallway like he was headed for the front of the school and might not stop until he was a long way away from how mean she'd just been to him.

***

"Call me when you get the chance, Mr. Beaumont," Kristen said to Law's voice mail. "I should be available for the rest of the school day."

She'd checked in with Daphne during third-grade recess, and discovered that things with Chloe and Fin seemed worse today, likely because of Kristen's meddling. She glanced toward Mallory as she hung up the phone. Mallory was sitting in one of Kristen's guest chairs, the one closest to her office door, wearing pink scrubs today, covered in a pattern of yellow rubber duckies.

"I thought I was doing the right thing," Kristen said, crossing the room to her filing cabinet. "But neither of the kids have spoken much all morning, not to Daphne or any of the other students—except for when Chloe lost her cool with her friends at recess. I thought getting her dad to coach would be a good thing."

"*I* think you're in way over your pretty head." Mallory had been patiently listening for half an hour to Kristen recounting her reasons for yesterday and the success she'd thought she'd achieved. "And considering how tall you are, that's saying something."

"Fin looked excited yesterday, didn't he? It really looked as if Mr. Beaumont had his attention."

Mallory rubbed a hand down the cute little baby bump that was growing cuter and curvier by the day. She reached behind her to massage her lower back. She was the epitome of a glowing pregnancy, no matter how sick she still got some mornings.

"So, he's *Mr. Beaumont* now?" she asked. "When you were educating Daphne about how she shouldn't doubt the man's suitability to mentor one of our problem students, I distinctly remember it being *Law*."

"He's a parent and a part of this community." Kristen slapped a file she'd retrieved onto her desk and sat. "And he took time out of his morning to come down here and let me pester him for a colossal favor. Why shouldn't I defend him? It was amazing of him, considering everything else he has on his plate."

"A plate I couldn't help but notice that you've been *considering* quite a bit lately." Mallory weathered Kristen's glare, and then she ruined it by smiling. "You wanna tell me how you knew he was the perfect person to help with Fin, or how you knew he'd say yes, even when he looked like he wanted to flip you off for asking? Or why you're calling him again today, when we don't know for sure there's anything wrong with Chloe? Not to mention, isn't Libby the school's first point of contact?"

Kristen opened her notes for the finance committee meeting about the cafeteria renovations—ignoring her friend's very valid, very annoying logic. She closed her eyes, remembering Law's scathing parting glance when he'd headed off to talk to Fin. She resisted telling Mallory that, for just a moment, he'd also looked as if he'd wanted to kiss her.

She laced her fingers together and opened her eyes, still not seeing, remembering Law's larger hand wrapping around hers, making her feel dainty and feminine.

You're never going to be as refined a lady as your mother, her diplomat father had said when Kristen had been in middle school.

She'd just fallen in love with basketball—more than anything else as a way to escape her parents' toxic relationship. Within five years, her *refined* mother had left them both, running off with the latest in her parade of boy-toy dealers, an international gigolo this time, never to be heard from again.

You might as well find something else to do with yourself . . .

The memory of his disappointment in her feminine assets still stung, no matter how much distance she'd put between herself and the utter vulnerability of that moment. She refocused on her hands, remembering the spark of desire she'd seen in Law's eyes yesterday morning. The warmth of his touch was still with her, eclipsing the insecurities of a long-ago, unwanted girl. It hadn't lasted more than a second. But the recognition that had passed between them had felt more real, more intimate, than entire relationships she'd shared with other men.

"That's a nice look for you," her friend said.

"What?" Kristen smoothed her palms over the file.

"Smiling."

"I smile all the time."

"Of course you do. But some smiles are better than others."

"What are you talking about?"

"You, stumbling out of your comfort zone yesterday, and having no idea how to find your way back inside." Mallory's grin grew wider. "Befuddled and frustrated suits you."

"What I did yesterday was clearly a mistake. Fin's even more detached than ever, and Chloe—"

"Chloe's problems aren't your fault. And neither one of us believes they're Law's. And even if they were, it's not *your* responsibility to solve them."

"No. It's my job. I'm supposed to look out for my students, not to make their lives harder."

"You were looking out for Fin. You were scrambling to find a solution for a student who even his foster parents can't figure out. But that's not my point."

Kristen stared at Mallory, refusing to ask the obvious question.

"My point is," Mallory continued, "that your job doesn't include keeping tabs on a man you've never officially met. It doesn't explain that when we run in the park Sunday mornings, you take an extra lap or two whenever Law's out on the soccer field. Or why you look like you want to smack Libby Beaumont when she says something nasty about him, or is clearly using her daughter to get back at Law for whatever ax she still has to grind with the man."

Kristen's stomach did a panicked kind of flip-flop. "I stay as tuned in to the community as I can, so I can be whatever help I can be, whenever school resources are needed."

Mallory nodded. "You're a master at bringing people together for the common good."

It had been a long year for both of them. Chandlerville had only recently regained its footing after a rocky ten months. Ron Griffin had read the handwriting on the wall after mishandling the fallout from their school shooting. He was moving on, parents and staff were overwhelmingly behind the Board of Ed's intention to have Kristen take over as principal, and she'd thrown everything she had at the chance to cement her place amidst this amazing network of friends and families.

Working at Chandler was a good life. She'd made it pretty much her entire life. No problem was too great, no solution too daunting, to keep her from tackling it with all the creativity and energy she possessed. She was determined to succeed at being the educator this town deserved, as successfully as she'd pursued her college basketball career.

So how could she have misstepped so badly yesterday?

"It's in everyone's best interests that Fin settles in," she reasoned out loud, "both here and at home with the Dixons. And that Chloe not lose herself completely in the confusion her parents' divorce has made out of her life."

"Naturally. It takes a village."

"Stop patronizing me, Mallory."

"Stop avoiding the conversation, Kristen. I'm not talking about how you handled that scene on the playground as an assistant principal. I'm talking about what's going on with you as a woman. There is a difference, you know. At least, there is where you and Law Beaumont are concerned."

Kristen sighed at her friend, who'd grown up with nothing, literally, and had found it within herself to fight for the life she had now—no matter how terrified she'd been of letting herself believe in it. Mallory was just about the least sentimental person Kristen knew. She had been up till now, anyway. And she'd been Kristen's practical, realistic touchstone, especially since January's shooting.

Truth be told, there'd been days this year when Kristen had longed to walk away from the confusion and the mess and the mountain of work that had needed to be done to keep the rest of her staff and their students focused and safe. When things were at their roughest, Kristen knew how to keep her head down and keep fighting. But that didn't mean the stress didn't affect her. It had been nearly impossible at times not to let her emotions get the best of her.

It was one of the things Mallory had said she admired most about Kristen—that she never crumbled or shirked responsibility. No matter the obstacle, she got the job done. Mallory was the same way, and it took a kindred spirit to tolerate the space Kristen often needed when she was off the clock and longing for the isolation of her private life.

From practically the cradle, she'd learned to separate herself from first her mother and then her father and then her past entirely. Others might find her private life as an adult too quiet, too solitary. But distancing herself from the complications of being too emotionally entrenched in any one thing or person meant she avoided the highs and lows and dramas that families around her—like the Beaumonts—endured. It had worked for her, all these years.

Except since the shooting, her no-frills life hadn't felt nearly as satisfying. And her recently expanded role in the community was making it harder to turn outward things off once she *was* home—particularly the longing that had begun to whisper deep inside her, for the day-to-day companionship that most everyone else found so easy to invite closer.

"You want to talk about it?" Mallory asked.

"What?"

"You and Law."

"There is no me and Law."

"Of course not."

"There isn't."

"Do you want there to be?" Mallory looked as uncomfortable with the topic as Kristen felt, but she sat forward in the guest chair—as forward as her pregnant belly would allow her. "You seem to understand an awful lot more about him than the rest of the staff, when we've all been working in the same school as his daughter and living in the same town as his whole family."

"I've heard enough of what people have been saying to know it's mostly crap. He's a good man."

"You don't gossip, Kristen. And you never listen to people who do. Except when it's about Law."

"I've been concerned about Chloe. A lot of people are, the way Libby's been carrying on."

"I heard you defending Chloe's *father* yesterday, not just looking out for his little girl."

"I was trying to help. I'd never intentionally do anything to make her situation more difficult than it already is."

"Of course you wouldn't. Or Law's. In fact, I'd say you're feeling downright protective about both of them."

"I . . ." Kristen was pretty sure what she'd been fantasizing about doing with Law since yesterday—since that first Sunday she'd caught sight of him in the park—didn't fall within the classic definition of *protective*. She cleared her throat. "I . . ."

"You're smitten. I've known it for a while. Ever since you heard he was a musician once upon a time, and I swear I saw stars in your eyes. That was your tipping point, after being intrigued with him since he moved to town. From what I'm hearing through the rumor mill, other people are starting to catch on, too, so gird your loins. Things are about to get bumpy. Your interest in him isn't the only reason you dote on Chloe the way you do, or how you knew Law was the best parent to help with Fin. But it's a big part of it that you need to start dealing with. Instead, you've spent the last thirty minutes of my life that I'm never going to get back talking *around* your messy emotions for the man—emotions you're convinced you shouldn't be having. Maybe it's time, Kristen."

"Time for what?" Mallory was way off base. It wasn't wrong for Kristen not to let the things she felt drive the choices she made—the way her parents had put their needs first every day of her childhood.

"It's time for you to let someone all the way into your heart," Mallory said. "No matter how much it scares you to think about trusting someone that much, and maybe being wrong."

Kristen shook her head. Her entire body was shaking. Evidently her friend wasn't nearly as off base as Kristen had hoped.

She had never talked about her past, but Mallory had guessed enough to back off when the worst of Kristen's memories had attacked and put the brakes on practically every other relationship she'd attempted to build since they'd met. Mallory hadn't judged or asked prying questions. She'd always been there to listen, or just to keep Kristen company when in the last few months being alone had begun to feel far too lonely.

But something *had* shifted inside Kristen yesterday as she'd talked with Law. Something out of control and dangerous that was refusing to shift back.

"It's not the end of the world, you know," Mallory said.

"What?"

"Letting yourself want someone."

That's because you've never known my world, Kristen almost said, before she remembered just how much Mallory had lost—and won—in her own life.

"It's . . ." She grappled for the right words. "It's . . . terrifying."

Mallory nodded and rubbed a gentle hand across her belly. "Tell me about it."

Kristen's answering smile felt bittersweet.

Mallory had fought her way out of the isolation that had kept her safe for so long. Marrying Pete and becoming a second mother to Polly and now having their new baby was her reward. Kristen was happy her friend had found somewhere to belong. But not everyone got their fairy-tale ending.

"I'm not looking for a family of my own," she reminded them both.

"I know that." Mallory suddenly looked as sad as Kristen had felt last night, when Kristen had walked into her quiet condo and wished someone else had been there waiting for her.

"I have a job to do," she said, "figuring out what's going on with Chloe and Fin."

"Just keep in mind that Chloe's been upset for months, and it was already getting worse."

"Yesterday didn't help."

Who knew what the girl's friends had been saying since her dad's visit, or what had happened when Chloe had gotten to Law's place last night, or the damage Libby might have inflicted if she'd heard the rumors about Kristen defending Law to Daphne. And of course Libby would have heard.

What had Kristen done . . . ?

"What would help?" Mallory asked. "Chloe seeing her dad with someone who doesn't want to make his life a living hell? Her seeing her father smile?"

"Smile?" Kristen remembered again the moments during their conversation when Law had seemed to be enjoying himself. But then there was the scorching look he'd cast her as he'd beaten a path away from the playground. "I'd settle for him not wanting to cut out my spleen when he returns my call."

"Oh, I'm betting doing something a lot more fun with you might have crossed his mind, no matter how steamed he is." Mallory smirked. "Don't tell me you didn't feel it, too. You may be careful with men to the point that I want to get you drunk before your next date, just to loosen you up." Mallory held up her hands to stop Kristen from stating the obvious—that she didn't drink. Ever. "But you're not blind."

"No." Kristen wasn't blind. But she was evidently a fool when it came to Law. She threw down her pen. Why *hadn't* she called Libby, instead of him?

"Don't dig yourself any deeper into the Beaumonts' problems," Mallory said. "Not unless you're ready to deal with Law as something other than the father of one of your students. That's clearly not all he is to you, Kristen. Either disentangle yourself from the man's life again, or figure out how to do a better job of handling how you feel about him."

Kristen stared at the cafeteria redesign proposal and began flipping through the folder. Law wasn't anything to her. She wasn't anything more to him than a school administrator who had just become a very prominent pain in his ass. There were too many variables, too many things that could go wrong, too much beyond her control, for there to be any more going on than that.

So why was she absurdly aware of the passage of time, of each minute that had gone by since she'd left her ill-advised voice mail?

"I have a meeting at two I need to prepare for," she said, the pages before her blurring, her thoughts consumed with wondering what Law's rough yet gentle touch might feel like as he spread his hands all over her body.

"Got it. Conversation over." Mallory struggled to extricate herself from the chair. "Just know I'm here, if you ever—"

A knock on the door interrupted them. Before Kristen could answer, it swung open.

"We've got a problem." Bethany Adams, the head secretary, rushed inside. "Daphne's here. Fin Robinson's run away."

***

Marsha Dixon loved Chandler Elementary.

The sound of children growing and learning and enjoying life was a delight every time she was here. It didn't matter that today she was seeing after one of the most difficult kids she and Joe had taken in.

Well, it almost didn't matter.

Even after the horror of the shooting in January—when eleven-year-old Troy Wilmington had vented the pain and fear and loneliness that had been eating him up, at the expense of another sixth grader—Marsha hadn't gone more than a week without being in this place, and relishing every second she got to stay.

She'd have been a teacher, if life hadn't made other choices for her and Joe. Instead, her job had become raising the ragtag brood of children she and her husband had fostered for decades and then helping them leave. Their very first generation of kids was grown and gone now, and yet her family was still going strong, thriving through daily challenges and unconditional love that came with adding new children to the mix almost yearly.

She was a teacher after all, she'd learned. It was just that the lessons she and Joe had mastered were about living, instead of math or science or reading. The two of them were far from perfect. They'd made their share of mistakes early on. But they'd made a difference in the young lives entrusted to them. Some of their kids brought baggage and special needs that couldn't be loved away in the few short years she and Joe were given to help. But she and her husband had yet to lose a mind or a spirit. They'd never had a child returned to the system because they simply couldn't make it work.

The young adults who aged out of their home were prepared to face life in their own ways, stronger and more confident and prouder of their individual gifts than when they'd first arrived. The world wasn't always easy to live in. But her kids learned how to do what they had to do, to live honestly and claim the future they deserved. Even the most damaged of the children she and Joe worked with could learn how to hope. That was their goal with each and every one.

Only this time, maybe they'd met their match.

They'd been warned that Fin would be a challenge. His detachment disorder was an obstacle, as was his track record of running from earlier residential homes he'd been placed with. While she and Joe had firmly explained the ground rules for living with them, they'd privately grieved for Fin's losses. His very early childhood had shaped the distrustful, isolated young adult he'd be growing into soon, if something didn't get through to him.

How could it not damage a six-year-old boy to lose his mother to the drugs he'd watched her take day after day, and then to have no one to turn to once she was gone? The father had never been in the picture. There were no grandparents. Fin's mother had been a product of the foster care system herself. There'd only been a small child, already too cynical and self-dependent for his age, not thinking he needed anyone but himself. Because what was the point, when he was only going to end up like his mother had, when she'd aged out of the system?

Marsha and Joe would do whatever good they could for Fin, for as long as they could. They'd try to make their home a place he knew he'd always be welcome, no matter how old he got or when the county stopped sending money for his care. But would he ever be ready to believe them?

In the month they'd had him so far, not so much.

She sighed and tried to tune back in to what Chandler's assistant principal was saying about Fin's latest rebellion, this time running out of the lunchroom and the school and to who knew where next. It was entirely possible that their eighteenth foster child was worse off now than when CFS moved him to Chandlerville from a nearby community.

"We knew his behavior at school had become increasingly disruptive to Mrs. Glover," she said to Kristen.

From the very start, the AP had taken a personal interest in Fin's situation. And Marsha had taken a personal interest in Kristen long before that. Especially this year, Chandler's very efficient, very professional assistant principal had seemed more in need of mothering than most any other adult Marsha knew. And surprisingly, the younger woman hadn't altogether balked at the support and encouragement that Marsha had tried to subtly offer while things had been so horribly chaotic. They'd formed a tenuous, unspoken friendship that Marsha checked in on each time she was in the school for whatever latest hands-on attention one of her kids needed.

When Kristen had called just a while ago, she'd sounded genuinely distraught.

"But Fin's misbehaving has been harmless enough until now," Marsha continued. "He and a few of the other boys have been too rambunctious and teasing some of the girls."

"Well, there's rambunctious," Kristen said, "and there's bullying. And after what happened in the lunchroom and at recess yesterday, Mrs. Glover is concerned Fin and his friends and a group of the girls in their class may be crossing that line. I'm sure you can understand why we're speaking with all of the parents about it, not just you. And in Fin's case, we have records of him becoming physical with students at previous schools he's attended before he came to Chandler. Which means that even if Fin hadn't cut class after lunch, we'd still be dealing with his behavior issues in a more formal way from here on out. Perhaps he knew that, and that's why he took off?"

"I don't think so. Authority issues aren't what spook him."

Love was, but Marsha stopped short of sharing that insight.

The boy's sense of betrayal was a soul-deep wound they might never fully understand. The last thing she and Joe could afford was to add to that. And maybe she already had—with her conversation two days ago with Kristen, searching for answers for Fin that she hadn't found on her own.

"I spoke with Law Beaumont yesterday about coaching," the AP said, her voice shaking a little, when Kristen was usually the calmest port in an emotional storm. "He was here, and he spent a few moments with Fin."

Marsha scooted to the edge of her chair. "He actually came to school? I don't think I've ever seen him at Chandler."

"I haven't either." Kristen wasn't quite making eye contact. "Having him show up in the middle of recess evidently wasn't easy for either Chloe or Fin."

Marsha couldn't help being pleased. Was something brewing between Kristen and little Chloe's father? "Easy isn't always what gets things done."

"I think I made a mistake." Kristen's gaze steadied. "When you mentioned Fin's love for soccer, I was so sure . . ."

"Are you certain it was Law's visit that upset Fin?"

Marsha wasn't going to bother Kristen, asking for details about what had happened on the playground. She was certain she'd get an earful of gossip at tonight's grand-opening party for what would likely become Chandlerville's newest family hangout: a bowling center that had been dubbed Pockets by its proud owner, Walter Davis.

"Fin and Chloe have been agitated ever since," Kristen said. "Daphne saw them talking together just before Fin ran from lunch today. Some of their friends joined them, and things got ugly, just like they did at the end of recess yesterday."

"After Law showed up."

Kristen nodded.

"So, we have Fin's attention now." Marsha squared her shoulders. "That's a change, at least. Joe and I haven't been able to get anything out of the boy. He's hardly said a word since he came to us. He shows practically no emotion at all, no matter what trouble he's in, or how much we explain the consequences if he doesn't settle down."

"This isn't the kind of change we were hoping for."

"It's a change. And I choose to believe it's a good thing. That boy loves soccer. And he's remarkable at it, from what we've been able to gather from Family Services. If Law offered Fin a chance to play on one of his teams, I think we're making progress. Now we wait and see what Fin decides he wants most—to keep going through life alone, or to become an actual part of this community that's clearly scaring him as much as every other foster home he's been in."

"He may have good reason to be afraid after today, Marsha."

Kristen looked miserable. Which pretty much described how Marsha always felt when she had to address the unavoidable consequences of one of her kids' poor choices. But dealing with life was dealing with life. There was no running from the good or the bad of it.

"Okay." Marsha sat taller in her chair. "Hit me with it. What's the damage?"

"I need to file a formal report with the county this time. He's in their records as a runner. It's a pattern, and I can't sweep that part of this under the rug, no matter how responsible I personally feel for contributing to what's upset him. I'll also have to let them know about the disruptive behavior in Daphne's class. Given Fin's history, we can't afford for things here to escalate without the county weighing in."

"I understand. Joe and I fully support Chandler's no-tolerance bullying policy."

After what their close-knit town had been through—healing from January's tragedy—everyone was committed to preventing anything similar from happening again. That desire was even partially responsible for Walter Davis, a former corporate CPA, building and running a bowling alley as his new career path—in addition to freelancing accounting services to every business and family in town who'd hire him.

Walter wanted what they all wanted: to bring their community back together. He wanted to see folks building one another up again. He wanted to believe that was what Chandlerville would always be about—caring for the people who lived here, even lost little boys who didn't want to be cared for. Marsha believed that, too. And she believed that the woman sitting across the desk from her was equally determined to help Fin and the rest of Chandler Elementary's children.

But that passion for helping kids was also tormenting their AP at the moment.

Kristen sighed. "I've made a mess of things."

"Nope." Marsha suspected her friend was talking about more than Fin. "I think you've struck just the right balance between Fin wanting more and the sheer terror of believing he belongs." She laughed at Kristen's surprise. "When everyone's out of their comfort zones, that's when the good stuff in relationships starts to happen. Fin's off balance. He's been biding his time, and maybe he was already planning to run from school like he has from everywhere else. Except we've given him something to think about coming home for. Joe and I have our chance now to make something good happen when the boy does make it back."

"I should have had you and your husband talk with Law, instead of doing it myself."

"I'm not sure we'd have made any more of a dent with him than we have with Fin." The only time the boy had ever shouted at Marsha and Joe had been when they'd suggested he start playing again. And no one around besides Libby and Chloe—and now Kristen—had gotten much of a reaction out of Law before yesterday, not even the man's brother. "You're looking at this all wrong. Your reporting what happened today to the county will be a bit of a setback. But the fact that Fin didn't pitch a fit the second Law started talking to him about soccer is remarkable."

Kristen sat straighter and rested her forearms on top of Fin's file. "Daphne and I both swore we saw Fin apologize to Law for picking on Chloe."

"That's marvelous."

"He ran away, Marsha."

"He'll be back."

"You don't know that."

"He's come back every other time." Three times, to be exact, though Marsha and Joe had kept that bit of trivia to themselves.

Kristen's shock was immediate, as was the type of scolding glare that must work miracles keeping rowdy kids in line. "Marsha . . ."

"I know we should have reported it to Family Services already, and I wouldn't blame you if you do now. But Joe and I didn't see the harm. Fin's come back to us each time—the same day he's run off. And he never willingly returned to any of his other homes. Something different is happening for him in Chandlerville. I can feel it. Like something different happened for him here yesterday, thanks to you and Law. Now we give him time to figure things out, and to accept that his life doesn't have to always feel as bad as it has since he lost his mom."

Kristen nodded. She rubbed a hand over her eyes. "He's going to have to stop running. The county won't let him stay if he doesn't."

"He'll stop, here with us. I'm sure of it. You've tempted him with just the thing he'll want badly enough to finally make somewhere a real home."

"Do you have any idea where he's gone?"

Marsha shook her head. "But he's always come home before dark. He never says where he's been. A kid that smart's probably got places to disappear to all over town. You said he was talking with Chloe before he ran. Did he say anything to her that might help?"

"Not that Daphne can tell. But Chloe's pretty upset. She's not talking with her friends this afternoon, or anyone else in her class."

"I'm sorry," Marsha said, when she wasn't completely certain she was.

"I pushed Law to try to get Chloe to play, too. Another bad idea."

"You suggested it because you care about the child."

And about the father?

It would do Marsha's heart good to see Kristen happily settled with someone who did *her* heart good. Law might be too intense and brooding for most other woman to tangle with. But Marsha had to wonder whether his unfailing loyalty to Chloe wasn't just the temptation to attract someone like Kristen, who'd proved time and again that she'd give everything she had for their community.

"You had the best of intentions," Marsha said. "Trust that. That's what Fin needs, to find himself a better path. Trust and time."

Kristen's next nod was less than enthusiastic.

Marsha's heart sank.

"Joe and I trust you completely," she made herself say. "You do what you think is best, reporting about all of this to the county. We'll stand behind you and Fin for as long as CFS lets us have him."

Kristen flashed a fierce smile and leaned back in her chair. Marsha could almost see her typically all-business companion considering each alternative.

"How about I hold off on informing Family Services about Fin's latest outburst until he comes home? Call my cell when he does. Hopefully by the time school opens in the morning, you'll have him safely back with you and Joe, and I'll be able to limit my report to what happened at lunch today."

"Thank you. Mrs. Sewel, his caseworker, has pretty much said that we're his last shot. If Family Services hears that he's run again, that he's not attaching to our home, they're talking about moving him to a more institutionalized setting where he can be monitored around the clock. I think that would be the end of anyone being able to reach him." Marsha gripped her hands together, refusing to believe that it might already be too late. "We'll call you as soon as we find him. Then we'll see if we can make some real progress, after what happened with Law and Chloe. If he's home in time, we'll bring him and the other kids to the Pockets grand opening this evening. We'll see you there."

Kristen shook her head. "I can't make it. One of my girls' teams has practice."

"At the YMCA?"

Kristen nodded. "And I'm already leaving work earlier than normal to make it."

Kristen coached girls' basketball every season, often several teams in the same season. Marsha had suspected for some time now that it was one of the many ways Kristen got to participate in the community without having to invest too much of her heart.

"It's a school night," Marsha said. "Practice should be over early enough to free the kids up for dinner and bedtime."

"Around six or so."

"Then stop by Pockets on your way home. Hopefully we'll have Fin with us by then."

"I . . ." Kristen shook her head, but she said, "I'll see what I can do."

"I expect one of the Beaumont parents will be there with Chloe." Marsha couldn't stop hoping that something had sparked between one of her favorite people and a man she believed deserved better than the hassles he was patiently enduring with his ex. "Don't you want to see for yourself how Chloe's doing, once she's away from school for a few hours?"

Despite Marsha's best effort to hide her enthusiasm, Kristen's eyes narrowed. The AP flattened her palms on top of her desk.

"Marsha . . ." Kristen inhaled, not finishing whatever she'd begun to say. Her professional mask slipped back in place. "I'll see what I can do about tonight. But let's plan on regrouping here in the morning, hopefully with Fin, to discuss things more formally before I touch base with Family Services."

Chapter Five

"Whatever you got on tap's fine," Vic Creighton said to Law. "I've gotta finish up quick and get back to the site."

"Sure thing." Law pulled a beer for the foreman of the Pockets construction project.

The Davises' grand opening bash tonight—free bowling and food and games and door prizes and even dancing—had been the talk of Chandlerville for weeks. Everyone was going—everyone who liked that sort of thing. Law had pretty much burned out on *good times* when his and Libby's bad choices earned him eighteen months in prison for DUI and reckless endangerment, after an accident that left another driver severely injured.

When he'd been called into McC's at noon to cover the midday rush, after he'd worked until midnight again last night, Vic had been right behind him, raring to turn his soon-to-be stressful afternoon into an excuse for having a beer and watching a half hour of ESPN, all while he expensed the bill to the Davises. He'd said his final responsibility before he signed off on overseeing the near-completed Pockets build was to manage the last of the landscaping installation.

Law handed over the mug. "I thought the construction on Walter and Julia's place was complete."

"It is." Vic raised his beer in a toast and sipped. "Mostly. The nursery put off handling the border plants and shrubs for the beds out front until this afternoon. You know, because no owner is going to get nervous that the landscaping for the entrance to their building still looks like rot the day of the opening. Julia's having a cow. I'm promising her everything will be taken care of by five, after promising it would be done by ten this morning. My new ETA for delivery of her handpicked shrubs is one o'clock. Between you and me, I'm guessing we're looking at closer to two. Maybe three."

He drank again.

Law shook his head, recalling the endless list of other misfires and off-schedule details Vic had come into McC's to good-naturedly rant about over the last few months. "Landscapers. Can't live with 'em. Can't—"

"Shoot 'em?" Vic pulled off his Atlanta Braves baseball cap and rubbed his hair back from his eyes. "It's no big deal. They're just plants that no one will notice."

"No one except for Julia."

"So my job's to make sure her pretty border shrubs show up and are installed without another hitch."

"Except there's always another hitch."

"Hell, *hitch* is my middle name." Vic took another swallow. "But come later tonight, I'll be sleeping like a baby for the first time since I took the gig. And Friday, I'm taking my bonus and my wife on a long weekend down to the beach." He held his mug up in a salute. "It's all good."

Law envied the other man his confidence, his contentment, and his plans, even though Vic had been frustrated beyond bear-

ing more than once on this project. The end of his troubles in
sight, Vic was looking past the crazy afternoon ahead, and forward to the good things waiting on the other side.

Law couldn't remember the last time tomorrow had loomed
before him with that kind of optimism attached.

"Crystal will have your Reuben out in just a few." He kept his
tone conversational, when he felt like pouring a drink for himself and finding a silent corner to stew over everything that had
happened at school yesterday, and since.

The impulse to use alcohol to cope with problems would always be there, even though he'd been sober since before his
daughter's birth. He'd never again give in to it. But that hadn't
stopped Libby—a recovering alcoholic herself—from using his
past against him to convince a judge to award her primary custody of their child.

No one in Chandlerville knew she'd been the one who'd
fallen off the wagon the year before they'd moved here. Law's
reluctantly reaching out to his brother, asking Dan to hook him
up with the job at McC's and a house Law and Libby could lease,
had been Law's last-ditch attempt to support his wife's recovery
and give their marriage a final chance. She'd begged him for the
change. He'd done it for her, for his daughter, for them, even
though he'd happily have gone the rest of his life without dealing
with his family. And then he'd refused to make her blip in sobriety an issue during their divorce, against his low-rent lawyer's
advice.

Not that either concession had earned him Libby's goodwill.

After making a complete disaster out of the world Chloe'd
been born into, he was willing to live his life under a microscope
and let people in town think what they would of him, rather than
publicly challenging Libby's accusations. Chloe's finally having

some peace at home was all he cared about now. But that wasn't going to happen until his ex-wife stopped demanding more— more that he owed her, while Libby refused to lift a finger to help herself.

His mind veered toward images of a true fighter, toward thoughts of Kristen and the voice mail she'd left a few hours ago. All she'd said was to call her back, most likely about yesterday. He had no idea how things were going with Fin, and he wasn't sure he wanted to know. Chloe had been giving him the silent treatment since last night, Libby was still giving him hell, and he shouldn't be wanting Kristen to continue contacting him about anything.

Except he did.

He thought about her genuine concern for his child and Fin, and her seemingly sincere belief that Law was a good guy despite the bad rep Libby had worked so hard to hang on him. And heaven help them all, he really, *really* wanted to listen to Kristen's voice mail again and return her call and see her again. Touch her again.

"Can't believe how hot it still is outside." Vic took another sip of his beer and wiped his mouth with the back of his hand. "It's November, man. It's just wrong to be thinking of running the air-conditioning in a few weeks, when my wife's got half her family over for Thanksgiving. The kitchen will be going full-steam. If this weather doesn't break, the house will be like a sauna."

Law had an unwanted flash of how the holiday season would likely go for him. The prospect didn't improve his mood.

His and Libby's newly minted custody agreement said they were to share Chloe for the holidays, alternating Thanksgiving and Christmas. But Libby was already complaining. She'd been dropping hints, mostly when Chloe was around to hear, that *her* daughter should be able to spend both holidays in her own home. Law would either have to put his foot down and force his ex to abide by the judge's ruling, dragging their daughter into yet another melodrama, or he'd cave, and let Chloe have Thanksgiving and Christmas with Libby, while he cooled his heels in his empty apartment.

"At least you won't be freezing your butt off doing your day job this winter," he consoled Vic. "That's not such a bad trade-off for wearing Bermuda shorts while you fake being up for things like turkey and cranberries."

His customer chuckled. "Plus when the kids and their cousins get on our nerves, we can toss 'em outside without worrying about anyone catching cold."

"Now you're talking . . ." Law poured himself a glass of seltzer, thinking how much he'd love to spend all of Thanksgiving outside with his daughter, playing the game they both enjoyed.

When he'd first discovered soccer, at about the same age as Chloe was now, he'd found something else in life that he was good at besides getting on *his* parents' nerves playing his guitar and drums at all hours of the day and night. That fresh taste of freedom, no matter how much the adults in his world continued to try to control him, had been a godsend. And even though music was now no longer an option, the sport that had saved him, the same way as composing and performing his own songs once had, was still his. Every winter or summer day he got to head outside and lose himself in kicking a ball around, especially when he was doing it with his kid, was one more than he deserved.

But had his and Chloe's time together, just the two of them on the practice field, made a difference at all to his daughter? Chloe no longer wanted anything to do with the sport.

Vic threw back a handful of peanuts from the bowl Law had placed in front of him. "Yeah. I guess there could be worse things than living in paradise."

Paradise...

The word seemed to hang in the air around them.

Law's memories served up another image of Kristen, decked out in yesterday's pale blue pantsuit, so professional it made him long to see what she looked like bedraggled and out of control. Then he pictured Fin's face, the boy looking up at Law with a desperate mixture of panic and excitement at the thought of joining a soccer team he wasn't supposed to have cared about playing on. Then of Libby, and then his parents, and all the times they'd made sure Law knew just how little he'd accomplished with his life.

Law drained the last of his seltzer, wishing for about the tenth time that day that it was something stronger. He'd done his time for the reckless mistakes he'd made in his twenties. He'd never again give the family of his childhood or his ex-wife the power to mess with him to the point that he'd screw up his future by thinking he needed alcohol to deal with them.

His hand was reaching for the whiskey, and he was pouring two fingers into a shot glass, before he realized what he was doing and stopped himself. The shock of it had his ears ringing, numbness spreading through him. He pushed the booze away. He braced his hands on the oak bar on either side of the glass and stared at the amber liquid inside.

Thank God Vic had lost interest in their conversation. He was enjoying the lunch Crystal had brought out from the kitchen, fully engrossed in whatever was on the flat-screen hanging on the wall above Law's head. All while Law's mouth was watering for a taste of the escape that awaited him at the bottom of a bottle.

Well, hell.

Every sponsor had warned him that working in a bar was off-the-charts risky for a man who could never take another drink, or he'd relapse back to the lifestyle that had already ruined him once. But bartending was the only job Law had ever held down and done well. And when he'd finished serving his time, it was the only job an ex-con college dropout like him could find that paid enough, with tips, to support his family.

It wasn't as if he'd started out planning to do this forever. He'd thought a time or two about going back to school. But he barely made enough as it was to cover the bills. And besides, serving alcohol to a million people wouldn't be enough to tempt him. He'd had a secret weapon these past eight years that every one of his well-intentioned mentors had underestimated.

He'd had Chloe.

His daughter was his second chance. Parenting her and doing it right had gotten him through the rest. It would keep getting him through whatever he had to do. He could give up anything, he'd discovered, as long as he saw Chloe's life become everything it should be—even if it meant no longer having her with him every day, now that he and Libby were done. Compared to being what he should be for his child, surrounding himself with all the temptation in the world didn't have a shot in hell of screwing him up.

At least it hadn't before today.

In a lot of ways, his job had become a daily reminder of the new life he'd claimed. Every drink he served someone else and didn't take himself was a victory—proof that he could do this for his little girl. Every night he fell asleep sober and free of the haze that had engulfed his world around the time Chloe was conceived—even a bitch of a night like the last few—gave him another day to look forward to. Another day that his daughter was the unforgettable melody of his life.

The door from the parking lot swung open. Sunlight pierced the bar's dim interior. Walter Davis strolled in, exuding friendly excitement.

"How the hell are ya, Law?" He stretched his hand across the bar to shake Law's, and then slapped Vic on the back. "How much is lunch costing me today?"

Vic took a bite of his Reuben and grunted as he chewed. "Not as much as the big gaping holes in those flower beds will cost you in curb appeal, if I'm not back on the site in half an hour to supervise the last of the landscaping going in."

Walter settled onto the stool beside his foreman and grabbed a fistful of peanuts. "You're golden, as long as by the time we cut the ribbon on the front door and let in the masses who are showing up for free food and fun, Julia's dwarf nandina are perky and thriving and brimming with berries, smiling at everyone like they've been living there their whole lives."

"You want your usual?" Law reached for a glass, while Vic got busy finishing up his lunch. At Walter's nod, Law scooped up some ice, filled the glass with it and Dr Pepper from the fountain, and handed Walter his soft drink.

"I sure do appreciate you and Rick hanging up the flyers about the opening." Walter smiled, the way he'd been smiling for months—since he and one of his Mimosa Lane neighbors, architect Brian Perry, first designed the new bowling center from the skeleton of a deserted strip mall everyone in Chandlerville had given up for lost. "It means a lot, the way you two have talked up tonight's opening to folks. I've heard from a lot of your regulars. You tell your boss I'll be sure to return the favor and send as much business your way as I can."

"We've been happy to do it, Walter." Rick had initially balked at displaying one of the flyers Walter had circulated to businesses all over town, but Law had talked him around to it.

"Tell Rick his ads are welcome anytime he wants something up at the bowling center. I'll link over to the bar from the website, too, once we have the page fully designed."

"I'd be surprised if he doesn't show up tonight with something he'll want you to hang."

"I hope he does. Julia and I want this to be a community place. Pockets belongs to everyone. That's the idea, at least."

It was an amazing concept, from a man who not too long ago—just this last April—had been one of the few McC's regulars Law had ever found himself concerned about.

Chandlerville wasn't the kind of place where locals drowned their sorrows every night. Not like some of the dives Law had worked in early on, when he and Libby and Chloe had lived in a string of small towns in southern Virginia.

Before he'd pimped his estranged older brother for the connections Law had needed to make the move to Chandlerville, it had been an almost nightly ritual for him to finagle people's car keys from them and call a cab, because they were unsafe and unaware, and he wasn't about to let them out of his sight until they couldn't hurt themselves or anyone else. Folks around here tended to mind their limits a bit better. But a lot of people in town had been through a lot of loss recently, and loss could do bad things to good people like Walter.

The man had taken January's shooting at the elementary school hard. Walter had personally known most of the kids and families involved, and he'd dealt with his grief by drinking. Over the course of just a few months, he'd ruined his reputation at his big-time downtown Atlanta accounting firm, alienated his own kids, and had nearly broken up his marriage.

Now he was in AA. He was running a one-man accounting service out of his home that was by all accounts thriving. And Pockets, his dream come true, had become a reality lightning fast, thanks to a silent partner and financial backer Brian Perry had hooked him up with. Walter's entire family was involved in bringing the place to life.

"Everyone's dying to see what you've done," Law said. "You've worked your butt off making tonight happen. You'll have to let me know how it goes."

Walter nodded, but he looked puzzled. "You're not coming?" he asked. "Chloe's going to love the games and prizes we've got planned for the kids. Or is she with Libby this afternoon?"

"Nope, I've got her after school for one more afternoon. I'm only doing a half shift here until three. I don't drop her at her mother's until eight. But—"

"Then bring her over. She'll know lots of people there, and you can meet a few more folks besides the ones who wander in here or hang out at the park."

Walter took a sip of his soda. He glanced down to the counter in front of Law. He zeroed in on the untouched shot glass of whiskey.

"That's what we're trying to make happen," he said. "Julia and I want people to have somewhere to hang out and relax and hook up with friends and families, on their way to and from all the stress that we spend most of our time chasing every day. We want to give folks a chance to decompress from the stuff that drives them crazy."

Law dumped the whiskey down the drain and set the bar

glass in the open dishwasher with enough force to leave it rocking back and forth on the rack. Decompressing. Relaxing. What
did that feel like—besides drunk, or running on the soccer field
until he was too exhausted to feel anything at all?

Walter nodded, even though Law hadn't said a thing. "I
know Dan and Charlotte are coming with Sally."

At the mention of his brother, Law flipped the dishwasher
door closed and turned his back on Walter and Vic to towel down
the counter. He didn't need this. He was already sorting through
enough emotional backwash today. He rubbed a hand over the
back of his neck. His head felt like it was going to explode.

Estranged was too mild a word for his complicated relationship with his big brother. He and Dan had been tight once,
maybe, when they'd been kids and before their parents, their father mostly, had decided to pit them against each other, with
Law forever falling short of Dan's example. By the time Dan and
then Law had headed to Duke for college—Law on a soccer
scholarship that had quickly dried up because he'd been partying too hard to get his butt to practice, and Dan on their parents'
dime, because he was prelaw and their dad couldn't have been
prouder—Law hadn't wanted anything to do with his perfect
brother or their aggressively disapproving parents.

Then, despite Dan's repeated attempts to get him to straighten
up, Law had gotten himself cut from the team, then booted from
school because of grades—after which their parents had been
sure to point out during Law's last phone call home that they'd
been expecting him to screw up all along. He always did. He always would. They were washing their hands of him.

Dan, on his way to law school, had tried to keep in touch. But
Law and Libby had been drinking most every day and night by
then. They'd moved to Virginia to live in a rattletrap trailer in a

mobile home park. They were traveling with his band, recklessly indulging in mind-bending excess that had felt like freedom. Meanwhile Dan kept busting his ass making grades, eventually marrying Charlotte, a perfect girl from another perfect family like theirs, who'd been so much more acceptable to their parents than Libby would have been. Law had been invited to the wedding. Stupidly, selfishly, drunkenly, he'd burned that bridge, too, and refused to go.

That had turned out to be the weekend the unthinkable had happened to him and Libby. Law had been jolted out of his adolescent, self-destructive bitterness over his lot in life. By then he'd made certain that except for *his* new wife, whom he'd married only because she was pregnant, he'd been utterly alone in the world.

He'd gone first to jail and then to prison because the prosecutor had been dead set on making an example out of his case and the previous DUIs he'd racked up, establishing a clear pattern of recklessness. His powerful lawyer father had offered to broker a deal with the DA if Law promised to shape up, go back to school, and devote the rest of his life to becoming a carbon copy of Dan. When Law had refused, their parents had gladly left him at the mercy of his inexperienced, court-appointed public defender—interceding only to ensure Law served his eighteen months in minimum-security.

Law hadn't spoken to his mother and father since, and he'd reached out to Dan, an established Atlanta lawyer now, only out of desperation—hoping the years of silence between them hadn't obliterated the loyalty Dan had once felt. Dan had come through. He and Law had reconnected, if you could call being distant, civil acquaintances living on opposite ends of the same small town connecting. But the damage had been done.

They were strangers now. And maybe Law still needed them to be. That made him a bastard, after his brother had gone out on a limb with Rick, securing Law a great gig at McC's, and with the owner who'd offered Law a lease on the house far below market value. But with the freak show Libby had been making out of his life the last few years, dealing with Dan, too . . . *That* might just have been the thing to shove Law back over the edge.

"The Perrys and their boys are coming to the party," Walter continued with forced enthusiasm, pushing the Pockets opening as if one night out would solve all Law's problems. "Lots of people from the school will be there, like Mallory and Daphne. Lots of Chloe's friends and their families, too. She'd have a blast."

And what about Kristen? Law asked himself.

Would Chandler's spunky, sexy, caring AP be there, driving Law crazy? He couldn't get her out of his mind. He couldn't stop wondering if a guy with an advanced degree and an establishment job like his brother was more her style. Or how that could possibly be the case, when she'd responded so sweetly yesterday to a burnout like Law. Not that she'd seemed all that thrilled by her reaction to him. Not that he should have let himself notice—then or now.

Walter was a good man and a good friend to a lot of people. He was a wealthy man, if his fancy house on Mimosa Lane, not far from Dan's, was any indication. But if he didn't stop pushing Law about coming tonight, Law was going to have to throw one of Chandlerville's favorite citizens out of the bar, the way he would a drunk and disorderly.

Vic stood and wiped his mouth with his napkin. "I've got to hit the john and then get back to it."

Walter stopped him from reaching for his wallet. "I've got this. Just take care of my wife's landscaping before she has a panic attack. If you can get pictures of the finished result up on our Facebook page so she can see it from home, where I've banished her until later this afternoon, there's another bonus in it for you."

"I'm on it." Vic slapped his boss on the shoulder and headed for the back of the bar, where the restrooms were tucked away.

Once the other man was gone, Walter locked gazes with Law. He glanced toward the dishwasher.

"You doing okay?" he asked.

They'd discussed their individual sobriety and recovery only once. After a month in AA, Walter had stopped by McC's toward the end of May to apologize and make amends. Law had stopped him before he'd gotten too far. Without sharing details, he'd let Walter know he understood, no apologies were needed, and he'd been happy to help. They'd sealed the deal with a drink—Law and his seltzer, Walter with a Dr Pepper.

Every week or so since, Walter would stop back by, no matter how busy he'd gotten with everything else. An easy friendship had settled between them. And even though Law wasn't a friendship kind of man, he hadn't minded a bit. Until this very moment.

"I'm as okay as I always am," he said.

Walter nodded. "I don't pay any mind to gossip, and even if I did I'd believe only about half of what I hear. But we know a lot of the same people . . ."

Law scanned the bar. Vic had slipped out a moment ago. The place was empty now except for the two of them. "What's on your mind, Walter?"

The other man took a sip of his drink. "It's none of my business. I get that."

"But . . ."

"But there's a lot of different kinds of family besides the ones most of us have waiting for us at home." Walter hitched his thumb over his shoulder, toward the door. "There are lots of people in this town who'd like to get to know you better, now that you're on your own and maybe can make some time for yourself. People who admire everything you're doing for Chloe. Anyone can see that girl means the world to you."

"She does."

Chloe meant so much to him, he'd put pressure on a third grader yesterday to stop acting up, on the off chance that Fin could drag Chloe back onto a soccer field. Law had felt lousy all morning, remembering how he'd strong-armed Fin, the same way Law's parents had once tried to control him. The unwanted comparison made him want to crawl out of his skin.

He wiped down the counter some more, feeling the itch again. The itch he'd felt as a mixed-up teen, when he'd taken his first drink, thinking it would be strong enough to deaden the emptiness inside him, the way nothing else had.

"Come tonight," Walter said, "and bring Chloe. It's not your thing. I get that. But it's the sort of thing I've seen Chloe do with Libby—except Libby's not exactly worrying about your daughter enjoying herself. Not the way you do. You make the most of every minute you have with Chloe. Do that tonight. Make Pockets something else the two of you enjoy. The place won't be a big deal for long. After a week or two, things will settle down into something everyday, something good I hope will last. Make it something that has nothing to do with your marriage, something that you and Chloe have to look forward to, no matter how much Libby misbehaves."

Law tossed his towel down on the bar. "What gives, Walter?

Since when are you an expert about how other people live their lives?"

"Since you've looked like you're ready to take someone apart the last few weeks or so—and to more people's thinking than just mine. Libby's pushing your buttons left and right, even though you two should be done with all of that. She's still talking trash about you to anyone who'll listen, including Chloe. And that sucks. But it doesn't have to be your whole life. Not if you don't let it. I was just thinking that bringing your daughter by my place tonight might be a nice break for the two of you, in the midst of all the other crap." He glanced back at the dishwasher. "Hunkering down alone and enduring doesn't seem to be helping. Come and meet some new people. Really talk with your neighbors—for you *and* for Chloe."

Law gave his friend his full attention, while he craved his Jameson more than he had in years. "A round of bowling with a bunch of people who may or may not want me there after what they've heard about me isn't going to undo the mistakes I've made."

"What mistakes, man? Your parole was almost a decade ago. You've been a free man trying to do right by your family ever since."

It was on the tip of Law's tongue to say that some mistakes could never be made right.

From out of nowhere came a vision of Kristen's beautiful face again, this time as she'd talked with Chloe yesterday and coaxed a smile from his daughter. What would Chloe's life, his life, have been like all this time if he'd been smart enough and sober enough to have handled things differently with her mother from the start?

"Change things up," Walter said, carrying the conversation on his own. "Give Chloe something good to remember about her time with you this week, after how rough yesterday must have been."

Law pushed away from the counter. "Yesterday?"

Walter took a sip of his drink and tried to look nonchalant. He didn't pull it off.

"So it's all over town." Law could almost taste the smooth bite of whiskey in his mouth. "The scene at the school playground?" When Walter kept fiddling with his drink, Law sighed. "Of course. Merely busting my balls about it would never be enough to satisfy Libby."

"Who cares what your ex is doing or saying about it. What are *you* going to do about it?"

"I'm *not* coming to Pockets tonight."

Walter smiled. "I'm just saying that if the woman's going to be pissed at you whatever you do—and she seems hell-bent on it these days—why not *do* whatever you want? You know?"

Whatever Law wanted . . .

He wanted to see Chloe happy again, playing with her friends because she liked to, doing what she liked best instead of what her mother thought she should. He wanted her glad to be with him again, smiling at him the way she had at Kristen for just a moment yesterday—even if it meant going to a community gathering that at the moment he'd rather lose an arm than endure.

"I don't know, man," he said.

"She'll hang out with her girlfriends. She and Brooke and Summer are giggling together every time I see them around town. You'll get to know folks better. We'll keep you occupied and out of her sight line, if that's what you're worried about. But you'll still be there, being part of her fun night. It'll be good."

Not too long ago, a fun night with Chloe would have been as simple as a trip to the zoo. Now, it wasn't just the divorce confusing her. She was growing up, which was hard enough. The pressure he hadn't been able to keep Libby from applying, her wanting Chloe to want everything the way Libby wanted it, was making things worse. How long would it be before Chloe decided she didn't want anything to do with either of her parents, the way Law had written off his?

"When does everything start?" he asked Walter.

"Six." Walter grinned. "But come by whenever you like, no matter how early. We'll make a fuss over Chloe. She'll have a blast. And we'll find some way to keep you occupied so you don't notice how much fun you're having, too, even with a ton of people you think you don't know around. We wouldn't want to shock your system on your first try at being sociable."

Law made himself smile back, confused at the anticipation flooding him. And not just in hopes of doing something Chloe might enjoy before he dropped her off at Libby's for the night. Wasn't the Pockets opening exactly the sort of thing an administrator at Chandler Elementary would attend?

Call me when you get the chance . . . Kristen's message had said.

It was crazy how much he wanted to do just that. Kristen's maybe being at Walter's opening should be an argument against Law showing up. He didn't need more complications in his life. Except he was also craving the freedom Walter was going on and on about—Law doing something good for himself and his daughter, regardless of how complicated things might get.

"So"—Walter stood and pulled bills from his wallet to cover his drink and Vic's lunch—"I'll see you and Chloe there?"

Law nodded, trying to believe he wouldn't regret it.

***

Kristen was staying at the grand opening for only a few more minutes. She'd arrived even later than she'd expected. Basketball practice had run long. A few of the parents had wanted to chat afterward. She felt hot and sticky after being in the gym, even though it was finally cooling off outside. The temperature might dip into the fifties overnight.

She really shouldn't have stayed at Pockets as long as she had. She'd pretty much been telling herself to leave for close to an hour—since the moment she'd arrived. But each time she tried, her attention would stray across the café from where she was standing, to the bowling lanes and a familiar face she hadn't exactly been surprised to see there. Not that she'd known what to do with him or her excitement at seeing him.

And each time she'd looked, Law's gaze had been fixed on her as well.

He was leaning against the wall closest to the lane where Chloe and Summer and Brooke were bowling. He'd been talking off and on with Rick Harper, the owner of the bar where Law worked. And he'd appeared to be completely out of his element amidst the happy-go-lucky family fun rocking around him—except for when he looked at Kristen. Then she could almost feel him settle into whatever he was thinking about her or yesterday morning or them. And each time, the safe distance between them had seemed to shrink, even though neither of them had moved.

He leaned down to say something to Chloe, who'd transformed back into a laughing, happy girl, while she hung out with the same friends Daphne said had been giving the kid such a hard time since yesterday. Law nodded in agreement to whatever his daughter had asked, and then Chloe launched herself into hugging him.

Kristen's eyes misted at the touching sight.

She turned back to Julia Davis, who was keeping the café counter stocked with baked goodies donated by the pastry chef who worked at Lavender Bistro on Main Street. It was now or never. Kristen needed to get herself out the door and on her way, before she shamelessly threw herself at Law in front of the entire town.

Maybe it's time . . . Mallory had said. *Do a better job of figuring out how you feel about him . . .*

Figure it out? It didn't take a genius to know Kristen had already risked too much where Law was concerned. She needed to follow up about Fin and be on her way.

"Have you seen Marsha or Joe?" Kristen asked. The Dixons' brood of foster kids should be crawling all over the grand opening.

Julia handed over a paper cone overflowing with the cotton candy that one of her staff was spinning. She'd insisted that Kristen try it, even though Kristen was a bit of a fanatic about eating healthy. *Everyone eats junk food tonight* had been Julia's not-taking-no-for-an-answer response.

She shook her head. "Joe called. They're not going to make it."

Something in the other woman's smile had Kristen stepping closer so she could be heard over the music a DJ was blaring through his speakers. Usher had just started rapping "Yeah!"

"Is it Fin?" she asked.

Julia nodded.

Kristen's heart sank. "He's not home yet?"

Julia shook her head. "They don't want to call the police. He's been gone this long before. But Joe's been all over town looking for him, and there's no sign of the boy. They're starting to get worried."

"Of course they are." And if they called the authorities, Family Services would be notified. Fin would likely be back in the system by morning. "I feel terrible."

"It's not your fault." Julia sighed at the dubious look Kristen shot her. "I talked with Marsha after Joe put her on the phone. She told me what happened at the school yesterday, and that you were just trying to help, and that Fin's been acting out from the beginning and seems forever on the verge of running off again. Don't blame yourself for trying to get Chloe's dad to coach him. It was worth a shot."

Kristen nodded, to be polite. She picked off a piece of cotton candy and popped it into her mouth. It melted, and it should have felt like childhood trips to the circus and fair, where she'd always begged for the pink or blue confection. But instead of feeling nostalgic for one of the few happy memories she had from her youth, she felt like kicking herself for how she'd bungled things for Marsha and Joe and Fin.

"You do too much of that, you know," Julia said. "You take on causes no one else would, and you blame yourself when things spin sideways and something slips out of your control. You've been torturing yourself about the Wilmington shooting since January. Now it's Fin and Chloe. You can't keep pouring your heart into saving the world, thinking it's all up to you, whether or not people decide to save themselves."

"Sometimes people don't want to be saved," a deep voice said from their right.

Kristen jumped.

She turned to find Law standing there, instead of staying safely across the bowling center with his daughter, where he belonged.

"Some people?" she asked with a rasp, the sticky sweet residue in her mouth refusing to let the words come out right. Or was it the realization all over again that big, tall, rough Law Beaumont—in addition to being a teddy bear with his daughter—had the most beautiful blue eyes and the longest, softest eyelashes Kristen had ever seen?

"Maybe some people are just lost causes," he said, "no matter how much you try to save them. If I'd known you didn't realize that, I'd have walked away yesterday as soon as you started talking to me about Fin."

"I see Walter waving at me over by the arcade." Julia slipped away.

Kristen glared after her friend, for both the desertion and the innocent smile Julia cast over her shoulder. She turned her attention back to the intense man who'd walked all the way across the bowling center to be intense beside her.

"So, you're an expert on lost causes?" she asked.

"My ex-wife seems to think so." The right corner of Law's mouth curled upward. "Besides her, there was my parole officer, and before both of them, my parents. The list of folks who've given up on me is far longer than the ones who've written Fin off. He's still got time. Maybe everyone just needs to back off and let him figure things out on his own."

Law was putting her in her place for dragging him into the Dixons' situation. She deserved it. But he was also breaking her heart, talking so casually about the setbacks in his own life that helped him identify with Fin. His thin smile looked almost painful while he catalogued his faults. She longed to trace the contours of his mouth with her finger, to see if she could coax something softer out of him.

"So you think Fin is a lost cause?" she asked.

"I didn't say that."

"Then what did you say?"

He shook his head, looking down at her—actually looking *down* at her, because he was so tall. She couldn't remember the last time that had happened. She couldn't remember the last time she'd cared enough to notice whether or not a man she was talking with was her height or taller.

"This is a really bad idea," he said, "both of us being here, hoping the other one would be here, too."

She nodded. She didn't bother to pretend he wasn't the main reason she'd come. She could have called the Dixons to ask about Fin. She could have waited until the morning for their update. But despite Mallory's warning, maybe because of it, Kristen hadn't been able to stay away from Pockets.

She and Law were standing a respectable distance apart. But having the entire bowling center between them hadn't been far enough. They were getting closer. Neither one of them was going to back off this time, good idea or not. She could feel it, thinking about everything she thought she understood about this man's past and everything she didn't. But there was so much goodness in him, it pulled her in every time.

"You wanted to talk with me?" he asked.

She blanked on the question. It took her several seconds to remember the voice mail she'd left.

"About Chloe," she said with a start. "She had a rough morning at school. But she seems to have rallied."

"For now." Law grinned. Or was it a grimace? "She refused to talk with me today, until I mentioned coming here. All is well in her life again, at least for the next hour or so."

"Have you heard from Fin?"

"Heard what?"

"He's not reacting much better than Chloe to me pushing you at him." Kristen swallowed, choking on the cotton candy sweetness in her mouth. "He's run away, actually. I never should have . . ."

Law reached for her. The warmth of his fingers brushed the side of her neck. He folded down the collar of the crisply ironed oxford shirt she'd thrown on with a pair of jeans for basketball practice, and then his hand fell away.

"You did the right thing," he said. "I . . . I really hope he comes back and settles in at the Dixons', so he can play. I may have put too much pressure on him yesterday. I was pushing him to talk Chloe into playing, too. When I get a chance, I'll make sure he knows that's my problem, not his. I'll coach the kid, regardless of whether my daughter wants to be on the team."

"Oh . . ."

Kristen was suddenly blinking back tears. She wanted to reach for him, too. She didn't. This part of them—the Chloe and Fin part—was still her job, regardless of her growing feelings for Law.

"That's . . ." she fumbled. "That's wonderful. And I really do hope you can bring Chloe around. She needs something steady right now. She needs . . . you, so much."

"Yeah." He nodded. "I need her, too."

An awkward pause stretched between them. This was it. Were they going to be anything but *this*? Did she dare? Did he?

"I need to ask you a personal question," he said, "if that's okay."

"Um . . ." How did she form a complete thought, let alone speak, when her heart had stopped beating?

"Can you tell me if you'd have kept staring at me all night from over here, the way you've been staring at me on Sundays from across the park? Or would you have worked up the nerve to talk to me again? It's important, Kristen. I need to know before I push this any harder. And believe me, I want to push just as hard as you'll let me. Maybe a lot harder than I should. But I can't seem to stop. If it weren't for Fin, if it were only about this thing between us that we've been avoiding, would you have worked up the nerve to get closer to me?"

Chapter Six

Law was frozen, waiting, hoping, telling himself he was a fool for saying and asking what he had.

He watched Kristen swallow again, hard. She gave a shaky nod, *Yes*, and he found himself starting to believe, for the first time in a long time, that something good just might have found its way into his life again.

Music swirled through his thoughts as he stared down at one of the most beautiful creatures he'd ever seen. Rock music this time. Metal-band stuff that throbbed and overwhelmed, and promised to make a girl yours, so she'd never leave you.

"I've been telling myself a lot of things today," she said. Her voice was shredded—maybe with embarrassment. Maybe the blush on her cheeks meant something totally different. "Mostly that you'd been so pissed by my meddling yesterday that you'd never talk to me again. So what did it matter what I wanted? Or how much I wanted to talk with you again, just to apologize, even before I heard about Chloe's difficulties in class and left you that voice mail. When you didn't call back . . ."

"I wasn't ready to deal with what you might say. What I might say." He still wasn't ready. But he was there. That had to count for something.

"What . . . what would you have said?"

He'd wanted to say that each time he'd caught sight of her in the park, tall and lean and amazing-looking, he'd wanted to know if all of that confidence and composure and perfection tasted as good as he'd imagined. He'd wanted to tell her that especially since the divorce he'd lain awake nights thinking about her, when he couldn't sleep because he was worried about Chloe and pissed at Libby, or just wishing he'd made the kind of choices that would have made a life with someone like Kristen possible. He'd wanted her to know that she'd become somewhere clean and free for his thoughts to escape to. Somewhere nondestructive, maybe a little addictive, but always healing. That she'd become a harmless fantasy he was dying to make a reality.

"I'd have asked," he answered, instead of overwhelming her with the rest, "if yesterday morning was really only about the kids. I totally understand if it was. For the record, I respect what you're trying to do with Fin, and how kind you've been to Chloe, even if ambushing me to get me to coach wasn't the smartest move. You might have noticed I don't respond well to being cornered like that. But if that's all this was for you, if the kids are all you called about, I'll walk back over to the bowling alleys, and we'll pretend none of the rest happened. We'll politely stare at each other from time to time. People will talk if they want. What do I care what anyone thinks about me? But if there's something else here for you, too . . . We should probably try to figure that out."

Law was breathing hard, as if he'd been sprinting. It was more than he'd said at any one time, to anyone, including Libby and Chloe, since moving to town.

Kristen seemed to almost melt before his eyes. Her expression softened. Her lips parted, just enough for him to see her bubblegum-pink tongue. Instead of answering, she was staring at his mouth, then up at his eyes, drinking him in as if she needed to. The way, while he'd been watching her from across Pockets for the last hour, he'd suddenly needed to be beside her, no matter how much he'd warned himself to take things slow.

She jerked when he reached for her hand. He wrapped his fingers around hers, trapping her, except she wasn't trying to get away.

"You're right." She lifted her chin, her expression honest, a challenge. Damn, he liked that. "This isn't a very good idea."

"This is trouble." And surprise, surprise. Chandler Elementary's ultra-professional soon-to-be principal liked herself a little trouble.

He stepped closer, telling himself that he was a free man, and as far as he knew she wasn't dating anyone. They were just getting to know each other. Perfectly harmless. He needed to be sure if she was sure, before he let himself want more. But for now, he needed to be closer.

"What has a woman like you . . ." His free hand brushed against the softness of Kristen's long sleeves. Hers came to rest against the muscles of his arm. Totally innocent. Sexy as hell. ". . . who goes out of her way to do everything right all the time, been doing all these years, staring at a wrong man like me?"

Her eyes lit up even more. Her lips curled confidently.

"Maybe I see a lot of good in an intelligent man like you"—

her fascination with his mouth tortured him some more—"no matter how determined you seem to be to lead with your past and let people believe the worst."

"Right about now, I'm inclined to let you believe just about anything you want."

For an *intelligent* man, he'd officially lost what was left of his mind.

They were in public. His daughter and her friends were laughing it up across the room, and who knew where Julia Davis had gotten herself off to so she could act like she wasn't watching everything he and Kristen did and said, along with the rest of the adults.

But the Pockets opening was fading away from him. His world was narrowing like it used to when he'd latch onto a new song that would consume everything until it was done with him. All he could see or feel or hear now was Kristen.

"See something you like, Law?" a high-pitched, slightly slurred female voice said.

It echoed with a bitterness that had been Law's constant companion for most of the last ten years.

He closed his eyes, mentally kicking himself. Of course Libby had shown up tonight. Of course it had been to give him hell. When Kristen tried to draw her hand away, he held tight. He inched back from her, but he didn't let go. He grimaced and squeezed her fingers, silently apologizing.

Walter had been right. Law had to start living a life with Chloe that transcended Libby's jealousy and unhappiness. He couldn't protect his daughter and make sure she thrived, living the life of a hermit because otherwise her mother might make trouble. What Libby had been doing since she'd heard about his visit to Chandler—not just bitching to him over the phone, but texting and calling Chloe and instigating a flurry of rumors about him and Kristen as if they'd somehow done something wrong—had to stop.

"You've met my ex-wife, I presume?" he asked Kristen.

"Of course." Kristen's chin went up again. She set down her cotton candy. She firmly removed her hand from his and offered it to Libby. "It's a pleasure to see you again."

"I just bet it is." Libby didn't shake.

Behind her were Brooke's mom and Summer's mom, and behind them were the girls and Chloe, who'd walked away from their bowling to watch the show.

Libby redirected her anger from Kristen to Law. "When I heard you'd made an ass out of yourself yesterday, doing this sort of thing in the middle of the school playground, even I didn't think you were stupid enough to try it again someplace like Pockets."

Kristen did a double take between Libby and Law. "Mrs. Beaumont, I assure you that there was an official reason for me to ask Law to meet with me yesterday. I—"

"About Chloe?" Libby craned her neck so she could stare daggers up at Kristen. "I have primary custody of my daughter. If you have anything to discuss about her schoolwork, then—"

"Yes, ma'am. But this matter didn't concern Chloe, at least not directly. I wanted—"

"You don't need to explain anything," Law said.

"But—"

"Stop picking a fight, Libby," he said to his ex. "You should know by now that doesn't work with me. I assure you, it's not going to work with someone as levelheaded as Kristen. Let's step outside so everyone can get back to Walter and Julia's party, and you can rip me a new one about whatever you want—in private."

"I *want* my daughter's father not to be panting over her assistant principal in the middle of school." Libby checked behind her to find her two best friends with their arms crossed and their expressions set in matching glares. "I *want* him not to be pawing over one of Chloe's school faculty in a public place, with her and her friends and everyone else watching, because my girl can't look away any more than the rest of the town can. God, Law, at any moment I was expecting the DJ to start playing a sappy love song. Could you be more indiscreet? If you want to do her, at least have the decency to take her over to the EZ Sleep for an hour."

Law did step away from Kristen then.

He moved toward his ex with a burning need to put his hands around her neck. He dug his fists into his pockets to keep himself from making an even bigger mistake than he had the day Libby had told him she was knocked up and he'd taken her to a justice of the peace and married her—instead of doing whatever he had to, *including* crawling back to his parents, to take Chloe away from Libby then, and raise his daughter on his own.

"You need to shut your mouth," he ground out, his voice hard and unforgiving, just the way she liked to describe him to anyone who'd listen. "We need to step outside, so we can take care of this *discreetly*. You're making a scene, Libby, and it's not going to do any good. The divorce is over. The judge made his ruling. You have no claim on my life anymore, and I'm not the one whose behavior is hurting our daughter. You're—"

"I'm what?" She cocked her head sideways, daring him to say more. She glanced back at Chloe this time. She was cowering beside her friends, as she hung on every word Law and Libby said.

Law braced his hands on his hips. He stared at his boots. He counted to ten and reminded himself that no matter what he wanted, no matter what he needed, traumatizing Chloe wasn't a price he was willing to pay. Libby always found a way to hurt their child, every time she went after him. That seemed to be the point lately—if Libby even had a point anymore. And that was what he needed to stop first. Dealing with the rest of his ex's increasingly poor choices would have to wait.

"Outside," he said between clenched teeth. "You're drawing a crowd."

"*I'm* drawing a crowd?" Libby's voice grew louder. "If I hadn't shown up once I heard you'd brought her to the opening, thinking I could save you a trip and pick Chloe up here, I'm guessing you'd have Kristen laid out on one of Walter's pool tables by now. Have you lost your senses, Law, or have you been drinking the afternoon away, the way you boozed your way through our marriage?"

He saw red.

He grabbed her arm. "I haven't had a drop to drink since before Chloe was born, and you know it. That's enough."

"Dad?" Chloe asked.

Law glanced her way, to see his brother, of all people, emerge from the crowd of onlookers. Dan hugged Chloe to his side.

"Let your momma and daddy talk, honey," he said. "Come have some pizza with Sally and your aunt and me. Then we'll check out the dunking booth. I hear the Perry boys are up next. And Josh is just a grade ahead of you at Chandler, right?"

Chloe nodded at her uncle. Her attention didn't move away from Law and Libby. Dan locked gazes with Law, his expression hard, judging, disappointed . . . just like old times.

"Bring your friends with you," he said to Chloe. "We won't stop until both Perry boys are soaked head to toe. Maybe we can get their daddy to give it a go, too. Brian owes me big-time for that trip to Charleston he bid out from under me at the Founders Day silent auction."

Chloe hesitated. She let Dan lead her away. After a few seconds, Brooke and Summer took off after them, whispering like mad, casting glances over their shoulders at Law and Libby and Kristen.

"Let's go," Law said, half dragging Libby away from her own friends and toward the door. And for once he didn't care what she had to say about it or how loudly she said it.

"Turn me loose," she yelled.

"You first." He pushed her through Pockets' double doors and headed around the building to the alley that ran alongside it, keeping a tight grip on his ex the whole way. "When are you going to stop this, Libby? When are you going to finally be satisfied? When you've made sure our daughter hates us both as much as you hate me?"

***

Kristen shouldn't be there.

This wasn't her family, it wasn't her drama, and Chloe wasn't her child to protect. Not to mention that Kristen showing up at Pockets had been the catalyst for the horrible scene between the Beaumonts that half the town had just witnessed.

She most definitely shouldn't have followed Law and Libby out of the bowling center. Just as earlier she shouldn't have let herself get lost in Law's touch, or the honest and downright endearing things he'd been saying before Libby interrupted them. She shouldn't be standing at the corner of the building now, watching the man confront his ex, hearing things nobody but the two of them should ever hear.

But she couldn't walk away, any more than she'd been able to resist Law inside. If she was going to own her feelings for the man, it was time to own them, including backing him up with Libby.

This is trouble . . . Law had said about the two of them, while he'd held her hand and touched her arm, his body language and his voice communicating how much he'd like the kind of trouble they could make together. Her defenses against him had bottomed out so completely, she wasn't sure how she'd ever rebuild them. How did she walk away, when he'd just unknowingly given her something her oblivious parents had never figured out how to?

He'd wanted her. It was just that simple, and that life-changing—to feel wanted so completely. What woman could resist having that kind of need focused on her?

"Let me go!" Libby shouted. "Or I'll call my lawyer."

Her voice sounded not quite right, Kristen realized—in a not-quite-right way that Kristen had no problem identifying. She was, after all, the daughter of a woman who'd almost always been drinking—not quite drunk, but most of the time too far gone to be completely careful about the things she said or did.

Law let Libby go. "I have your lawyer on speed dial. I'll call him for you. What do you want now? Tell me what it's going to take to get you to stop this."

"I want it all." Libby's tone was close to hysterical, each word louder than the last, making Kristen wince.

They might be outside. But they were next to one of Pockets' side exits. The walls of the strip mall the bowling center had been built into were likely paper thin.

"There's nothing left to take," Law said.

He'd rammed his hands into his pockets again. His expression was unreadable. His body looked relaxed, nonconfrontational, in control. But when he glanced at Kristen, there was hell in his eyes.

"That's where you're wrong." Libby pointed a finger at his abdomen. "Your brother's rich. Your family's rich. Where's my piece of that?" The top of her head barely reached his chest, even though her brunette hair was teased into a frenzy that rivaled the crazy swirls of Julia's cotton candy. To emphasize her point, she poked Law with her manicured fingernail. "Dan was right there, stepping in to protect Chloe tonight. Wasn't that sweet? Even after the shitty way you've treated him, your brother would do anything for you and our kid. *Anything.* But you never loved him either, did you? Just like you never loved me. Well, if you want to keep seeing Chloe as much as you are, and you want to whore around town with Ms. Thing over there while you've got my daughter with you, then maybe you better buddy it up with good ol' Dan, and see if he'll finance whatever it's going to take to make sure I can swallow watching you leave me behind for the first skirt to come along before the ink's dry on our divorce!"

"You're . . ." Law peered closer, into Libby's eyes.

Then he hung his head. He took another step back from his ex-wife. Not that the woman still looked inclined to get away from him. It seemed to Kristen that Libby had Law precisely where she wanted him.

"I loved you," Law said, "at least, I tried to. A lot more and for a lot longer than you ever tried to love me, Libby. And Dan's got nothing to do with this. *You* threw it all away. You did this, not me, because you never trusted me; you never really wanted me. I'm not even sure you know how to love or be happy, but you sure as hell don't know how to be a wife, or even a mother, if this is how you think I'm going to let you keep treating me and our daughter."

"You don't know the first thing about being happy either, you son of a bitch," said the woman who acted like a paragon of motherhood when her friends or anyone else from the community was watching. "At least not with me. It was never about me, was it? None of it. Maybe you've just been biding your time in Chandlerville all these years . . . If you wanted Kristen so badly, why did you stay with me as long as you did, huh?"

"You're the one who asked for the divorce, Libby. I was committed to us from the first moment I heard Chloe was on the way. And then I held Chloe in my arms, once I was paroled. From that moment on, my heart was hers. And yours, if you'd decided anywhere along the line that figuring out how to love, no matter how much both our parents screwed us over, was worth your time."

Kristen pressed her fingers to her lips and blinked to keep her tears from falling. She'd never heard a parent's unconditional love for a child described more beautifully. And she'd never seen anything more disturbing than the toxic impatience that had washed over Libby's features.

"Love?" she asked. "*You* know how to love? Is that what you call living in the same town as your brother all these years, and never once trying to make things right with him?"

"You don't want things to be right with Dan, Libby. All you've ever wanted from my brother was his money."

"And you wouldn't even let me keep that, would you?"

"You never should have taken it in the first place. I asked you not to. You lied to me and said you wouldn't."

"He kept me from having to work three dead-end jobs while our infant was in day care, while you were on the inside."

"And I've worked my ass off ever since to take care of you both. Dan's money is off-limits now, just like it was when I was in prison. Leave him out of this."

"You better hope I don't." She lifted her hand and rubbed two fingers against her thumb, as if she were brushing paper money together. "My daughter deserves the best things and the best friends and the best connections Dan's money can buy. And you're going to get them for her and me. If you want me to sit by and watch you chase another woman all over town, then you're going to pay." She glanced at Kristen. Her eyes were glassy but piercing. "I've got connections, even without a judge. I can make both your lives a living hell. Don't you forget that."

Law twisted Libby's arm behind her back and pulled her onto her toes, her body flush with his. "That's enough. You're out of control, and don't think I don't know why. I can smell it on your breath. I don't know how it could have taken me so long to figure out why you've been more off the deep end than usual. But you're going to stop it, now. Stop embarrassing yourself and our daughter in public. Stop coming after me. And don't you dare drag Dan or his family or Kristen into this. You understand me?"

The threat in Law's voice, no matter how justified, took Kristen off guard. Despite his size, the rough edges to his personality, and his reputation as an ex-con, she had known him to be a gentle, loving man. Even to Fin, when he hadn't wanted to talk with the boy at first. But he was something else now. His energy had shifted into something threatening that should be given a lot of space.

Kristen stepped closer instead.

"Law?" At his side, she was reaching for his arm, ignoring Libby's glare, when the bowling center's side door opened and Dan stepped out.

"You three need to keep it down out here." Law's brother glanced at Kristen briefly. He zeroed in on his brother and ex-sister-in-law. "Half of Chandlerville is on the other side of that door, trying not to listen to your shouting. The other half practically has their ears plastered to the wall, trying to make out everything you say—while Chloe's acting like she doesn't mind that her girlfriends are eating up the scene you're making like it's candy."

It was the most amazing thing to watch, how from one second to the next Law forgot about Libby, let her go, and squared off against Dan, fully prepared to vent his frustration at his brother. While Libby turned docile and sweet, smiling at Dan and clutching her hands in front of her, her eyes as soft as a fawn's in a Disney feature.

"Oh, my," she simpered. "What was I thinking? I don't know *what* came over me. I had no idea we were being so loud, Dan. Thank you so much for letting us know. Is Chloe okay?"

Dan had always struck Kristen as the passive, conservative type, except for the one time he'd taken on the school board along with several other parents, demanding reform after Sally had been one of the kids who'd witnessed—and very nearly been injured in—January's shooting. The outrage and disgust Kristen had seen in Dan's temperament at the board meeting was back—and to his credit, it was aimed solely at Libby.

"You've got to be kidding me, lady," he spat.

He studied her carefully made-up face and hair, and then her camp shirt and chic tailored pants, rounded out by three-inch gold platform sandals. All of it was in stark contrast to the simple golf shirt and jeans Law wore.

"I don't know what you're after," Dan continued. "But I know for certain that my niece's feelings and well-being aren't even on your radar." He smiled when Libby stiffened in outrage. He peered into her eyes. Only then did he look to Law. "Is she safe to drive?"

"Give me your keys," Law said to his ex.

He pinned his gaze on Libby, not his brother.

Libby hugged her tote bag to her side. "You think you're some kind of an expert about other people, just because you're a drunk and went to AA and have everyone convinced you haven't stepped a toe out of line since?"

"I'm sick and tired of this." Dan grabbed her purse and dragged it off her arm. He glared back and forth between Law and Libby. "All of it. You two are torturing a little girl, because you can't deal with the mess you've made out of your own lives."

The first thing he pulled from Libby's bag looked like a flask. He tossed it to Law, who had the reflexes to catch it out of the air without looking away from his ex-wife. He stuffed the thing into the back pocket of his jeans. Dan plucked up Libby's keys next, then handed her back her purse. She snatched it to her chest, and then she turned to Kristen, of all people.

"You saw them," she insisted. "You saw them take my personal property and invade my privacy. My lawyer will be calling you, and you better not be considering lying to him. I assure you, you don't want to join my husband on the court's bad side."

Kristen considered the other woman's threat.

Then she considered kicking Libby's ass, the way she knew Law was dying to.

Then she smiled her sweetest, emptiest smile—she'd learned it from a master, her mother—and shook her head. "I saw Law and his brother making certain you and Chloe get home safely."

"What do you know about what I do or don't do for my daughter?"

"I know I've thought I smelled alcohol on your breath more than once at school functions this year."

Law's attention resettled onto Kristen. Something in his expression said he realized she was bluffing—that she was guessing

Libby hadn't waited until tonight to start drinking—but that Kristen was backing him up and forcing Libby to back down at the same time. She watched him inhale deeply, soundlessly, as if he were taking her words deep inside him.

"And if your lawyer or the judge were to ask me questions about what just happened," she continued to Libby, "I'd be happy to make a statement about *everything* I've seen and heard tonight—as well as each and every time I've run into you at school and wondered if you'd been drinking that day, too."

"Let's go," Dan said. "My car's around front. I'll take you home. Law can bring Chloe over later. She doesn't need you back inside, doing even more damage than you already have."

He left without waiting for a response. Libby cut a killing look at Kristen and then Law. She headed after Dan, digging in her bag for her cell phone, pressing a button and putting it to her ear.

Kristen watched Law, dazed and worried and wondering how they'd gotten from the intimacy of the moments they'd shared inside to this dark place, with him suddenly feeling light-years away.

He was looking at the ground, his hands in his pockets again so she couldn't wrap her fingers around his in support, the way she longed to.

"I should go check on her," he said to the dirt beneath them.

"Chloe's with her friends." Kristen didn't pretend that she thought he was worried about Libby. "If this morning was any indication, she'll be acting like nothing happened, and that the three of us don't exist, while Summer and Brooke harass her for as long as they find it entertaining. She's going to keep acting like she doesn't care until she's alone, and then everything that's eating her from the inside out will be all she'll be able to think about . . ."

Kristen sucked in air so fast, it made her dizzy.

Or maybe it was the wave of mortification crashing over her, because her own childhood memories were becoming mixed up in all of this.

"I'm sorry," she said, not expecting him to understand—and she'd rather die than explain. But hadn't she just witnessed his deeply personal exchange with Libby? She brushed her hand down his arm. "You're not the only one who didn't grow up with the kind of loving home people in a place like Chandlerville think everyone has known."

"Your parents?" Law asked, accepting her revelation as if it were nothing, identifying with her, the same as he had inside.

He seemed so distant and solitary and apart from a lot of what happened around him, *because* he felt so much of it, she suspected. Because he needed *not* to feel, perhaps, only he couldn't stop himself. Which was likely why drinking had become a problem when he was younger. Now he coped by not giving away too much. Not letting anything in that he didn't want to handle. Not getting close enough to feel more than he could—except close was what he'd said he wanted with her.

"My mother," she admitted. It was more than she'd shared with anyone, even Mallory. But with Law, it suddenly didn't feel like enough. "Most everyone in the town I grew up in thought she was a good mother. My father did, when he was home long enough to notice, which wasn't often. The problem was, she was good at hiding her addictions, her excess. Too good. No one realized she was throwing her *fabulous* life and my childhood away, drinking and taking prescription drugs and living it up with her latest lover-slash-dealer-slash-knight in shining armor."

"Libby's evidently good at hiding, too." Law nodded, acknowledging Kristen's past with an easy acceptance that floored her. "I had no idea my ex was drinking again. She was off the wagon the year before we moved here. She promised me she'd sober up for good if I gave us a fresh start somewhere like Chandlerville. I wouldn't have put up with all this if I'd known . . ."

"Of course you wouldn't have."

"We promised each other, when we both dried out before I was sentenced, when she was first pregnant and we'd gotten married, that we'd stay clean and do the best we could for our child, no matter how hard it was going to be for a while. And she's tried. I know what you heard just now must make it sound like—"

"It sounds like you've done the best you could, Law."

His fists were still dug so deeply into his jeans, it was a wonder the seams hadn't ripped. His expression had hardened to a mask of control. Gone was the sensitive, charming, almost playful man he'd been with her inside. In front of Kristen was someone in pain, a father at the end of his rope who desperately needed something to hold on to.

"We were both drunks when we met," he said. "We were just kids, but we were full-on addicts already." He sighed. One of his hands emerged and took hers, his touch so light it was like a dream. "I really did try to make it work. I did everything I could to make up for the fact that Libby and I were never a good match. It was fun while we dated, how careless and irresponsible and out-of-control she could be. She was the life of every party . . ."

"And then the party stopped?" Kristen asked, empathizing more than she wanted to. "When I was thirteen, my mom took her party on the road, with Mr. Wonderful number six or seven, and she never looked back. My dad hardly missed her. Then again, his work for the State Department kept him out of the country so much, he never really noticed if I was there or not. As long as the housekeeper didn't complain about me, it wasn't worth his time to notice—except that I paled in comparison to my flamboyant, petite, exotically beautiful mother. I was too much like him, as it turned out. Too tall, too plain, too—"

"You're gorgeous, Kristen." Law squeezed her hand. He brought it to his lips and kissed her fingers. "Inside and out, you're drop-dead gorgeous and generous and kind—and so fiercely aggressive when you need to be, you take my breath away. What you said about Libby's drinking . . ."

"Yeah, that was a bluff."

"But now I pretty much know that tonight wasn't the first drink, and that she's blown her sobriety. And I owe that to you. The things she said about Dan and my family . . ." He nodded after his brother and ex-wife. "It's complicated, my brother and me. It's about our past, long before I hooked up with Libby. But lately she's decided to make it about—"

"Money?" Kristen said for him. "That's pretty much how my dad and both sets of my grandparents tried to control me once I was old enough to get away from them. They had a lot of money. They tried to make me believe I was nothing without it or them. And all I had to do to get it was become whatever I had to, to fit into their world. I couldn't have cared less."

Law nodded.

And then he shook his head.

"You didn't just get away," he said. "You've triumphed. Look at your basketball, at what you've done for Chandlerville and the elementary school. This place is just as lucky to have you as your family would have been, if they'd bothered to be what you'd needed to stay."

"I . . ." She wiped at her eyes, hating the vulnerable puddle of memories she'd let herself become. But she was mesmerized by his admiration, too. "I don't know why I told you all of that. I don't usually ramble like this. I'm not making a bit of sense..."

Law brought her hand to his lips again.

"You're doing all right," he said against her skin. He was looking at her again in that hungry way of his, a look that could consume her if she let it. Then he gazed past her. "I should see if Dan needs help with Libby."

He let Kristen go and stepped away.

It was all she could do to watch him leave without insinuating herself further into his personal problems, or asking him what she was supposed to do now, after what he'd said earlier and what had just happened with Libby—and how he'd somehow in a single conversation managed to ease for her a lifetime of her feeling invisible to the people who'd raised her. The man's family was imploding—still—and she'd played a prominent role in tonight's disaster. Once he was certain Libby was on her way, he had to try to explain to his understandably upset daughter what had happened. Pacifying Kristen's insecurities was the least of his worries.

He stopped before he rounded the corner of the building and turned back.

"You're an amazing woman," he said. "You let me hear that you're blaming yourself for a speck of what's gone on tonight, and you and I are going to have to talk again. And God knows where that would take us."

"I've put you and Chloe in an awful bind," she forced out.

"I put myself in this bind a long time ago." His voice hardened. "Libby wants someone to pay for the disappointments in her life. I have to make sure that's no longer going to be me or Chloe. This isn't about you, Kristen. Don't take on my problems, because that's what you've done your entire life to make up for whatever damage you're still carrying around from what your parents did to you. You can't fix this by worrying yourself sick, just like you couldn't fix Fin yesterday no matter how much you put on the line to get me to help him."

Kristen could feel her heartbeat all over her body. She shouldn't say it. She absolutely shouldn't say it. But how could she not, when it sounded as if he was saying good-bye?

"I'm not trying to fix you or anything else," she said. "I'm not expecting anything from you, and I know you need to do what you need to do now, without thinking about me. I'm just trying to care, that's all. Like you care, a lot more than you want people to know. I see that every time I see you with Chloe. I saw it in how you handled Fin, even if you talked to him at first just as an excuse to get away from me."

"What?" Law stepped toward her. He stopped. He stopped way too soon. "What did you see?"

"You never stopped caring, Law, no matter how many times you might have tried. Trust me, I know what it looks like when a person cares only about himself. That's not you. No matter what's happened in the past"—and Kristen didn't give a damn about his prison sentence or the mistakes he'd made before he'd grown up enough to make something more for himself—"you're a good man doing right by his daughter and his ex-wife. You're fighting a hell of a lot harder to do right by both of them than a lot of people would."

She paused, expecting him to say something, needing him to in a pathetic way she despised. When he didn't, she accepted that it was time to bow out. It was past time. But he seemed so alone, standing there as if her words had fractured something inside him. He couldn't seem to move now. So Kristen did, toward the parking lot.

She slowed on her way past him, holding herself still for the few seconds it took to say, "I think you're amazing, too. If you ever need to talk with someone who has just as hard a time trusting her feelings as you do yours, give me a call."

Chapter Seven

"You're late," Libby bitched, after opening the door to Law and Dan and Chloe. "My daughter's supposed to be returned to me by eight on Thursday nights so I can deprogram her and get her ready for school the next day. I've had dinner waiting for almost an hour, since you forced me to come home without her."

"She ate at Walter and Julia's place," Law said.

"And let's discuss *why* she's an hour late getting home," Dan said, "namely because you were in no condition to drive her yourself."

"Because you refused to let me." Libby gave Law's brother a scathing once-over, her attempt to charm him history.

Dan looked as angry and ready to take someone apart as he had around back at Pockets, before he'd driven Libby home. He'd insisted on following Law and Chloe back over to Libby's, after Law had found Chloe inside and tried to speak with her about what had happened, not that she'd said a word in return. Dan had wanted to be there when Law dropped his daughter off at the house, in case there was another altercation and Law needed a witness. Law's easygoing, never-step-a-toe-over-the-line older brother, who'd given Law space since helping him relocate his family to Chandlerville, had looked ready to fight it out if Law resisted.

He looked even more eager to do violence now.

Law gritted his teeth. He kept his own temper under control for his daughter's sake. How could Libby have started drinking again? How could he not have noticed?

"Whatever you do when you're alone is up to you," Dan said to Libby. "But from here on out, what you do with my niece is my business, too. This is the final straw. You're out of control. Knock it off, or—"

"Or what?" Libby tilted her head. She reached out, her fingers smoothing provocatively over Dan's half-undone necktie, more in control of herself than she'd been at Pockets, but still too bold, too brash, too reckless—exactly the way she'd been when she and Law first hooked up.

Dan took a queasy step away from her.

"Or we'll find a family court judge," Law said for his brother, "who's more inclined to see reason than the one your lawyer's dug up."

We.

The word slammed into him. From the stunned look on Dan's face, he'd been rocked by it, too.

"I'll be in my room doing homework," Chloe muttered.

She didn't hug Law or Libby or say good-bye to her uncle. She slipped away too quickly for anyone to stop her. She looked so fiercely fragile, Law was afraid to reach for her. Not that Libby had made an effort to even acknowledge their child. She never seemed to these days, unless she was in public and she was playing for the crowd.

She and Chloe had been close once. Even though Libby and Law had never quite fit, Libby had loved her daughter the best she could. She'd petted and pampered her and dressed her like a doll and wanted to do every girly thing with Chloe that Law could afford for them to do—to compensate, Law eventually realized, for everything Libby had missed with her own single mother, who'd gotten pregnant as a teenager, too, and had worked herself to death to support her child on her own.

Libby had tried to give Chloe the kind of motherly love Libby had never known. But then she'd relapsed back into her disease, and her world became dominated by a constant need for attention and reassurance. She'd promised the move here was the answer. Chandlerville was a beautiful place where she'd never thought someone who'd grown up in a trailer park could live, she said. It had been exactly what she'd needed to get right and stay that way for the daughter she loved with all her heart.

When was Law going to learn that the only person Libby would ever care about with all her heart was Libby?

Law caught a whiff of mint or mouthwash or breath spray, or whatever she'd used to freshen up, likely as soon as she'd heard his truck and Dan's Mercedes turn into the driveway. It hadn't been enough to mask the lingering notes of vodka on her breath.

Had she had more to drink since she'd gotten home? She sounded more in control now. Law had no legal grounds to challenge her or to try to keep Chloe with him. All he could do was leave his daughter in his ex-wife's care and trust Libby to do the right thing. It was killing him.

Dan looked worried, too. Libby had never been reckless with Chloe's safety. But her erratic behavior over the last year, which Law had thought was about their marriage ending . . . Had it been about this? How long had she been drinking without anyone knowing?

"Are you going to be okay with her?" he asked Libby.

"Why wouldn't I be?" she asked, fiddling with the dangling gold hoops hanging from her ears and determined to behave as if nothing had happened.

"I'll let you two sort this out," Dan said. "I'll be in the driveway when you're done."

"Have you been drinking all day?" Law asked, once his brother was gone.

"What I do with my days away from being a full-time single mother is none of your business."

"It is if it hurts our daughter. You can't drink, Libby."

"I had one drink, Law. I'm not drunk. And I wasn't the one cozying up to Chloe's assistant principal in front of the entire town."

"I was talking to Kristen. That was all."

"*Kristen?*" Libby mimicked. "That's Ms. Hemmings to you from now on, buddy, if you know what's good for you."

Before, he'd have ignored her over-the-top threat, the way he ignored ninety-five percent of her rants. Now . . . He'd ignored too much. He'd refused to deal with Libby for too long. And in her warped reality, that neglect had given her more reason to up the stakes, until she'd finally grabbed his attention.

"This evening was supposed to be a treat for Chloe," he said. "She deserves to have a normal, fun time with her friends. We all do. It's been a hard couple of years. That's my fault as much as yours. But I need you to take care of yourself, so you can look out for our daughter when she's with you."

"*I* do look out for her, every day. I'm the custodial parent. I'm the one who's involved in her life, not you. Don't act like you've ever understood what either of us needed. You never cared."

He rubbed a hand across his forehead.

Before tonight, Libby's accusation might have taken another

bite out of him. He'd let her low opinion of his attempts to be a husband and a father hurt for a long time—the same as he'd once let his parents convince him that he was a lousy son and brother and student, and whatever else he'd tried to do right to please them. But Libby's hatred didn't hit its mark tonight. Tonight there was another, softer, kinder voice in his head, helping him push his ex's selfishness back where it belonged—onto her shoulders.

You never stopped caring, Law . . . I know what it looks like when a person cares only about himself. That's not you.

And maybe if he'd believed that sooner, if he'd stopped fighting long-dead battles from his past before now, he could have kept his own family from becoming as broken as the ones he and Libby had fled.

"How could I let us get here?" he asked himself. "All I wanted was for Chloe—"

"*Here* . . ." It wasn't a good look for his ex—the sneer that sliced across her face. "You mean me walking up to a social gathering and finding my husband flirting with another woman while our daughter watches from the other side of the room?"

"*Ex*-husband," he reminded her, the rage he'd been controlling for hours spilling out. "I'm not dating Kristen, Libby. I was talking to her in a public place. I'm not angling to date her or any other woman. But even if I was, that's my business. Not yours. Get your own life together and stop obsessing about mine. Pathetic and needy were never your most attractive features."

On cue, tears welled in her eyes. A chorus of a down-on-your-luck gambling song came to mind while he watched her try to make him feel like a bastard for telling it like it was.

He stood there for close to a minute, watching her make a fool of herself. She must have realized she was getting nowhere.

She blinked back her play for sympathy. She crossed her arms over the chest she'd already gotten another man to augment by the time Law met her.

"You're a loser, Law Beaumont." She looked so proud each time she said it. This time she was speaking so loudly there was no chance Chloe wouldn't overhear in her room, unless she had on her earphones. "With all your connections in this town and the money you could access from your family, we could have been swimming in the best circles for years. We could have been happy, like folks who live over near your brother on Mimosa Lane."

"I came to Chandlerville to give us a better life. I didn't give a damn about my brother's money or his lifestyle. I still don't."

"If you cared about us, you would have. You'd have gotten us the same things."

"I cared." And now he knew that at least one other person in town believed that. Kristen's admiration back at Pockets had felt solid. Real. So real it was helping him see himself clearly, maybe for the first time since he was a kid. "I've always cared."

"Never enough," his ex said. "You never cared enough."

"Nothing's ever enough for you. A better place to live. Better things my money couldn't buy. Better friends and activities for Chloe, even if she didn't want them. None of it was enough. But that's on you now, not me. You're the one who told me to get out."

She'd expected him to crawl back, begging her to try again. They both knew it wasn't because she'd wanted him, as much as she'd wanted to keep her claws in someone she thought she could manipulate into getting her even more.

Her eyes filled with real tears this time. "If I have a drink every now and then to get through this—my ex-husband not giving enough of a damn to fight for his family—that's my business.

You and your brother stay out of my life, Law. Nothing that happens here matters to you anymore, remember?"

Law looked around the house. He thought of his one-bedroom dive half a mile away, and he smiled. His place was small. He slept on the couch the nights his daughter stayed over. But it was peaceful. He and Chloe were happy there, when he had her to himself. She'd realize that eventually and stop blaming him for the divorce, no matter how long Libby kept shrieking about it.

"I may be a loser to you," he said to the soulless woman who'd once held his heart, back when he'd valued himself so little. "But I'm a good parent. And you're going to be one from here out. Be the mother my daughter deserves, Libby. I hope you're hearing me. I didn't make a scene back at the bowling center, for Chloe's sake. I don't want to upset her. But I've trusted you with her. That's the only reason I didn't fight you on the terms of the divorce. Don't push me now, or I'll push back, and Chloe will just have to be upset about it for a while until I fix this myself."

"Fix what?" Libby laughed. "Fix me? No one's going to believe you over me. I don't care how much you kiss up to your perfect Ms. Hemmings."

"I wasn't . . ." He rocked back on his heels, remembering just how much more of Kristen he'd wanted to kiss. "We were talking."

"Is that what you call drooling all over her?"

"Leave Kristen out of our problems."

"So you can slide right into her big-girl panties?"

Law shoved down the instant image that came to mind of how amazing Kristen would look in her panties . . . and just her panties.

"Stop it," he said. "Stop drinking. Stop dumping your problems on me. Stop all of this for good, and find something else to do with your life besides torching mine, before someone gets hurt."

"Well, we're the experts on hurting ourselves and anyone else who gets in our way. Aren't we, my love?"

"That's enough."

It was always between them.

The accident and the damage that night had done to them. For the last nine years—and especially for the six months just after the collision, when the other driver had been in rehab learning how to walk again—that night had haunted Law, and Libby knew that. Throwing it in his face was her final low blow whenever they fought. It was his greatest regret, and she seemed to enjoy hurting him with it.

"It's not going to work anymore," he said, the same moment that he realized it was true.

No matter what's happened in the past, you're a good man . . .

"I've done my damnedest to make up for my mistakes," he said. "Now you're going to do the same. Stay sober. Get yourself into rehab, if that's what you need. Our daughter's paid enough for the disaster we've made of our marriage. I'm not going to see her hurt anymore."

He started down the driveway, not waiting for a response.

"She's *my* daughter," Libby yelled after him. "And don't you forget it. You're the one who's hurting her, Law. You're the one who's screwing this up, not me. You're always screwing up. You hear me!"

Law kept walking.

His brother, true to his word, was leaning against Law's truck, waiting. Dan's rumpled lawyer's suit looked comically out of place framed by the dust and battered dents that came with Law's less sophisticated lifestyle.

"So," Dan said. "That went well."

Law laughed.

What was he going to do but laugh? He was a desperate man. Only it didn't feel as desperate as it had other nights, walking back to his truck after dropping Chloe off and knowing it would be days before he saw her again. This time he wasn't alone, and that felt good—even if not being alone meant dealing with his brother's sudden determination to ignore the KEEP OUT sign Law had hung on his personal life since moving to Chandlerville.

"How high's the water?" Dan asked. "Is it over your head? Because I know you, whether you think I do or not. When you're spoiling for a fight, you come out swinging, and you don't take prisoners. You wanted Mom and Dad off your back, and they haven't been in your life for close to a decade. You wanted me gone from having a chance to help you, and every new check I tried to send Libby once you were paroled came back uncashed. If you wanted this divorce mess with Libby over, you'd have handled her by now. So, what gives?"

Law laughed again, a shorter, angrier sound. His brother was pulling a tiger's tail. He had to know it. Which meant he was raring for battle.

They'd always been about the same size, intimidating the hell out of most people at first sight. But Law's big brother was the calmer, more reasonable one, always trying to mediate the conflict between Law and their parents. Law had never known him to be a confrontational kind of guy. Then again, he hadn't really known Dan in a long time.

"The water's right at my head," Law said. "It's nothing I haven't handled before."

Dan shook his head. "You don't really believe that, or you wouldn't be standing here. We haven't shared more than two or three words at a time since your parole, even though you live three miles away from me and drop your kid off at my house to play with Sally at least once a month. If everything's fine, why are you still talking to me?"

"I'm doing the best I can."

"Tell me you're done with letting Libby use you as a doormat because you think you deserve it. Tell me Dad and Mom didn't screw you up that badly."

Law glared back. "What do you know about it?"

"What do I know about it?" Dan squared off, his hands on his hips, his well-muscled biceps bulging beneath his Brooks Brothers or whatever dress shirt. "I lived it, the same as you. You left me, blamed me, the same as you did them. And all I'd ever done was try to be a brother to you, no matter how much they seemed to want us to hate each other, thinking that would make us stronger men or something. But I never gave up, Law. Hell, when Mom and Dad washed their hands of your life, and your baby came along while you were in prison and they still didn't step up and help, I sent money to Libby to get her through until you came home. I'd hoped that you'd see that I wasn't the enemy. No matter what you said the last time I saw you, I'd be damned if I wasn't going to try to do something. But as soon as you got out and saw my first letter in the mailbox, I was out of your life all over again."

"You're damn straight you were. I didn't need your money then, and I don't need it now."

"It's not about the money, damn it! Or the strings I pulled to help you get set up here. I wanted to help my brother. I wanted to help you. I still do. I knew things had to be rotten with you and Libby, especially after you'd sobered up and realized what you'd married. I've always known. But I kept my distance, hoping you'd come find me one day. And you did. But strangers was all you wanted us to be, still, no matter how much you needed me. Or how much I might have needed you... I've had my own problems, man. My family hasn't been on the best footing this year. And it's not like I had Mom and Dad to depend on, either. Where were you when I needed *my* brother?"

Law's urge to punch something evaporated. Dan was talking about the Chandler shooting. Sally had been in the line of fire. She'd been in the cafeteria that day when everything went down. Even though she hadn't been injured, Law knew exactly how terrified Dan must have been for his child. Law had felt the same about Chloe, until he'd been certain she was safe.

"I'm sorry about that, but ..." Something else his brother said registered. "What do you mean, you didn't have Mom and Dad?"

"They've been out of my life since Dad let you go to prison, instead of helping you—because you still wouldn't agree to kiss his ass and live your life his way. That was it for me, too, Law. The only time I've spoken with them since, the shooting had made national headlines and Dad called to criticize me, not to ask about Sally. Why wasn't I after the school and the county and Troy Wilmington's parents for everything they're worth? I hung up on him telling me I was a waste of a lawyer for caring more about my daughter and family than I did about making a name for myself in the legal community, grandstanding in court while I had national media coverage. So don't stand there and act like they haven't judged me just as much they have you."

"Maybe *you're* the one I didn't want judging me!" Law threw back unfairly, but it was all too much to take in. "Did you ever think of that? Maybe I didn't want my perfect brother knowing any more about my crap life than he already did. Mom and Dad weren't the only ones pushing me to straighten up when we were in college. Maybe I didn't want *you* to have been right about how screwed up I was, getting myself into this situation. And I sure as hell didn't want to give you the chance to lord it over me. Or to be the one to say you told me so, when I finally admitted that I couldn't make my own family work!"

All this time he'd walled himself away, Law had still cared about his brother. It had been Dan's approval he'd still longed for, not their parents'. It was Dan he'd worried about disappointing, while Law's life continued to fall apart in Chandlerville.

Now his hands were clenched into fists at his sides. Dan's were clenched at his waist. They were practically nose-to-nose, eager to fight. Because wouldn't that make everything better?

"That's just great," Dan said. "I tell you our parents have moved on from their favorite pastime of making you miserable, to blaming me for not making the most professionally out of my daughter almost getting shot earlier this year. I tell you you're not the only one hurting. It took Sally months before she felt safe enough to go back to school. Did you know that? We had to get her into therapy just so she'd be ready to start middle school, instead of begging us to homeschool her. Charlotte and I nearly split up once or twice from the stress of watching our little girl suffer and not being able to do a damn thing to help her. But does that make a dent with you? Of course not. All you've got to say to me is that you've ignored me so I wouldn't keep giving *you* a raw deal? Not a phone call, Law. Not a visit. Not even a note to say you were glad Sally was alive . . . When are you going to realize that all of this isn't just happening to *you*?!"

Law froze, the fight in him drying up. Dan was making him sound like . . . Libby.

He finally heard, really *heard* his brother. More than that, he was feeling the emotions right along with Dan—the helplessness and fury, and the kind of hopelessness no parent should feel. It was the same depth of fear that Law had been enduring all this time, as Chloe slipped farther and farther away from him. His own confusion and panic were standing in front of him now, reflecting back from his brother's blue eyes.

"Dan . . ." He started to say. Then he didn't know what to say.

"Hell, man," Dan said. "Chloe was in the school that day. You had to have been just as terrified. Did you even think about Sally or me or Charlotte? Did you even give us a moment's consideration?" Dan's voice broke, making Law's gut clench. "I could have used my brother. I could have used someone who understood how much my family means to me, after the nothing our parents gave us to live with growing up."

Law had thought about Sally. He'd made sure she was okay. He'd kept asking people like Julia and Walter and Rick about her, people he knew weren't likely to say anything to Dan about his asking. He'd kept his distance, figuring the last thing his brother needed in a crisis was Law barging back into his life.

It was the last thing Law had thought *he'd* needed.

"I was . . ." The words he'd never said came to him then, because they felt absolutely vital to get out—for both him and his brother. "I was drowning. I guess I still am. And I guess that made me about the worst brother I possibly could have been to you when you needed me the most. I'm sorry, Dan. I've been a total prick to you, and you're right. You don't deserve it."

"Well . . . " Dan ran a hand across the back of his neck. The gesture was so familiar, it tugged at something inside Law, a memory of seeing his brother doing that when they were kids and their dad had been on their cases, which even then had been pretty often. "Just so we're clear, I never sided with Mom and

Dad against you. Ever. I've always been here for you, even when you didn't want me to be. *Especially* when you didn't want me to be. And I'm not going anywhere now. If you are ever drowning again, if you can let yourself need a lifeboat, you know where to find me."

Law watched Dan head to his big-money car, throw himself inside, slam the door, and peel out of the driveway.

Their parents had treated Dan like the golden boy. At least, Law had let himself think so. He'd even let himself get angry a time or two since January—while he was dealing with the worst of his divorce—imagining his parents swooping in after the Chandler shooting to coddle his older brother through his crisis. As status-obsessed as Libby had become, she'd been going on and on about Dan and Charlotte's perfect life in their perfect Mimosa Lane house with their perfect daughter. All of it making Law feel like even more of a screw-up by comparison. So he'd tuned out Dan and his crisis . . .

He climbed into his truck and stared at the house he'd lost. He let the last ten years wash over him. The life he'd wasted chilled him to the bone, like the November wind swirling outside.

Had Dan really wanted to help from the start? Law's mind scrambled backward, to early memories from his boyhood with the brother he'd given up, the way he'd given up so much else so he could be free. Only he didn't feel free now, any more than he'd yet to feel free of Libby. Until tonight—when he'd had Kristen close and understanding him and wanting to understand more.

He started his truck, slammed the transmission into gear, and checked in his rearview for the traffic he knew wouldn't be there this time of night. He floored it out of the driveway the same as Dan had. Damn it! It was all circling too close, like the leaves kicking up in his rearview mirror as he drove away. He couldn't tune out thoughts of Dan and Libby and Chloe and Fin and Kristen.

Kristen . . .

If you ever need to talk with someone who has just as hard a time trusting her feelings as you do yours . . . give me a call.

If you are ever drowning again . . .

He laughed.

He had people tripping all over themselves today wanting to help him. And that was the reality, not Libby's tantrum, that had his fingers itching again to curl around a whiskey bottle, so he could drink so deeply he stopped wanting to talk with anyone.

Cursing, he pulled over to the side of the road and stared through the windshield into the starless night, as if the darkness beyond held more answers than the turmoil inside him.

***

Chloe had heard everything her mom and dad said. She always heard. Her parents fought more every day, no matter how much her dad tried not to.

It was like her mom wanted them to keep arguing. Chloe sometimes still thought about her parents getting back together, even though she knew it wasn't going to happen. But at least that would have meant things going back to normal. Most of the time now, she wished her mom and dad would never talk again.

And all her mom seemed to want anymore was to never let Dad go. Otherwise, why would Mom care if Dad talked with Ms. Hemmings? But Chloe knew what her mom had really cared about tonight was everyone at Pockets seeing her argue with

Dad. That was all Mom ever wanted now: everyone looking at her and talking about her and siding with her against Dad. Mom would do just about anything to have that, and she was scary when she didn't think she was getting it.

Was she trying to totally destroy everything?

As much as Chloe had been mad at her dad for starting her friends talking about her at school yesterday, he'd at least tried to make things up to her, taking her to the party tonight. He was a good dad. She didn't really care about what had happened before she was born, or if he did boneheaded things like at school yesterday with Fin, or talking with Ms. Hemmings tonight, even if it was totally embarrassing to Chloe.

But Chloe's mom . . .

Most days Chloe could ignore the worst parts of being in her family. Most days she'd do almost anything to ignore it. She'd do whatever her mom wanted her to, if it meant Mom wouldn't do things like she'd done tonight. When her mom totally lost it like that, especially in public, Chloe hurt so much she wanted to be part of someone else's family, anyone's family but her own, or maybe part of no family at all.

She wished she could tell someone how she felt. But who? She didn't even know what she'd say. Did she say that her mom drank? A lot? And that no one but Chloe had known for a long time before tonight?

It had been getting worse for months, since the divorce had gotten so bad, and Chloe hadn't told anyone. She hadn't wanted her dad to know. Mom had been making people think her dad was the one drinking again, after Mom had made sure the divorce judge and a lot of other people knew why Dad had gone to prison. Only now Dad knew—Chloe had heard him say it tonight—that Mom was really the one who'd been messing up big-time.

So what now?

Dad had told her mom to stop drinking, or else. He hardly ever said *or else.* When he did say it, he'd always meant it, and he didn't even know how bad it really was.

Chloe didn't know if her mom *could* stop drinking. Mom had probably been drunk the last two nights, when she'd kept calling Dad over and over while Chloe was with him, saying mean things and crying. She had been drinking a lot today, or she wouldn't have done what she did in front of everyone at Pockets. She was probably drinking now, even though Dad had just told her to stop.

What if she never stopped?

It made Chloe scared, thinking about that on the nights she wasn't staying with her dad and her mom was really bad and passed out on the couch or in her bed, and all of Chloe's friends were asleep, and no one was up texting or chatting online anymore. She couldn't stand it sometimes. When her mom was totally out of it, Chloe stayed up all night watching TV, to keep herself from calling her dad to come get her.

Because then her family, what was left of her life, would be over for sure.

But sometimes even TV wasn't enough to keep her quiet. Keeping her mom's secret was too hard some nights, like tonight, when Chloe couldn't think about anything but the bad things that would happen if her dad knew more—after all the bad things that had already happened this year.

Everyone in town was already looking at her and her family like they were nuts—especially her friends, especially tonight. Brooke and Summer had spent the rest of the night at Pockets talking about Chloe and her parents with all the other kids. Laughing about Chloe again, after she'd finally gotten them to let up at school. After Chloe had been mean to Fin to make things better for herself, even though she'd kinda wanted to be nice to him.

Now things were even worse.

Her mom had to knock it off. Her family had to stop being the town joke. Somehow, Chloe had to make sure that happened.

But not tonight. All Chloe wanted to do right now was forget everything.

She listened at her door. She didn't hear her mom moving around anymore. She grabbed her jacket and opened her window and scooted through it, into the perfect, quiet night that would help her stop thinking about anything, especially her family, for just a little while.

Chapter Eight

"That poor child," Kristen said to Mallory over the phone.

Mallory and Pete and Polly had stayed home tonight. Mallory hadn't been feeling well. And even though Pete and his daughter would have had a blast at Pockets, and Mallory had wanted them to go, she'd had no luck trying to talk them into leaving her.

The honest, loving way the Lombards stuck together and supported one another, no matter the obstacle, left Kristen a little envious sometimes. It would have been too perfect to believe, if she hadn't witnessed for herself just how real their bond was.

"Julia said it was quite a scene," her friend agreed. "She and Walter tried to keep everyone distracted. But it sounds like half the party, including Chloe, watched Libby go for Law's jugular before he dragged her outside."

"Someone has to do something to help Chloe." Kristen's heart was breaking for what the eight-year-old and her friends had heard and seen.

"Just Chloe?"

"And Law. He's clean and sober, and he's being the best father he can be. Libby's the one who's out of control. Everyone should be figuring that out right about now." Kristen closed her eyes. "Not that it's any of my business . . ."

Mallory chuckled. "Sounds like after tonight maybe it could become a little more of your business, if you wanted it to."

"I . . ." *If* Kristen wanted it to?

"Julia said you and Law had a bit of a moment near the café before Libby showed up. I guess that means you've made up your mind how you feel about him."

"And didn't that work out so well."

"And after you followed him and Libby out of Pockets, Julia heard you defended Law, like—"

"Like I couldn't stay out of his personal business? Which is only making things worse for him with his ex, right?"

"You don't know that."

"No. I don't." And Kristen didn't know how Law felt about any of it.

Or did she? He'd let her walk away. He'd let her go tonight, after she'd said she'd always be on his side. As feelings went, Law's about her, about them, seemed pretty clear at the moment.

"What are you going to do?" Mallory asked.

"I . . ." She was going to wait and see if a man who seemed to understand her so effortlessly could trust her to do the same for him. "I told him he has my support and admiration for how he's trying to care for Chloe."

"Admiration?"

"I thanked him for stepping in and at least wanting to be there for Fin." Kristen checked the clock on her stove and winced when she realized it was after nine. "Though as far as I know, no one's seen Fin since lunchtime at school. So much for my plan there."

"You *thanked* him."

"I encouraged Law not to let Libby's outburst make him doubt himself."

"You encouraged him?"

Kristen was going to hyperventilate if Mallory didn't stop repeating her rationalizations back to her.

"I said he could call me if he ever wanted to talk, okay? Does that make you happy?"

Mallory didn't chuckle this time. She didn't push again. Her silence fell over Kristen like a soft, understanding hug. And then she said, "I'm not happy that you're doubting yourself about offering to help a man who clearly thinks as much of you as you do of him—maybe more, given Julia's description of how Law was looking at you tonight before Libby interrupted. But I think it's hopeful that you've reached out to him, without something like Fin's and the Dixons' situation for camouflage. You've left things open, Kristen, and I'm glad. That had to be hard."

"Don't you think you're exaggerating? We've barely even held hands." Except Kristen's fingers still tingled from his kiss.

"Sometimes that's all it takes. With Pete and me, it was coming together to help Polly. It was seeing each other at our most vulnerable. It was not hiding anything, none of the worst things we hid from everyone else. For some reason, we couldn't do that with each other. That's how we fell in love, long before we'd touched each other physically."

Kristen's chest hurt, hearing her friend talk about helplessly trusting someone. For so long, Mallory had given up on being able to take that kind of risk. Longer maybe than even Kristen had.

"I'm not sure I know how to love like that," Kristen admitted. "I'm not sure—"

Her phone beeped.

"Hold on," she said. "I hope this is Marsha with news about Fin." She glanced down at her call-waiting display. She read the number, and her heart stopped. She pressed a hand to her mouth. "Oh, no."

"What?

"It's him."

"Fin?"

"No."

"What's wrong?"

"Law." Seeing his name on her phone was so . . . *wrong*. Because it felt too right, having him call her so soon after she'd told him he could. "I have to go."

She didn't wait for Mallory's response before clicking over to the incoming call. But then all she could do was stare down at the portable handset.

"Kristen?" The faint sound of his voice blew away her ability to do anything but lift the phone to her ear.

"I'm here," she said.

"I . . ." He didn't sound steady, either. "I'm not sure why I called."

"Is Chloe okay?" She hoped it wasn't bad news.

"I don't know . . ." He sighed. "I think so. But I need . . . I don't know what I need."

Kristen heard Mallory's rueful chuckle escape her own throat. "Well, then, you're in good company. Neither do I."

"I'm sorry," he said, without saying why.

"Me, too," she responded. "I'm sorry this is so hard for you."

He'd been feeling the same restlessness, maybe the same confusion, and he'd called. He'd called *her*. He wanted to talk. It was exactly what she'd hoped for, while she'd been telling herself and Mallory she wasn't hoping for anything at all.

"You were amazing back there," he said, "the way you went to the mat with Libby for Chloe . . . for me. I can't stop thinking about it. I didn't even thank you. You're going to catch flak about it in the community. Libby will find a way."

"It was worth it if it helps Chloe. Maybe her mother will settle down, knowing someone outside your family has called her on her drinking, even if there's no proof."

"She made another scene when I dropped Chloe off at the house. I told her to back down, get her act together, or . . ."

Kristen waited, but he didn't finish the sentence. She understood. And she didn't. It wasn't exactly healthy, the way he'd let things rock on for so long with Libby. The way he'd let their problems hurt Chloe. But who was Kristen to instruct anyone on how healthy families should behave? The pause between them lasted so long, she was afraid she'd already said too much.

"It helped me, though," he finally said. "Confronting her and drawing a line in the sand. I'd like to think I made headway tonight. I'd like to think Libby heard me, at least a little." He grunted. "God, my life is a disaster."

She clutched the phone closer. "Your life might just be starting to get better, you know."

"Or things could be getting worse," he warned.

"Some things have to get worse before they get better." Jeez. She sounded as sappy as Mallory had.

"Better sounds more fun."

"Better it is, then." She remembered the touch of his fingers on her cheek, the brush of his lips. And suddenly, having sounded like her friend, when Mallory had talked about finding Pete, didn't feel so sappy. There was another pause, an even longer one than before. "I should let you go . . ."

"No, you shouldn't."

"Okay," she instantly agreed, unable to hold the word in, even though her fingers were once more pressed to her lips. The silence between them stretched out, for so long this time she checked the phone's display to make certain he hadn't hung up. "Law?"

"So can I call you again . . . even if it's not about Chloe?"

Kristen nodded.

All they were doing was talking over the phone, for heaven's sake. But that wasn't really all this was. She'd been intimate with half a dozen men since her early twenties, and nothing with any of them had felt this close, or this terrifying.

"I . . . I'd like that," she finally said.

"Me, too." He didn't sound any steadier than she did. "I'm glad I called. I don't know why I did, except I needed . . . I needed to hear your voice again tonight."

"I'm glad, too."

"Good night, Kristen."

"Good night," she breathed, not begging him to keep talking, no matter how much she hoped he would.

The line went dead.

She hung up herself and looked around the quiet condo that she'd loved from the second she'd walked inside with her real estate agent. This was her sanctuary, nestled on a quiet residential street in a small town that had become the home of her dreams.

At the end of a long day—and there hadn't been many days in her stint at Chandler Elementary that had felt longer than today—she was instantly at peace in this place. It was her retreat away from being the positive center for every situation her staff and students and ballplayers and basketball teams challenged her with. She cared about her community, but she could only take so much before she needed time away.

Except tonight, *alone* had turned out to be lonelier than she'd let it feel since she was a little girl and had first protected herself with solitude. And even though tonight's scene with Law and Libby had been hideous and Kristen would hear about it tomorrow, regrouping on her own wasn't what she needed.

More of Law's touch was. More of Law's voice. More of him wanting her just as much. The secret, lonely part of her was definitely falling for the man.

I'm not sure I know how to love like that, she'd told Mallory.

Now she wondered if she knew how to stop.

***

You're a loser . . .

Law dribbled his soccer ball through the shadows, running another lap across Chandlerville's park field. The voices in his mind followed him as he kept moving, covering the same ground over and over.

Change things up . . .

You're out of control, lady . . .

Your life might just be starting to get better . . .

Dad? . . .

Years of playing—since he was a child—meant he didn't have to see the ball to keep it rolling back and forth between his feet. Good thing, because even if he could make out the white and black of it through the darkness, the images that had joined him while he drilled, backlash from his day, were all he could focus on. The memories rushed with him through the night. And the past was there, too: the disappointment Libby had made the bedrock of their marriage from practically the moment he'd slipped a cheap, pawnshop-bought band of gold on her finger.

They'd been wild then. Drunk on their youth. Addicts, first and foremost, to the belief that they were invincible, and that calmer, safer, more conservative people like their parents and Law's brother, and then his coaches and the professors at college, were all saps who didn't know how to live life to its fullest. They'd both been arrogant and reckless. He'd played his part in life's crueler realities crashing down on them so hard they were still reeling from the aftershocks.

He turned at the edge of the soccer field and kicked the ball ahead of him, sprinting to catch it. Music from the early days of his marriage was his sound track tonight. Things between him and Libby had turned darker and darker, beginning soon after the day they'd said "I do" at city hall and let their families know what they'd done. Followed swiftly by telling his parents that Law was in jail, that his record of driving under the influence meant there was no way to bond him out, and that he had a court date pending.

He lifted the soccer ball in the air in front of him and juggled it between his knees, continuing down the field, his lungs burning from the frigid night air. He'd been running nonstop for the last half hour. His heart was pounding, and not just from the damage he and Libby had done to each other. The worst was that he could have prevented all of it, including what Chloe was going through now, if at the very beginning he'd sobered up enough to *not* throw his life away.

Instead, he and Libby had been in a downward spiral since his conviction.

He stopped dribbling at the edge of the grass. He was nowhere near finished burning off the frustration and regret and confusion. He'd driven to the park after talking with Kristen. He'd wanted so much to make a U-turn and head to her house instead. Not for sex, he'd told himself. Just to talk some more. Just to be near her while she said more supportive, hopeful things about his chances to make things right for himself and his daughter and maybe even Libby, if his ex would stop thinking only of herself long enough to cooperate.

Libby's demands that he stay away from Kristen weren't idle threats. She might retaliate in the community, and he didn't want to see that happen. But as soon as he'd heard Kristen's voice over the phone tonight, and the compulsion to drink himself senseless had instantly receded, he'd accepted that he wanted her in his life somehow.

Not because he needed her help not to drink. He'd made the choice not to, before he'd called. He'd keep making that choice whatever Libby did next—for himself, not just for his daughter. But Kristen . . . hearing her caring about him and his daughter was what he'd needed tonight, the same way he'd needed Dan's help.

Both of them had challenged him today. Walter Davis, too. It was like Law was waking up from a lifelong sleep and realizing how lucky he was to have these people on his side, Kristen most of all, after years of not letting himself need anyone.

He flipped the ball high over his head, trying to shake the confusion he'd hoped a grueling workout would silence. He juggled the ball with his forehead. Doubts and memories and flickers of hope for the future remained as he worked his way back down the field, alternating heading the ball with juggling it between his knees, pushing his body and his mind, focusing on not letting the ball hit the ground until he'd reached the opposite end.

"That's freaking amazing, man," a young boy's voice said from the sideline closest to Law.

Law trapped the ball beneath his right foot, breathing hard and soaked to the skin despite how cold it was. He shoved up the sleeves of his sweatshirt and stared through the moon-shot night to find Fin watching from the aluminum bleachers beside the field. The kid was dressed only in the jeans and T-shirt he must have worn to school that morning.

"Aren't people looking for you?" Law asked.

Fin shrugged, as if it were no big deal that he was lurking about a public park well after dark, after disappearing for half the day.

Law didn't like to think that the way he'd acted yesterday had made things even harder for the boy. His mind replayed the image of Chloe slinking off to her room tonight—away from Law and Libby, because he hadn't handled that situation any better than he had Fin's. But at least Chloe still had parents to despise and a home and her own room to disappear to.

Kristen had asked Law to help Fin because the boy didn't seem to realize he was throwing away his chance to get the same security for his life. Law understood how impossible it could be to believe in a fresh start like that.

With his toe, he flipped the soccer ball into the air and toward Fin. The kid trapped it with his knees and feet without breaking eye contact. He stared across the playing field at Law, as if he might run again. Law wondered if he'd looked that scared himself when he'd been staring at Kristen after he'd first walked up to her tonight at Pockets, hoping she wanted him closer.

I'd like that, Kristen had said to the idea of his calling again.

And because she had, his world had felt good tonight, despite his memories. Good seemed possible again for him, mostly because of her. Could just spending time with Law and soccer really help Fin get to the same place?

"Let's see what you got," Law said to the kid. "Show me your best stuff, before I take you home."

Fin flipped the ball into the air with the tip of his sneaker. He began to juggle it with his knees, the way Law had.

"I'm not going back if I don't want to." He side kicked the ball out of the air, sending it straight at Law's face.

Law headed it away, keeping his eyes on Fin and letting the connection he felt to him settle deeper. Law had been in the same place. He'd thrown his own chances away. He'd made so many stupid mistakes he couldn't count them all—all of them avoidable if he'd spent less time enduring and resenting his lot in life, and instead, early on, focused his energy on making something better happen.

"If you want to blow whatever you have with the Dixons," he said, "and keep flipping Family Services the bird, I can't stop you. Nothing anyone says is going to change your mind, if you refuse to listen. But you'll have to get away from me tonight if you want to stay out here on your own. I hardly know you, and I care enough about you not to let that happen. And I'm pretty sure which of us is the fastest. So don't waste my time, Fin. You're not going anywhere, unless I want you gone. And I want you safely back where you belong, with good people who can make a good home for you if you give them half a chance. So I guess the only question is, do you want to have our first workout before I take you back?"

Fin took a step closer, scowling at Law. They stared at each other, measured each other, and then suddenly the kid smiled an eat-shit grin Law knew all too well—he could remember smiling the same way at Dan, when they'd been young and they'd first discovered the freedom of soccer together.

"Race you to the ball," Fin said, taking off before Law could respond.

***

Chloe had been standing at the trees around the back of the soccer field for like half an hour. She'd wandered over to the park because it was close to her house—but it *wasn't* her house, so maybe she could stay there for a while until she could stand being in her room again. And she liked the park and the fun she'd had there with her dad and the soccer teams she'd been on, even though she'd let her mom talk her into telling her friends and her dad she didn't want to play anymore. She'd expected the park would be empty this late on a school night.

But the soccer field hadn't been empty after all.

Her dad hadn't turned on the lights, even though he'd had the key to the circuit box since he'd started coaching years ago. He and Fin didn't need lights.

They were dribbling and juggling the ball up and down the field like it was the middle of the day, drilling like they knew exactly where the other one would be. Like she and her dad always knew what each other was going to do next. Sometimes, when he didn't play with the guys he usually met up with at the park, she and her dad had spent entire Sunday mornings just running up and down with the ball. Chloe would get so hot and sweaty she thought she was going to die, even when it was cold like now. And she'd get so tired she'd want to quit. But she never did. Playing with her dad was too much fun to quit.

She'd let herself forget that. Mostly because her mom had said she should, that she'd never stay friends with Brooke and Summer if she didn't change. Chloe had been so stupid, thinking that becoming like Brooke and Summer—trying to like cheerleading same as her girlfriends did—might make her mom happy enough to stop drinking.

And now, while she watched her dad and Fin have so much fun together, she realized she didn't want to sit on the sidelines and cheer for boys while they played sports. She wanted to be out there, kicking their butts and playing with them, while people cheered for *her*. While her *family* cheered for her. And then suddenly, she was crying like a baby.

She'd been such a brat when her dad had tried to talk with her about soccer yesterday and this morning, like she'd been with Fin at lunch. And now they were out there on the field together, where she suddenly wanted to be more than anything. They looked so amazing together, running in the dark.

Her dad always looked amazing when he played. Like he sounded amazing when she'd heard him sing to himself in the shower, or in the mornings when he made breakfast and thought she was still asleep. Soccer and singing and when he took her to the zoo or for a milk shake were the only times she'd ever seen her dad smile.

Now he was smiling with Fin. And Fin was good. Really good, even though he wasn't as good as her, or nearly as good as her dad. He would be in a lot of trouble for ditching school. But the kid could play, the way she'd been able to play better than all the other kids the first time Dad had gotten her to try. And her dad was having a blast out there with Fin now, *not* Chloe.

She'd been a natural, he'd said. He'd been so proud every time he'd coached her. She'd never seen her mom smile the way her dad did when Chloe played. Her mom, the one or two times last season that she'd come to soccer practice or games, had been too busy talking to the other moms about Dad to care what Chloe did.

Fin was having a blast doing what Chloe did best with her dad. She'd never seen Fin like that, happy and looking like she wanted to feel again. He laughed and stole the ball from her dad. Her dad stole it back and popped the ball over Fin's head. Dad raced ahead to trap the ball, dribbling it already before Fin could get there. Of course the kid chased after him, laughing even though he'd been beat. She loved it, too, when her dad did that.

He'd slow down next and dare Fin to try to steal the ball back. And he wouldn't let Fin do it, not at first. He'd keep playing as hard as always, making Fin try harder and harder to get the ball, until Fin learned something new about how good defense could win a game when the other team's offense was better than your team's was. That was something her dad said all the time.

He was so great when he coached and said stuff like that. Why had she stopped remembering that—or how proud she'd always been when he'd found something new to teach her, and then she'd done something great in a game because of it and made him smile even more?

Her dad's smiles were the best thing she could remember about playing, and about her family, before her mom and her drinking had taken even Dad's smiles away. Now Chloe wanted them back, the way she'd been wanting the rest of her life back for so long.

"Dad," she yelled, forgetting that she shouldn't be there and that he'd be mad at her and Mom. She rushed from the trees and onto the field. "Kick it to me . . ."

Chapter Nine

Marsha blinked at the ragtag band of sweaty ruffians standing on her front porch.

She couldn't help but laugh. Leaning back into the strength of her husband's body, feeling his hand settle comfortingly on her shoulder, she took in her first full breath since leaving school earlier that day. Fin was home. And he'd brought an unlikely duo of buddies with him.

Law and Chloe were a sight. They looked exhausted, and it was no wonder. It was after eleven o'clock at night. Marsha had nearly called the police twice already.

"Well, I guess quarter till midnight is as good a time as any to come home," she said to Fin, hiding how freaked out she and Joe had been all night, and not mentioning how many laps around town Joe had made looking for the boy. "I don't figure you finished your homework while you were playing truant, am I right?"

Joe squeezed her arm, his rumbling chuckle curling around her heart.

"You all had better come on inside," her husband said. "It's cold enough to catch a chill, especially when you're sweaty from running around. Been playing a little soccer?"

Three overheated bodies stumbled into the family room to the right of the door. Fin made a move to fling his filthy self onto Marsha's slipcovered couch.

"Do it," she warned, "only if you plan to stay up the rest of the night pushing the cover through the washer and dryer. In fact, none of you move a muscle until you kick off those grass-covered shoes and leave them on the hardwood."

She wasn't going to ask how Fin and the Beaumonts had ended up playing soccer. No point in looking a gift horse in the mouth. Their shoes off, the three of them stood side by side in front of Marsha and Joe in almost identical stances: legs shoulder width apart, heads down, and hands folded in front of them.

"This isn't a firing squad, folks," Joe said. "Why doesn't one of you get to the point, so I can salvage a few hours of sleep before I head in to work?"

It had been years since he'd taken a day's vacation from his job as a claims adjuster for StaySafe Insurance. Marsha had been after him to make more time for relaxing, but there were always bills to pay, stretching their monthly budget to the max. Her husband was perpetually exhausted. But her Joe would have stayed up with her all night regardless, until they had Fin back.

"I should have brought him home from the park," Law started, "as soon as I realized he was there watching me work out . . ." He glanced at Chloe. A world of worry and pain seemed to settle between them. "But I guess we got carried away. He's a fine ballplayer. And then my daughter showed up, too . . ."

"Chloe wasn't with you?" Marsha asked. Chloe had been running around town at night also, all by herself?

Law looked as if he might scream or break down.

"I wanted to . . ." Chloe started to say. She cut a look toward her dad, and then at Marsha and Joe. "I just didn't . . ."

Fin rolled his eyes. "It's no big deal. None of this is a big f-ing deal. Can I go to my room now?"

"What you can do," Joe said, "is mind your manners."

He never went out of his way to intimidate any of the kids. He didn't have to. Like Law, Joe was a tall, strong, overpowering man. He was as impressive at sixty as he'd been when Marsha had first caught sight of him at the University of Georgia, when she'd been a freshman her first day on campus. But underneath it all, he was more teddy bear than bulldog.

"I want you to thank Mr. Beaumont," Joe continued, "for bringing you home before we had to report you missing to the authorities. Apologize to Marsha for worrying her sick. And then go get washed up and catch a few winks before we haul you into Ms. Hemmings's office in the morning to see what she wants to do about all of this."

Fin opened his mouth. Before something smart-ass could emerge, Joe held up his hand.

"Do us all a favor," her husband said. "Don't make any more trouble for yourself tonight."

Fin scowled at Joe, looking for all the world as if he'd prefer to throw a tantrum and run again. But then something miraculous happened. He looked mutinous, but he turned to Marsha.

"Sorry," he said. And then to Law, he said, "Thanks for the ride and . . . you know, for not making me feel stupid when we were playing. You're . . ."

"You're not so bad yourself," Law said, sparing the boy. "Now let's see if you can't find a way to stay here with the Dixons long enough for me to teach you a few new things."

Fin looked as stunned as Marsha felt.

Law was saying exactly what she'd hoped he would when Kristen had first mentioned asking him to help. She watched Fin closely as his shock transformed into excitement. When he just stood there, saying nothing, Joe hitched a thumb over his shoulder.

"Shower," her husband said. "Bed. Set your alarm for six, because we've got some things to discuss before the three of us leave for school. Now move. I want you under the covers when I check on you in ten minutes. And don't even think about turning on a bunch of lights and waking the other kids up. You're already grounded until the end of time. Step out of line one more time, and you'll be filling the rest of your days here doing everyone else's chores."

***

Law listened to Joe gently but firmly lay into Fin, and he found himself smiling, despite the terror churning in his own gut. The mouthy kid had said "thank you" and apologized. And now he was heading quietly off to shower, instead of stomping up the stairs and slamming doors the way Law would have when he'd been the same age and in trouble.

At some point while he and Fin had been messing around with his soccer ball, he'd accepted that Fin was a younger version of himself. Grittier, tougher, and maybe even a little more reckless than Law had been . . . But Fin felt alone in his world. Law would like to see if he could help change that.

And like Law, the kid worked double-time to make it clear he didn't care about anyone or anything. But one thing he couldn't hide was his passion for soccer. Just like Law. Just like his daughter.

Chloe . . .

When she had run from the thick ring of trees on the south side of the park's rec field, she'd blown Law's world apart. She'd called for the ball—which Fin had promptly stolen, because Law had stopped dead in his tracks at the sight of his little girl out by herself so late at night. Before he could question her and begin plotting his ex-wife's demise, Fin had kicked her a leading pass that set the two kids off running together, and Law had been stunned by similarities between them.

Fin, who said he'd never play with a girl, had begun bickering with Chloe right away, while they ran down the field, and trapped and passed and dodged each other with the ball. They'd seemed so much alike as Law had watched them and eventually led them through more drills, he'd wanted to yell for them to stop. Because if his daughter was like Fin, she was like Law, too, lost and unsure and disconnected from herself in ways he hadn't wanted to accept.

Chloe couldn't really be like that: feeling out of step with everyone and everything around her. Except she'd run from her home and mother in the middle of the night, and he was betting Libby didn't even realize Chloe was gone.

God, my life is a disaster . . .

Your life just might be starting to get better . . .

Chloe glanced up at the same time that he looked down at her, as if she could feel him making the decision he should have made earlier tonight, when he'd instead trusted Libby, again, to do the right thing for their family. Chloe opened her mouth to say something—by the defensive expression creeping across her face, he'd guess some kind of excuse.

He held up his hand, the way Joe had. He hadn't pushed her for an explanation, not while they had Fin with them. But Law was about to insist on one. Too much was at stake. He'd let too much slide already, for too long.

"Wait for me in the truck," he said.

"But, Dad—"

"In the truck. Now. And you'd better be there once I'm done speaking with Mr. and Mrs. Dixon."

Her cheeks pink, she dug her hands into her jeans pockets. "I can walk home from here. It's only like a mile away. I do it all the time at night."

I do it all the time at night . . .

A panicked rush of adrenaline nearly sent him to his knees. He must have looked as stricken as he felt. Joe squeezed his shoulder.

Law pulled his cell from his jeans pocket. "If you're not in the truck when I get out there," he said to his child, "I'll have the police looking for you before you get a block away. And then I'll have them take you home to your mom, to see whether or not she's even conscious enough to answer the door."

It was Chloe's turn to look scared. She glanced at the Dixons. Law reached out to reassure her that everything was going to be okay. He had no idea how to make that promise a reality, but he was damn well going to do a better job of it than he had so far. His daughter shied away from his touch.

"I'll be in the car." She yanked the front door open. She slammed it behind her on her way out.

"I'm sorry about that," Law said to the Dixons. "I'm sorry about all of this."

"Don't be." Joe hugged his wife closer. "We're grateful that Fin found you at the park, and that you got him home."

Law nodded.

"I suppose," he said, not hiding from the truth any longer, any truth, no matter how difficult, "that you've heard about what happened at the bowling center."

"A little." Marsha shook her head. "I'm so sorry, Law. I hope Chloe's going to be okay."

"If there's anything we can do . . ." Joe added.

Law shook his head, prepared to beg off, but then he remembered Kristen making the same offer.

Good people—he was surrounded by good people who were willing to step in to help him and his child, no matter how much he'd said he didn't need anyone. Just like his brother had at Pockets, even though Dan had been royally pissed and Law had thrown his brother's generosity back in his face.

"I just might take you up on that," he said to the Dixons, "once I figure out exactly what's going on, and what to do next. And if you have trouble explaining what happened tonight to the school, I'd be happy to talk to Kristen for you tomorrow."

Marsha smiled, her heart-shaped features brightening. "Have you definitely decided to coach next season?"

Law considered the midnight phone call he was about to make, and the additional conflict it was going to invite into his and Chloe's life. Then he remembered the joy his daughter had found playing soccer tonight, when for months she'd refused to so much as kick the ball around with him. They'd been a family again, for those few minutes on the park field. She'd been happy with him out there—a lot happier than she'd seemed anywhere else for a long time.

Just as Kristen had suspected his daughter might be.

"It means," he said, "I'm thinking I don't have any choice *but* to coach, for Chloe's sake. And after what I saw tonight, I'd be willing to take Fin on, too, as long as he works on his attitude and makes an effort to get along with the other players. If soccer is what he likes, I'm at the fields most Sundays. Unless I'm totally misreading my daughter, you'll find Chloe and me there several afternoons a week from here on out, until winter season starts in February. I won't have details for a while about team registration and tryouts."

"Hang on . . ." Marsha grabbed a pad of scratch paper from the table beside a huge, worn recliner. She handed it over along with the pen that had been lying on top of it. "Give me your phone number. We'll be in touch once we talk to the school. I can't tell you how important it is to get Fin to commit to something, anything."

"You don't have to," Law said. "I understand." Soccer and music had saved him from making an even bigger mess of his life. He jotted down his cell number. "You'll be able to reach me here . . ." He handed back the pad and pen. "It's my mobile. I'm not sure . . . I don't think I'll be at my apartment much after tonight. Call when Fin's ready to start. Better yet, just bring him to the park at five on Monday afternoon, after school. Chloe and I should be settled in by then."

"He'll be there," Joe said, looking as if he wanted to ask *settled in from what*, but he didn't. "As long as we still have him by then." His brown eyes were worried beneath bushy white brows. He glanced through the den's unshaded front windows. "Are you sure everything's all right?"

"It will be," Law said. "Just as soon as I convince a judge to at least temporarily suspend Libby's custody rights, before her escalating drinking problem puts Chloe at even more risk."

Marsha's shock showed only for a second.

She rallied and reached out to squeeze his hand. "You be sure to let us know if there's anything we can do. If nothing else, we're witnesses that Chloe was out and about so late on a school night. That little girl of yours is special, and she'd be a pleasure to help look after, if you find yourself needing a spare pair of hands now and then."

Her touch was gentle and warm. She pulled back quickly, so Law didn't have to. He tried twice to find his voice, and then settled for simply nodding. He opened the Dixons' front door and carefully closed it behind him.

Law could see his *special* girl huddled in the front seat of his truck, staring out her side window with her arms crossed over her chest, angry and hostile and a lot of other things he understood too well—emotions he'd never wanted Chloe to feel. But she had been feeling them, and hiding the worst of what she was going through—the same as Fin had hidden all day from his problems.

How did Law explain to his daughter what was about to happen and why, when he'd gone for so long not really talking with her about the hard things in their lives, the toxic things, hoping he could fix everything, even Libby, before he'd have to?

Looking down at his phone, he scrolled through his contacts until he'd found the number he was looking for—a number he'd had since moving to town but never used.

Home or cell? he wondered.

Cell, he decided.

That way he hopefully wouldn't be waking up more than one person. He placed the call and raised the phone to his ear, a lifetime of confusing images kaleidoscoping through his mind again, along with the memory of what had happened out back of Pockets.

On the fifth ring, the call connected.

"Hello?" a gruffer, sleepier version of his own voice said.

"Dan . . ." Law swallowed the instant flash of resentment riding him to hang up on his brother, instead of asking the colossal-ass favor he was about to. "I'm sorry to wake you, man, but it's kind of an emergency."

"What?"

Rustling and a muffled curse brought to mind an image from their childhood: he and his brother sitting across the breakfast table from each other, eating off the crystal and china their mother insisted the staff set out, *even though my boys always look like ruffians,* she'd say, *because they refuse to wash up before coming downstairs in the morning.*

Dan cleared his throat. "Law? Is it . . ." A sigh followed, then a quick inhale. "What's wrong? Never mind. Where are you? I'll be there as soon as I can."

And just that quickly, Law's brilliant brother had engaged his brain, summed up the situation, and was on Law's side like he'd said he always had been. Law had kept his distance all these years, not wanting to need that kind of help from his family.

Indulging that fantasy was now officially over.

"Sit tight," he said, stalking toward his truck. "I'm heading your way. I hope you meant what you said, when you were chewing my ass out about Libby. Chloe and I need a place to stay for a while, with someone I can trust to help me keep an eye on her when I can't."

"What about your ex-wife?"

"She's out of the picture. At least, she's going to be. She has to be, for now. She's gone too far this time."

"You mean what happened at the bowling center?"

"I wish that's all it was." Law sighed, stopping beside the driver's door and lowering his voice.

He and Dan were going to have to talk about all of it. But before he moved Chloe onto Mimosa Lane, he and his brother needed to be on the same page about one more important thing. Something Law would rather go back to prison than ask Dan for. But he was going to ask, for his daughter's sake.

"I need another favor," he said. "Could you front me enough cash to hire a decent family lawyer? You specialize in contracts, right? I need someone who can kick ass and take names in family court."

Silence answered him at first.

"I've got cash," Dan finally said. "I know a few judges around here who'd be willing to listen to the right lawyer . . . judges who can see through whatever voodoo Libby did to get her everything she asked for in the divorce."

"I was kinda counting on your being able to reach out to someone tonight." Law was grateful, resentful, embarrassed, and a whole lot of other things he'd never wanted to be again with his brother. "It's that important. Libby's going to hit the roof in the morning, once she sobers up enough to read the text I'm about to send her."

"Send it." His brother inhaled again. "I'll make a few calls. What's going on, Law?"

Law opened the driver's door to the truck and slid behind the wheel. He started the engine and risked a sideways look at Chloe. She was crying, he realized, so quietly he wouldn't have noticed if he hadn't looked so closely through the dark. Rage rushed through him.

He reversed out of the Dixons' driveway and away from the

quaint, well-kept home that they'd given Fin and a host of other castaway boys and girls.

"I'm finishing growing the hell up," he said. "It's time to make decisions I should have made a long time ago. I'll be at your place soon. I'll explain the rest then."

He thumbed the call closed and tossed his phone onto his dash. He was going to make this right, if he had to beg for help from his brother, the Dixons, or anyone else in town. He reached across the cab for Chloe's hand. He wished he had Kristen there. She knew how to talk to people and relate to them and show them that she cared.

"I need you to talk to me, darlin'." He squeezed her fingers, not letting go when she tried to. "I know it's been hard, and I know I don't know enough about why. But . . . you scared me tonight. And I think you're scared, too. I think you have been for a long time, and your mother and I have been too busy with our own problems to really notice how much . . ." His voice cracked, failing him.

He ground his teeth. He was going to understand his daughter. She was going to know that someone was there for her, whatever else was going on.

"I want to help, Chloe. And I think you want me to, or you wouldn't have come out onto the soccer field tonight and let me know you were there. We're going to fix this—together. Tell me what's been happening at home. And I promise, I'll do everything I can to make it better. Trust me, darlin', please?"

Chloe's watery glance accused him of every single time he'd let her down.

"How much has your mom been drinking, darlin'? How many times has she been so drunk she hasn't known you've snuck out of the house in the middle of the night?"

Chloe stared out the windshield then, alone and resigned as she mumbled, "A lot."

Law focused on his driving, on the prettiest part of town passing them by as he headed for the unexpected sanctuary of Mimosa Lane. When he could trust his voice again, he glanced back at his daughter.

"How many of the things you've been wanting lately, like cheerleading instead of soccer, and being one of the popular girls at school when those girls don't seem right for you at all, at least started because you were scared that if you didn't do what Mom wanted, her drinking might get worse?"

Chloe scrubbed at her eyes. "A lot."

Law nodded. A part of him died, listening to his daughter sound so desolate. "We're going to make it better, Chloe. I promise you that."

"How?" She finally worked her hand free. She drew her knees up to her chin and wrapped her arms around her shins. "Where are we going?"

"Someplace where things can settle down a little for you. For us. We're going to be living with Uncle Dan for a while. We're going to be living together every day, you and me, until your mom agrees to stop drinking and start doing better for you. That's going to be hard, I know, and I'm sorry. We've already put you through so many changes. But I promise you, Chloe, I'm never going to let your mother or anything else scare you like this again."

Chapter Ten

Kristen reached for her customary calm.

This was a good moment, regardless of the difficult circumstances. Sitting across her desk from the Dixons and Fin at nine o'clock on Friday morning, she was convinced they finally had their chance to get through to the kid who'd returned to Marsha and Joe last night—even if he'd needed Law's help to find his way home.

Law . . . From what she'd heard had happened since their phone conversation, he was dealing with a fresh flood of problems. But he'd promised the Dixons he'd help with Fin.

"You've made a lot of trouble for yourself," she said to the boy. Marsha had just recounted what had transpired at the park and then the Dixon home. "But facing your mistakes the way you are now is a good first step. I admire that kind of courage."

It sounded as if Law had finally found the courage to take a firmer hand with his ex. Kristen and Marsha had had a very brief conversation before Joe and Fin joined them. Before that, Kristen had already heard from Mallory, who'd learned from early-morning school gossip that Law and Chloe had moved in with

Dan last night. Kristen's heart was hurting for both father and daughter.

"Don't you want to say something to Ms. Hemmings?" Joe asked his youngest foster child.

"I'm sorry," Fin mumbled. He actually sounded as if he was.

All of this had to be overwhelmingly confusing for a kid who'd already been through so much. It was baffling enough for Kristen.

I'm glad I called.

I'm glad, too . . .

For those few minutes, things had seemed so good, so possible for her and Law. Now, she had absolutely no idea what to expect from him, or if she wanted to expect anything at all. For the first time, she'd put herself out there—possibly her whole heart—and it was with a guy who came with even more emotional baggage than she did. And now it looked as if he was going to be in a custody battle with his relapsing alcoholic, jealous ex-wife.

Did she tactfully step back and give Law time to get his bearings and figure out what he wanted? Did she call him and thank him for his help with Fin, and casually feel him out about the rest? Or did she give in to the impulse to break all contact with him now, before he had the chance to dump her, and then her world could stop feeling as if it were tilting off its axis?

She studied Fin's file, struggling to focus on her job. She reviewed the long list of mischief Fin had been in just since coming to Chandler. The half-formed thought that had been nagging at her finally snapped into focus. The boy was being entirely too well-behaved this morning. Too calm.

He was saying all the right things. He was working them. Which made her wonder if he had any idea just how close he was to blowing his shot with the Dixons. Was he luring them into letting their guard down again, just so he could ratchet up his reckless behavior—until Family Services had no choice but to remove him from the kind of loving community he'd needed his whole life?

You're a teacher, K, she scolded herself. *Enough with the personal drama. Get in the game.*

"Are you sorry enough to stop this, Fin?" She folded her hands over his past. "Because I need to document something here. For starters, there's your escalating disruptive behavior at school. How far beyond that I take this with your caseworker at Family Services depends entirely on what your plans are once you're back in class. Are you going to stick this time? Are you going to settle down and try to learn something here, instead of looking for another reason to run?"

"If my friends keep being stupid and mean like yesterday," Fin said, sounding more like his disagreeable self, "I don't gotta take that. You can't make me. No one can."

"You're absolutely right," she said, before Joe could say whatever he'd inhaled to say. "No one can make you do anything. But the Dixons are your friends, and they've been anything but stupid and mean to you. You scared them to death running away again, but they're here now, going to bat for you. They've hidden all the other times you've skipped on them, at the risk of their reputation with the county and their chance to help not just you but all the kids in your home. When are you going to do right by them, and protect them the way they're trying to protect you, instead of fighting them?"

"I . . ." Fin wiped at his eyes. "I didn't ask them to do any of that. I didn't ask them to come here today."

"And yet you're a lucky young man, because here they are, right where they've been since you were placed with them. Do you have any idea how much they care about you?"

"I didn't ask them to care." Fin gulped, swallowing the tears he wasn't letting fall from those shiny green eyes. When Marsha's hand covered his, he didn't flinch away. "I didn't ask them not to tell Mrs. Sewel how much I'm screwing up. Go ahead. Put everything in my file. Tell Family Services. It's all going to end the same, anyway."

"It doesn't have to," Kristen said. "If you want things to be different, everyone in this room wants that, too. Even Mr. Beaumont does, or he wouldn't have stayed with you at the park and made sure he got you home."

A real home, which Law was now helping make a reality for the boy.

Kristen felt another piece of her heart slip beyond her control. She couldn't imagine not seeing Law again, not asking him about last night with Fin, about Chloe and how she was doing, about Libby and how he was handling learning just how bad her drinking had been for so much longer than he'd thought. She wiped at her own eyes and shared an understanding smile with Marsha, though she had no idea exactly how much the older woman understood.

"No one holds the mistakes you've already made against you," she said. "Not here in Chandlerville, not at this school. We're all focused on now. But we need you to be, too, so you don't repeat any of the stuff in this file. Is that what you want, Mr. Robinson? Or are you determined to give up on us before we give up on you? Because I can call Mrs. Sewel right now and make this a whole lot easier on everyone. You don't have to waste your time or ours acting up again. Do you want to head back to county and meet with her today and see where she'll put you next?"

Fin glared at her. "No."

"No, what?" If he said nothing else, instinct told Kristen it was important that he said this.

"I don't want to."

"You don't want to . . . what?"

"No one's giving up." Marsha fumbled to keep hold of Fin's hand.

"Is that what you want, Fin?" Kristen nodded at his physical connection with his foster mother. "Do you want people fighting to hold on to you? Or do you want to take your chances with another town and another bunch of strangers you won't trust to love you, any better than you've trusted us so far?"

Fin's watery eyes were jarring companions to his scowl. He looked young and afraid finally, instead of jaded and cocky. He looked like she'd felt so many times in her youth.

Please, she begged whoever listened to her when she identified with that kind of loneliness in one of her students. *Please help me help this child . . .*

"What difference does it make what I want?" Fin demanded. "So what if maybe I want to stay here? Who cares, right? Doesn't matter what I say. You people always get to decide. And so what if I go somewhere else? Whatever. Just tell CFS to send me away already. Stop . . ."

"Stop what, Fin?" Kristen asked. "Stop believing in you? Because it's too hard for you to believe you can have this school and your home with the Dixons, or that people like Chloe's dad want you around, too?"

Pain shot through Kristen at the stricken, panicked look on Fin's face. He pushed himself out of his chair and away from

Marsha. Before the adults could react, he was grappling with Kristen's closed office door.

"Fin!" Marsha reached for him. "Running doesn't do any good . . ."

But he was already gone, racing through the outer office.

"Slow down, buddy," said the deep voice Kristen had been longing to hear all morning.

"Let me go!" Fin shouted.

"Not a chance," Law was saying by the time she and the Dixons made it to the outer office. His attention immediately fixed on her, as he continued to talk to the boy he had a firm grip on. "We wouldn't catch another glimpse of you before nightfall, if I let go."

Law looked so good, and so exhausted. Chloe was standing beside him, staring at Fin, who was now openly, defiantly crying.

Kristen checked the clock over the door to the hallway.

"Late morning?" she asked Law, not sure of what else to say.

He nodded. His demeanor grew even grimmer. "I had an emergency meeting with a lawyer first thing, who'd already woken up a judge on my behalf. He gave me paperwork to file with the school, for Chloe's records. He said it was important to formalize a few things, in case my ex-wife contacts you, once she hears about the judge's temporary ruling."

Kristen nodded, not all that surprised, desperate to know more.

The Dixons moved to stand behind Fin. Joe rested his hand on the kid's shoulders. Fin swiped at his eyes with his jacket sleeve, looking across the office at nothing, as if that could take him away from all of them—maybe especially Chloe, whom he eyed suspiciously.

And then she did the most amazing thing. She stepped around her dad until she was shoulder-to-shoulder with Fin, standing next to him. When he still didn't look at her, Chloe nudged his arm with her elbow.

"Can we go to class now?" she asked Kristen, earning herself a glare from her classmate. She shot him a *don't be stupid* look.

"Can we?" Fin finally asked no one in particular.

Kristen bit the corner of her lip to keep from cheering.

We.

Like *I'm sorry*, the word hadn't made an appearance before today in Fin's vocabulary. His saying it about Chloe, after the trouble the two of them had had getting along, made the milestone even more significant.

"I don't know," Marsha said. "Can we trust you to stay put, and to keep out of trouble?"

"No more bailing like yesterday," Joe added. "Like Ms. Hemmings was saying, you either want to be here or you don't. You tell Ms. Hemmings and Marsha and me right now that you want to be with us, and that you're not just biding your time in Chandlerville, and we'll make this work with Family Services. Mr. Beaumont's even offered to help you become a fine young soccer player come February, when practice for the winter season starts. But you've got to decide if that's what you want, son. If *we're* what you want."

Silence filled the school office.

Even the administrative secretaries had grown quiet. There was none of the customary typing and shuffling of papers and files and low-voiced conversations. Phones were ringing. No one picked up the calls.

"What's it going to be?" Kristen asked.

Fin swallowed. He glared at Chloe again, as if it were her fault that she was there to witness this moment. He looked down, saying nothing.

"You just have to get through today," Law told him. "Forget the rest, and make today work. Don't run from it. Trust me, that's a lot. Sometimes that's all we can do."

We again.

Kristen knew enough to realize Law was talking about his sobriety, serving time in prison, and maybe even facing his problems with Libby. He was sharing his hard-won personal wisdom with Fin in front of the entire school office. He was determined to help the boy, and a determined Law Beaumont was something to behold.

Even Chloe was staring up at him as if she was seeing a side of her dad she never had before.

"Don't ditch school again," he said to Fin. "Get through today. Get your homework done. If you can manage that, I've called in sick for my evening shift at work. Chloe and I will be at the park at five."

"We will?" Chloe sounded scared, but excited, too. "What about Mom? She—"

"I'll deal with your mom," Law said. "You're taking the bus home to Uncle Dan's, and then you and I are spending the afternoon together."

"But—"

"Head to class," Kristen said, diverting more public discussion of Law and Libby's issues. "Both of you. That is, if you've decided that's what you want to do, Fin."

Two confused kids glanced at each other. Fin shrugged and opened the office door to the hallway, brushing against Chloe's shoulder in the process.

"Come on," he said. "Everyone's at social studies."

Without another word, they headed into the hall together.

***

I'll never let you have her, Libby had screamed over the phone at Law at six that morning, her voice sleep-heavy and not yet completely sober. *Moving her in with Dan and shutting me out isn't going to happen. She's my daughter. I'll fight you for her. I'll never stop fighting you for her. If you take Chloe, then what will I have? Even Dan doesn't have enough money to keep her away from me.*

Law couldn't get his ex-wife's threats out of his head as he watched Chloe trudge away, following Fin.

Libby didn't want Chloe. At least, not as much as she didn't want to lose her leverage with Law. Whatever natural mothering instincts his ex-wife had had, she'd sacrificed them long ago, by constantly indulging her own insecurities.

She hadn't asked whether Chloe was okay, not once that morning. She hadn't apologized for having no idea Chloe had been gone all night. Since phoning Law and going ballistic, she hadn't tried to contact their daughter at all.

He handed Kristen a folder of documents he'd read and re-read a dozen times since meeting with Dan's lawyers, for a butt-crack-of-dawn powwow in his brother's ridiculously opulent den on Mimosa Lane.

"These are for you," he said.

"Oh . . ." Kristen glanced toward the Dixons, looking worried. "Thank you."

"Marsha and Joe heard enough last night to guess what's going on." He checked out the administrative staff, who promptly ducked their heads and went back to their jobs. "I'm sure you have, too. Everyone in town probably knows what happened at Pockets, and likely some of what went on after I dropped Chloe off at Libby's." He pointed to the folder now in Kristen's hands. "That's a temporary stay to Chloe's custody guidelines. Based on Libby's behavior last night, which Dan substantiated, and the pattern of blackout drinking Chloe's described—not to mention Libby's complete spacing on the fact that our daughter's been running around town at night by herself for months—a judge has agreed that Chloe's better off with me for now. I'm asking for a formal adjustment, something that will stay in place until Libby gets the help she needs and I'm certain Chloe's no longer at risk when she's with her mother."

"I see." To her credit, Kristen made the nonsense reaction sound convincing. He could tell she was holding back a ton of questions, or possibly trying to find a nice way to say that he should keep himself and his problems away from her from now on.

And why shouldn't she?

Dan and Charlotte's upstanding reputation in the community had been enough to appease the court temporarily. But Law had a knock-down, drag-out fight on his hands, regardless of Libby's obvious issues. He couldn't afford a second's distraction from what he had to do now for his daughter. And what woman in her right mind, especially one with Kristen's responsibilities and high profile in town, would risk taking on the array of shit coming his way over the next month or so?

She looked so professional and pressed and perfect today in her curvy light pink skirt and matching jacket. She'd never know how much her support had meant to him last night. But now . . .

"Until a judge makes an official ruling in a day or so," he said, "I'm Chloe's primary school contact. All the information you'll need is in there, plus an affidavit from my brother about us moving into his house, and the supervision Chloe will have there with Charlotte when I'm at work." Law switched his attention to Marsha and Joe. "If you don't mind, I'll have Dan's lawyer contact you about a statement of what you witnessed last night when I brought Fin home."

"Of course," Marsha said.

"And I'd be happy to testify about the altercation in the alley at Pockets," Kristen offered.

Was she closer? Or was Law imagining that a moment ago he wouldn't have been able to reach out and cup her cheek with his palm, and now he could? He could smell the same citrus scent he had yesterday at Pockets, when he'd been tugging Kristen's hand to inch her closer.

If she didn't step back, there'd be no way he could do the rest of what he'd come to school to do.

"Dan's taking care of recording what went on outside," Law roughed out. He cleared his throat, hoping he didn't sound as desperate as he felt. "I don't think there will be a shortage of people who could account for what happened at the party. I'm pretty sure Walter Davis will give a statement if I ask him to. It's probably better for me if you just stay out of it."

"Oh . . ." Kristen looked toward the Dixons again—a sideways, mortified glance. "I see."

She really didn't.

"I didn't mean—" he started to say, when he'd meant every word, and he needed to stick by them.

She placed her hand on his arm, her skin warming his below the sleeve of his T-shirt, her gaze soft and anger-free.

"I do understand." She lifted the file. "We both have a job to do here. I'll make sure this goes into Chloe's records, and that the carpool staff is briefed on who's approved to pick her up and drop her off from now on, if she doesn't ride the bus." Kristen smiled at the Dixons next. "And I'll keep you in the loop on Fin's progress here at school." She stepped back, miles away it seemed, though she'd barely moved an inch. "Thank you for working with Fin," she said to Law. "You're going to make an amazing difference in his life. I just know it. You already have. Now if you'll all excuse me . . ."

She disappeared into her office, closing her door with quiet dignity.

Joe shook his head and slapped Law on the back. "Damn, son. You sure know how to sweet-talk a woman."

"Joseph Dixon!" Marsha swatted her husband's chest with her purse, pointedly looking over her shoulder at their audience. The school secretaries were working still, but not with much enthusiasm. It was so quiet, Law heard someone walking by outside the hallway door.

"Excuse me." He stepped toward Kristen's office. But then he remembered Fin and the promise he'd made to the boy. "Chloe and I will be at the park around five," he reminded the Dixons.

He opened Kristen's door without knocking and walked inside. She was standing before the window instead of sitting at her desk, staring through the blinds. She had the file he'd given her clutched in her hand.

She folded her arms over her chest and turned toward him.

He shut the door behind him, not knowing what to say. But he wasn't leaving until this was done, and done right.

"This is a really bad idea," she said—using his words from last night. "Open my door, Mr. Beaumont, or my staff will get the wrong impression."

"I wasn't brushing you off out there. I wanted to talk to you in private. And my name is *Law*." He sighed, willing the frustration out of his voice. "Whatever else we are now, I think we at least owe it to each other to use our first names."

"Okay." Her eyebrow rose. "What are we, Law?"

"I don't know. But I know I'm not in a place to figure us out. Libby's going to be on the warpath. I have to deal with her, and I can't do that and worry about how any of this is affecting you, or what you're thinking, or what I'm going to do if you decide you can't handle another minute of my crazy life being mixed up with yours. I'm digging myself out of a deep hole. Deeper than I'd realized. I can't afford to be distracted, the way I've tuned too many things out for too long."

"I'm not trying to distract you." Some of the rigidness eased from her posture. "What if I were to decide that being mixed up with your crazy life suited me just fine?"

Well, Law admitted to himself, that would be even worse, wouldn't it?

"I don't think that's likely to happen." There, he'd said it, because she wouldn't. "You've been great to me, Kristen. But I need to be free of this before we end badly, too."

She tilted her head to the side, as if she'd only now realized that he was nuts. "You barge in here, shut yourself in my office, and stay when I ask you to go, because you want to tell me we're over, before we've even done anything to *be* over, so you can be free of me before we end badly?"

"That didn't come out right."

"I would hope not."

This wasn't what he wanted: her confrontational and hurting; him trying to do the right thing, but being an ass to her all over again. None of this was what he wanted.

God, she was sexy, giving him hell in that teacher's tone of hers, in her prim little suit with a skirt that dared a man to run his hands all over and under and up her mile-high, toned legs.

"I never meant for this to happen," he said, suddenly needing to adjust the fit of his jeans. But he'd be damned if he was going to draw attention to his predicament. "I never meant to upset you or your life."

"I'm not upset."

He was close enough now—three steps closer to the window, by his count—to know differently. Her pulse was beating away at the base of her throat.

"Law . . ." She said his name breathy and half-formed, while his finger traced the soft skin beneath her chin. "What do you want from me?"

"I want you to be okay with me keeping my distance while I sort things out with Libby." He let his finger slide just a little lower, torturing himself, before dropping his hand to the waist of his jeans. To make sure it stayed there, he snagged his fingers in his belt. "But I want you to know that the last forty-eight hours between us is making it nearly impossible for me to let go."

"Yeah," she whispered. "I know exactly how you feel. But you are letting go, right? And here I was, thinking you'd trust me enough to let me help you sort things out."

"Kristen . . ." He *didn't* trust her. He didn't know how to trust anyone.

Her hand tangled in his shirt, tugging him closer.

He brushed her lips with his, softly, sweetly. It was a chaste first kiss. It was a gentle good-bye.

"I don't want to hurt you," he whispered, his hands still at his sides. Hers were on his arms now, running up the muscles that felt like they might never unclench from the strain of maintaining space between them.

"Then don't," she whispered back.

She held his gaze for a second, and then she closed her eyes and kissed him. Harder, out of control, her mouth open to his, her lips soft to his tongue, her body pressed to his as they lost themselves in each other. No groping. No desperate need. Just touching and being touched and needing stronger than anything he'd let himself feel in a long time.

She stepped back, leaving him grasping for the emotional restraint he'd kept up all morning. He was in the midst of the most destructive mess of his life since the accident with Libby that had all but destroyed him. His daughter needed all of him now, to get her through this. And yet . . .

He needed Kristen, too, and the way she was making him feel broken open and stitched up and full to brimming and empty, all at the same time. He stared at her answering confusion.

"What are you going to do next?" she asked.

He shook his head. He had absolutely no idea. "We'll be fine."

Kristen nodded, disappointed. He could feel her letting go. It was already undoing him.

"Fight for your daughter," she said, arrowing straight to the heart of the matter with her customary fearlessness. Yet there was sadness in her eyes. Desire, and loss. She gulped. She reached for him again, this time laying her hand over his racing heart. "I'll be watching, Law, and cheering you on—for the good I know you'll be doing for Chloe and Fin. I'd like to help. If you ever decide you really want me, and trust me not to bail on you the way you're so convinced everyone will when you need them the most, you know how to reach me."

Chapter Eleven

Now

"It sounds like you got to know Chloe and her dad, by first playing soccer with them," Mrs. Sewel says after I finish telling her about how I met the Beaumonts. "And it almost sounds as if you were glad to see them in the office when you and the Dixons were talking with Ms. Hemmings. Was that when you and Chloe started to be friends?"

I look around Mrs. Sewel's run-down office that feels like my world has always felt—leftover and unwanted, because that's why kids like me come to places like this. When you're a kid and everyone else gives up on you, there's nowhere else to go.

Mrs. Sewel wants the Dixons to work. I believe her, even though she's not happy with everything I've told her. But that doesn't change what's happened. So why keep talking about it?

So what if, after I saw the Beaumonts at school that day, I started playing soccer with Chloe and her dad. I started trying harder at school. I stopped being such a pain to the Dixons, because they were kinda cool. And I started liking Chloe a little, because she'd decided to like me first, no matter how mean I'd been to her. But that doesn't change last night.

"You and Chloe must have felt like you had a lot in common," Mrs. Sewel says. "You must have heard what was going on with her parents, especially her mom. You'd seen her friends treat her badly, and she was feeling like she didn't fit in. But her dad was helping you, and she got you to go to class that morning. I hear you two are great on the soccer field together. You must have felt like you owed the Beaumonts a lot. Was that it?"

I shake my head.

"You knew that if my office heard you'd tried to run away again," she says, writing more into her notes, "you weren't going to be able to stay with the Dixons. So why, Fin? Why run away with Chloe from last night's Valentine's party, after working so hard at your soccer and your foster family and school and making Chandlerville work?"

I shake my head again. I'm not going to cry anymore. And I'm not going to rat on Chloe.

I heard what Chloe's parents said to each other last night. What no one else knows. That's why we ran, after she listened to them fighting outside the party at Pockets. Chloe couldn't stay after that, and I couldn't let her go alone. Just like I can't tell Mrs. Sewel why now—because I promised Chloe I wouldn't. Chloe hates that everyone in town is going to know how messed up her family really is. I don't want her to hate me because I'm the one who tells.

"You said she was a mean girl at first, like her friends," Mrs. Sewel says. "But she wasn't that way at all, was she?"

I shake my head. "She's cool. She and her dad were cool to me."

"And because of them, you started to think the Dixons and school and other things here might be cool, too?"

I nod, feeling stupid. Feeling sorry. "Chloe's family was messed up, but she and her dad helped me. A lot of people helped me."

"Then why, Fin?" Mrs. Sewel pushes her notebook and pen

away. She's still in her chair on the other side of her desk. "You learned to like your new family and your new friends and being in Chandlerville. I need you to tell me why you threw all that away last night."

I shrug. The Dixons' house is loud and noisy and full of kids, but it's my house now. And I don't want to lose them, or Chloe, or even school. I don't want to lose any of it. I'm sick, just thinking about it.

Mrs. Sewel is suddenly beside me, on my side of her desk and sitting in the chair next to mine.

"I know you've been happy in Chandlerville," she says. "I can tell how much this is hurting you. Your permanent placement with the Dixons was green-lighted. It's what they want. It's what I thought you wanted. Except I can't make that happen for you if I can't tell my supervisors and the judge that you won't run again. Help me figure out what's the right thing for you. Talk to me about what happened last night."

I shake my head.

I can't. I've never had a friend before, not like Chloe and Mr. Beaumont. And if I tell, it would mean Chloe never should have trusted me at all. And I've already messed up enough.

"Come on, Fin," Mrs. Sewell says. "Certainly you can tell me more. Let's talk about what happened the day before your first practice with the soccer team . . ."

Chapter Twelve

Before

"You doing okay?" Walter asked Law, just before noon on the first Wednesday in February.

Law grunted.

Lunchtime at McC's was, as usual, a slow start. That had become the appeal for Walter over the last couple of months—getting away from Pockets before his and Julia's afternoon picked up. And Law usually liked having the man around at the start of the late-morning shift that was all he worked now most weekdays. But today wasn't the day for Walter to ask what Law had sensed him wanting to, several times before.

Is Mom better? Chloe had asked before school that morning. *Is she better enough for me to go back and live with her, and you to go back to your apartment, and for everything to go back to normal again?*

Law sighed instead of answering his friend. He thought of the warped version of *normal* his life had been last year, before he'd realized his ex-wife had relapsed. And the nothing-close-to-normal that he had to look forward to now, *if* Libby kept herself sober and he could trust her with Chloe again.

It was almost unbearable, thinking about coming out of the last two months only to watch Libby bottom out again. What would another relapse do to Chloe? To all of them?

He hadn't known what to tell his daughter this morning. They'd been living in limbo with Dan since November. Law still wasn't ready to commit to something more permanent. Right now it took all he had just to get them through each day.

His lawyer had secured him temporary sole custody. If Rick needed Law to work nights in a pinch, Charlotte was always at the Mimosa Lane house to supervise the girls, or she gladly took Chloe with her and Sally when they went places. But Chloe needed him around as much as possible, even when she spent most of her time at home in her room, pretending he didn't exist. She alternated between clinging to him and refusing to talk. She was confused and angry still, and not liking the way they were living. He could relate.

The holidays had been impossible. Libby had made certain of it.

She'd refused to take her sobriety seriously at first, demanding more time with Chloe than the supervised visits the court had granted her, while she spiraled deeper into her addiction. She'd found rock bottom on Christmas morning, which she'd spent drunk and entirely alone. By New Year's, she'd finally sobered up and promised to do whatever she had to, to make amends. And so it had started again: Law trying to believe her enough to get them all back to something resembling the stable family Chloe deserved. For their child's sake, he and Libby had to learn how to co-parent without being at each other's throats.

Which would mean more change, more limbo, more of him doing whatever he had to, to show Chloe that things would somehow work out.

Dan was helping out financially with more than just legal expenses. Law had broken his lease on his apartment. Most of his personal things were boxed up and banished to a storage locker on the outskirts of town. His brother was covering the fee for that unit, as well as helping with the alimony and child support Law was still legally required to pay his ex-wife—even though Chloe was with him full-time, and that meant he was clocking fewer hours at the bar.

Thanks to the skill of Dan's lawyer buddy, Libby's drinking had been formally documented for the court. She hadn't been able to talk herself out of the irresponsible behavior so many people had now witnessed. Since the new year, she'd worked hard to rehab her image, if not actually going to rehab. She was sober, she insisted. She was more attentive to Chloe. She was back volunteering at the school and mending fences with the friends who'd shunned her after her alcoholism had become public knowledge.

But was it a real change this time? Was she committed to making this last? Law wished like hell he knew. And he wished he really knew what his daughter thought about any of it.

Chloe seemed to be enjoying the several afternoons a week she and Law spent playing soccer with Fin. All she'd wanted, she'd told him that night after they'd left the Dixons, was for their family, their lives, to feel good again. Now that things were calming down, she was dealing with school better, according to the e-mails Law received each week from Daphne Glover. She was more like her old self than the wannabe mean girl she'd tried to become for Libby's sake at the beginning of the school year.

But Chloe was still too quiet with him. She was missing her mom. She was waiting, bracing for whatever happened next. His daughter sometimes seemed to feel as lost, still, as Law did.

He looked up from drying a load of glasses he'd just pulled from the bar's dishwasher, his gaze connecting with Walter's. How was he doing? On top of everything, he was missing Kristen like hell, so badly his chest physically hurt each time he thought of how sweet and understanding she'd been to him.

He braced himself against the memory of her the morning he'd broken things off. Angry and confused and resigned to him pulling away, she'd kissed him breathless and told him she hoped everything would work out. A haunting song poured through his mind, about capturing time in a bottle forever, along with dreams he had no chance of making come true.

Walter nodded at Law's silence, as if he'd heard the litany of regrets tumbling through Law's mind. He took a bite of his cheeseburger. He popped a fry into his mouth.

"You give any thought," he said, "to getting out a bit more, like you did that night at mine and Julia's opening?"

Law grunted again.

He knew exactly who his friend was thinking he might be *getting out* with. According to Dan, it sounded as if half the town was wondering the same thing—especially since no one had seen him and Kristen together since that morning in her office. Especially since Kristen had left Chandlerville for almost two weeks, once school let out for Christmas and New Year's. She'd evidently never done that before, not once since she'd moved to town. It had made people think there was something, someone in particular, she'd needed to get away from.

Law could be pissed at Walter for prying into his personal life. He could refuse to answer. But the truth was pressing up from somewhere inside, until it came tumbling out.

"Yeah," he said. "I think about it a lot."

He'd thought about following Kristen to wherever she'd

gone over the holiday. He'd thought about calling and telling her he'd made a mistake, and then begging her to give him another chance, to be there for him the way she'd said she wanted to.

Then he'd thought about Libby, and his still having to deal with her, and how many times he *hadn't* dealt with his life, and the pain that had caused people he'd cared about. Dumping on Kristen, after the way he'd treated her, wasn't going to change his reality one bit. And it would likely hurt her all over again.

Walter took another bite of his burger. "It's got to be hard."

"What does?"

"Doing all of this alone."

Law thought of Dan and Charlotte, supportive but in a hands-off way. Mostly because Law hadn't had it in him, after dealing with Libby and Chloe every day, to delve any deeper into the unspoken truce he and his brother had found. He thought of Chloe and how skittish she still was around him, ever since he'd pried the truth out of her about Libby's drinking. He thought of Walter, stopping by McC's so often when there were better places in town to get lunch. And Marsha and Joe Dixon, always making a point to ask how things were going when they dropped Fin off and picked him up at the park.

"I'm not alone," he said. The weight of everyone still seeming so far away settled heavier on his shoulders.

Walter kept eating.

Law wiped down the bar's already spotless counter.

"Kristen stopped by Pockets last night," Walter said, watching the flat-screen over Law's shoulder.

Law stopped wiping.

"What are you getting at?" Law wasn't talking about Kristen today, or any other day.

Walter crumpled his paper napkin and tossed it on top of his half-eaten burger. "She asked about you, is all. Actually, she asked about you and Chloe. She's as worried as the rest of us are."

"Us?" It should help. It should feel good to know he had the kind of support Walter was talking about. Only it didn't. None of it felt real yet. Maybe it never would.

"Julia and me," Walter said. "Dan and Charlotte. A lot of the families on Mimosa Lane would like to get to know you two better, and see you happier, now that you're living near us."

"We're only there temporarily." Everything in his life felt so damn temporary, Law suddenly wanted to smash every glass he was sliding onto the overhead rack.

"People around here aren't going to stop caring about you," Walter said, "whatever you end up doing about Libby and your family. Especially not a lady who's still as into you as Kristen is, if I don't miss my guess."

Law braced both palms on the counter.

Kristen had asked about him. She'd been looking out for Chloe at school, too. His daughter had mentioned how Kristen kept stopping by class or during recess or lunch, to check in and say something kind or just to give Chloe a hug. Kristen was still there every day, so close to his life it was maddening. She hadn't backed off one bit, even though she'd given him the space he'd said he wanted, not phoning or trying to see him again.

"I appreciate everyone's concern," he said to Walter. "But . . ."

"But what?"

Law couldn't get past it. He also couldn't say it. Not to his brother, not to Walter. Certainly not to his daughter.

"But you think Libby's drinking still?" Walter asked, right on the money, the relentless bastard.

Law almost told his friend where he could shove his insight. Instead, he nodded. "Yeah."

Walter rested against the back of his stool. He took a sip of his Dr Pepper. "Dan is figuring that, too. I think Kristen's wondering as well, though she'd never come right out and say it."

"I'd be surprised if everyone in Chandlerville wasn't thinking it."

"And?"

"And what? Of course my ex-wife's biding her time, waiting to yank my chain again once she has everyone believing she's past the mess she made out of last year. That's what she does, Walter. And she's Chloe's mother, which makes her part of my life for good, no matter what she screws up next. This is my family. I'm dealing with it."

"Are you?"

"Am I what?"

"Dealing with it? I see you scrambling. I see you dedicating yourself to not giving in to Libby again, no matter how hard it's making things. But I don't see you leaning on anyone for the kind of help you're gonna need to get through this. You and Dan are doing better, I guess, since you've made it this long living with him. But that's not all there is. This isn't just about having a place to stay while you wait Libby out, or lining up lawyers and dealing with family court, or getting Chloe through another disappointment. What about you, Law?"

"What about me?" Law wadded a bar towel in his fist. "I'm holding my daughter's life together with my bare hands, and I have no control over whether or not Libby lets her down again. Half the time I think Chloe still thinks her mom and I are going to get back together, and that that will fix things. Divorce is hell on a kid under normal circumstances. But this . . . Eventually I'll have to break her heart about the fact that nothing between Libby and me will ever be *together* again. All I can do in the meantime is try to control the damage. Libby's going to do whatever she's going to do next. She's going to get better once and for all, or she's going to hurt whoever she's going to hurt."

"So you just let her mistakes overwhelm every part of your and Chloe's lives? For how long?"

"However long it takes. If people think I should be doing more, then I'm sorry to disappoint them. There's no more of me to go around."

I'd like to help. If you ever decide you really want me, Kristen had said, *and trust me . . .*

Walter braced his elbows on the bar. He clasped his hands in front of him and leaned in. He looked frustrated and earnest and resigned, like a father giving advice to a troubled kid he knew wasn't going to listen.

"I asked Dan the other night," he said, "when he and Charlotte and Sally came to bowl without you and Chloe. I asked him how he thought things were going for you and your daughter. I've never seen him that way before, Law."

"What way?"

"He's worried sick about you still trying to get through this alone. He said that all your life you'd always done everything by yourself, until you met Libby. And then you insisted on doing everything with her, even after the accident, when he was desperate to help you, just like he is now. Only now . . . it's like you're still in this alone with Libby."

"I'm not *with* Libby, I assure you." The thought was chilling.

"Who are you with, then? You're living near all of us. Like you said, you're taking care of your responsibilities and doing what you have to for your family. But you and Chloe are still on your own. You're expecting things to get worse before they get better, is all I can figure. So why settle in and learn how to make something good happen for your life? Is that what you think your daughter deserves?"

"We'll be fine." Law was taking care of Chloe. He was going to get her through this.

Walter cut him a killing glance. He drew a business card from his pocket and pushed it across the bar. Law took one look. Al-Anon. He pushed it back.

Walter stared at him. "I'm sure Libby thinks she'll be fine, too."

"I'm not drinking again, Walter. I'm not a walking time bomb like my ex-wife."

"I never said you were."

"Then back off."

"Codependence can be just as destructive as addiction, if you don't deal with it. Julia had to learn that the hard way, remember?"

"Well, I don't."

"Then what's going on with you and Kristen?"

"Nothing," Law bit out. Not a damn thing.

Walter stared some more. "Give her a chance to help, Law. I saw the way the two of you were looking at each other at my opening. Dan told me how she stood up for you outside, when Libby first started to come unglued. She's your daughter's assistant principal. She has to know enough about your issues with Libby to make her own decision about being part of your life. And she's still asking after you. I could hear how much she cares in her voice. Why are you treating her like something you and Chloe can't have?"

"Let it go, Walter. I've already done enough damage to enough lives."

It was all Law could do each night as he lay awake not to call Kristen and beg her for another chance. He wanted her close again. He wanted to fall deeper into her and feel her understanding him, wanting him the way no one ever had. Only sooner or later, his world would explode again. And then they'd be right back where they were in November.

When he'd walked up to her that first morning on the playground, he'd told himself *he* was the one taking a risk by confronting her. If he acted on the things he'd been feeling about her for so long, it would threaten the stability he needed in his life. Then he'd gotten to know Kristen, touched her, kissed her. And when she'd taken a chance on him, risked knowing him even better, *he'd* cut and run. He'd been the threat all along.

"So, being around you means trouble, it's always meant trouble, so what's the point?" Walter asked. "Law, if it weren't for me falling apart on this very stool last April, if it weren't for that call you made to Julia so she could get Brian Perry over here to kick my ass out of my drunken pity party, both my boys wouldn't be thinking about going into business with me. They want to help me run the bowling center, when they could be off doing anything else. My wife and I are working together every day, even though I've put her through the wringer. Julia and I are celebrating our twenty-fifth wedding anniversary and renewing our vows at the Valentine's party we're hosting next week. The whole town's coming to Pockets to celebrate with us. Because of you, Law. None of it would have happened if you hadn't seen how much trouble I was in and gotten someone down here to help me when I couldn't help myself."

"And if it weren't for me being so out of control ten years ago when I hooked up with Libby"—Law felt himself unraveling—

"Chloe's first few years on this earth wouldn't have happened without me there. And the rest of her life—"

"Are you telling me you think could have magically changed Libby into a better mother from the start if you two hadn't been drinking yourself senseless? That if you hadn't gone to prison, she wouldn't still be drinking now?" Walter stood and threw enough money on the bar to cover his bill and a healthy tip. "Or are you saying you'd go back and not hook up with Libby at all, so neither one of you would be where you are today? Because then you wouldn't have Chloe, would you? But at least you wouldn't still be contending with her mother, right?"

"You go to hell for saying that." Law leaned over the bar, looming over a gentler, smaller man who'd never been anything but kind to him.

He was thinking of doing serious damage to a friend who was only trying to help. He was thinking about Libby and prison, and Chloe and Kristen, and all the mistakes he still felt powerless to fix. Because maybe Walter was right. What the hell difference did any of it make, when more each day it felt as if Law couldn't change one damn bit of his life or move forward to anything better?

And suddenly he was thinking about drinking again.

A lot.

Walter pushed the Al-Anon card toward him again.

"You're already in hell, Law. You may have divorced Libby. You've finally got the court on your side, dealing with her problems. But her disease still has a stranglehold on you and your daughter. If seeing Chloe settled and happy is what you really want, you have to figure out how to do that for yourself first. And your saying no to a stable, loving woman like Kristen, who obviously still wants to care about you, seems almost as destructive for you and Chloe as what Libby's doing. If you can't grab hold of something better for yourself than what you have with your ex, what makes you think you can teach Chloe how to believe she can have more?"

Law stared at the business card. He stared across the bar at his friend, and then back at every chance to break free that he'd wasted in the past.

"You called Julia for me last year," Walter said. "I'm callin' you on your denial now. You need help, Law, from somewhere. You need to deal with Libby. You need to get right with yourself. If not for you, then do it for your daughter. And if you could do that on your own, don't you think you would have by now?"

***

"How are you doin', honey?" Aunt Charlotte asked Chloe, in her fake cheery way. "What happened at school today?"

Chloe glanced at her cousin. Sally was sitting with her in the back of Aunt Charlotte's brand-new car. At least, it looked and smelled and drove brand-new, not like her family's cars—her mom's ancient Camry or her dad's forever-old truck. Sally was staring out her window. She'd been with Aunt Charlotte when they'd picked Chloe up at Chandler, since middle school kids got out before elementary ones.

Sally turned her head and stared at her mom in the rearview mirror. She'd told Chloe she couldn't believe her parents wouldn't stop asking the same questions over and over since Chloe and her dad had moved in. They thought it would make Chloe feel like part of their family if she knew they worried about her.

Did Chloe feel okay? Did her mom say something to upset her again? How was her Thanksgiving? Did she get anything special for Christmas? What did she and her friends do at school today? . . .

Chloe didn't want to feel like part of Sally's family, even though Chloe and her dad were still living at Uncle Dan's house. She'd thought that by now, at least, her dad would be back at his apartment and Chloe would be back to staying with him and her mom again. Except her mom had kept getting drunk all the way through the holidays. Chloe still didn't have her family back yet, no matter how much better things had been since Christmas. Dad had said she could trust him to understand and help. But so far, nothing was helping.

School was okay, she guessed. She and Fin were sort of friends now. Her old friends, and sometimes his, made fun of her a little still. But he never did. And she didn't really care so much anymore about everybody else, now that Mom wasn't bugging her to be nice to all the popular kids all the time. Dad had made Mom stop doing that. And even though Chloe was acting like herself again, Brooke and Summer still talked to her a lot, even when she didn't want them to. Not that having friends, especially ones who hadn't completely stopped making fun of her, helped the way it used to.

It didn't keep Chloe from thinking about all the other stuff. Her family's stuff. When she'd asked again that morning when things would be back to normal, her dad hadn't been able to tell her. He'd seemed really sad that he couldn't. And that had made going to school today and pretending she was okay for everyone harder. Just like it was hard to pretend for Sally and Aunt Charlotte now.

The one good thing about today was that the first soccer practice for her new team, the Strikers, was tomorrow. And she and her dad and Fin had their last workout tonight, before the season began. The new team was going to be great, Dad said, with a lot of the players he'd coached before moving up with them to the new age group.

And even though Thomas Kilpatrick, who was still a pest sometimes at school, was going to be on the team, and her mom still hated that Chloe was playing, and Summer and Brooke still thought she was nuts for being the only girl on the team . . . Chloe couldn't wait.

"Did something happen in class?" Aunt Charlotte's face didn't look cheery anymore, staring into the backseat through the rearview mirror. She sounded worried, not fake. "You're so quiet. Are you okay?"

Sally rolled her eyes at Chloe. Chloe didn't answer. Things were worse than ever. Didn't everyone know that she knew that? Didn't her dad?

He hardly ever smiled anymore, not the way she'd seen him smile the night at the bowling center when he'd been talking with Ms. Hemmings, or later when he'd first played soccer with Chloe and Fin. Even when they got to play soccer with Fin in the afternoons, because Dad had changed his schedule at work so he and Chloe could do more things together after school, he pretty much never smiled. He was acting so weird. How could anything be okay?

"Why didn't my dad pick me up?" she asked.

She'd seen her aunt in the carpool lane, and Summer and Brooke had been going on and on about how cool her aunt and uncle's car was, talking to Chloe nice today, when tomorrow who knew what they'd say. Today they'd told Chloe she was lucky to be living with her aunt and uncle. Only instead of feeling lucky, Chloe had started crying.

Because she'd thought for a minute something was wrong with her dad or her mom, because Dad had promised to pick her up today. She still thought something was wrong, even though Aunt Charlotte was acting like it wasn't. Maybe because so much had been wrong for so long.

"Your dad said he had something last-minute he needed to do after work," her aunt chirped, fake-cheery again, like she wanted to know what Dad was doing, too, but she didn't want Chloe to think she did. "He said to be ready for soccer at six. He'll be home by then for sure, and you guys can head over to the park after you grab whatever you want for dinner. The Dixons are still dropping Fin off. Sally has a basketball game, so she and her dad and I will be heading for the YMCA right around then. Are you excited your season's finally here?"

Chloe looked down at the display on her cell phone that no one had called or texted her on. Were Brooke and Summer together somewhere, laughing because she'd cried in carpool over nothing?

Only it wasn't nothing.

What's the use? Fin had said that day in the lunchroom, when he'd first tried to be nice to her. Now Chloe knew exactly how he'd felt. His parents were gone, and hers weren't. But sometimes, a lot of the time, it seemed like her mom, her family, was never going to get better.

So what *was* the use?

***

Kristen pulled into the YMCA parking lot in her bright red convertible Mustang. She'd tossed her overflowing tote and the bag holding her half-eaten lunch into the passenger seat. She'd left school earlier than usual, because it was Wednesday. And Wednesday afternoon this time of year meant cutting short her review of her grade team leads' reports so she could make a four o'clock play-off game for her twelve-and-under girls' basketball team.

No matter the demands Chandler made on her time, nothing would keep her from being there for her team. Long ago, sports had become her inspiration and her life and her desire to do and feel better, when the adults in her world had emotionally abandoned her as if she didn't exist. Basketball had taught her the transcendent power of believing in and being responsible for someone besides herself. It was likely why she *hadn't* followed in her parents' narcissistic, self-absorbed footsteps.

Which meant, no matter how many long nights it might cost her making up her work, she'd always be the first one to arrive at practices and games, and the last one to leave—so she could hopefully make the same difference in the lives of her players.

Just before she'd left her office, Daphne had stopped by to say that Chloe continued to have up and down days in class, and that she seemed more down lately than up. It wasn't an unexpected side effect of Law's continued legal struggles with her mother. Libby had been pulling her act together after the holidays. But Kristen still worried about Chloe, and Law, no matter how long it had been since she'd heard from him.

I don't want to hurt you, he'd said.

So don't . . .

With the kiss she'd initiated in her office, she'd let Law know she'd keep seeing him, despite his issues with his ex. Then she'd stayed out of his way, while she'd watched over his daughter at school, hoping he'd come find her when he was ready. But he hadn't. He didn't want to reconnect. He didn't want *her*, or trust her, or whatever else had spooked him.

And *this*—this waiting around and wondering what she meant to someone she cared about, and wanting him to care about her, too—this was why she didn't do long-term relationships. Enough was enough. It was past time to move on. And yet, she couldn't banish the warm baritone of his voice from her memories, or the feel of his rough fingers rubbing against her softer ones, or the flash of need that had sparked between them every time they were close.

She hadn't been imagining it. It just turned out that she'd believed in it—believed in them—more than he had. She cut her ignition and leaned back into the leather headrest.

"Law Beaumont . . ." she whispered, sighing at the longing that still seized her, each time she thought of him, or thought of calling him with an update about Chloe's day at school, or to ask if Fin seemed to be doing as well with his soccer as the boy was now at school.

Law had fascinated her from afar for years, mesmerized her in person in a matter of minutes. He might be an obsession that would linger forever, reminding her of how foolishly she'd mistaken the fleeting moments she'd been with him for being as priceless to him as they had been to her. He'd slipped past the emotional barriers she'd clung to since childhood. His rougher edges and that gentle, decent, loyal soul of his had found the emptiness inside her and promised to fill it up. And she'd carelessly believed she'd touched him the same way.

I don't believe in lost causes . . .

She dropped her head to the steering wheel. Lord, she still wanted him. She'd fallen for a man whose personal life was in shambles, and she couldn't get up. She'd known it was a risk, but she'd cared about him and his child anyway—she still did. At least she'd put everything on the line that morning in her office. She'd never have to look back and regret not doing more.

Since he'd walked away, she'd refocused on her friends and neighbors, the community that was strolling past her now on their way inside the Y. She'd consoled herself with the blessing that being part of Chandlerville and her job at the elementary school still was. Even her basketball teams had been a source of comfort, as she watched her girls shine and mature. She cared about them. A lot of people cared about her. She was a lucky, content woman, the same as she'd been before she'd met Law. Except it was no longer enough.

Because she wanted to at least have the chance to share even more with Law. He'd made her want to prove to herself, and to him, that belonging to something—to someone—*really* belonging, unconditionally, without limits, without protecting herself from how things could fall apart at any moment, might really be possible for people like them.

She should be pissed at him.

Not a word. He hadn't said a single word to her for almost three months. No phone call, no voice mail, no note or e-mail. He'd been honest. He'd said he had to focus on Libby, and helping Chloe. And he had, from what she'd heard. But it still stung.

He was an amazing man. He'd kept showing up for Fin several nights a week. He was protecting his daughter as best he could. He'd reconciled with his brother, for Chloe's sake, no matter how much scorched earth he and Dan had accumulated over the years. He deserved so much more from life than he was allowing himself to claim. And didn't that just make her afternoon—how much happiness and peace she still wanted for him, when by now he likely no longer thought of her at all?

She reached for the handle and pushed her door open. She was making herself late for the game. She froze halfway out of the car.

A smile, and then just as quickly a frown, tugged at her lips. Coach Beaumont—as she'd heard Fin call him at school—had parked his battered red truck on the other side of the lot.

And he was headed Kristen's way.

Chapter Thirteen

Law didn't have a lot of time.

He didn't want to be late picking up Chloe. He didn't want her worrying about whether he'd make their last night of playing for fun in the park before the season started. And in his latest brotherly bonding gesture, Dan had said he'd be stopping by the park, too, after Sally's basketball game. He wanted to help out with the coaching.

Law had all of that ahead of him tonight, and possibly another round of pleading phone calls from Libby begging him to give up his plans to petition for full custody. She'd woken him up in the middle of the night twice already this week, including last night. And he was dead tired from covering the first shift at McC's. But there he was at the Y, walking toward trouble, prepared to tackle Kristen in front of God and everybody, if she ran from him the way she looked like she might. Not that he had the first clue what he was going to say once he got to her.

He'd been stewing over Walter's parting shot since the man had left the bar, still thinking about the peace that had settled over him during his and Kristen's one phone call, and their con-

versation outside Pockets—when she'd shared some of her difficult memories of her parents, and it had helped him face more of
his past. They'd spoken about personal things only twice, but
he'd never before talked that candidly with anyone in his life, not
even his daughter these last few months.

And then it had hit him like a ton of bricks. The growing
distance he'd been feeling between himself and Chloe was beginning to resemble the empty relationship he and Dan still
shared, even though he and his brother were living under the
same roof again. It was as if he were becoming a stranger to his
own daughter, the way he was to everyone else in town.

That wasn't what was happening, he'd assured himself. Except Chloe's enthusiasm for life seemed to be fading more each
day, no matter how many people were trying to help her through
this. Almost as if normal, enduring, healing things like friends
and family and . . . love were never going to be hers—pretty much
the way he'd felt for too long that they weren't going to be his.

That awful moment of reckoning had propelled him to call
Charlotte. He'd sprinted to his car and driven to the YMCA,
where he knew Kristen would be this afternoon. He clenched his
hand around the Al-Anon card in his jeans pocket, and kept
walking across the parking lot toward her. She'd seen him as
soon as he'd driven up, and she'd frozen as if she was terrified.
And then angry. And then sad. It was the sadness consuming her
expression now that was the hardest for him to face.

She wasn't hiding her bombshell sexuality this afternoon beneath one of her prim suits. She'd changed into jeans and a jersey
like the one Sally wore on game nights—his niece was on the
team Kristen had a play-off game with. She still looked supremely
cool and put together. Effortlessly in control, no matter the situation. But when he looked into her eyes, instead of the generosity

he'd always seen before, or her willingness to help and give him a chance, all he saw was . . . pain.

So you just let Libby's mistakes overwhelm every part of your and Chloe's lives . . . ? Walter had said.

And Law's ex-wife had, from practically the day he'd met her. Until everything exciting and hopeful about who they might have been, and now who Chloe was becoming, was collateral damage.

He stared at the selfless, mesmerizing woman in front of him. Everything he'd thought about saying since he'd asked his sister-in-law to pick up Chloe evaporated from his short-term memory. He glanced behind Kristen at the flashy sports car he hadn't known she drove.

"A Mustang? On a school administrator's salary?" As soon as the words came out of his mouth, he wanted them back. He was poking at her like a nervous schoolboy Fin's age, trying to show a girl he liked her by pulling her hair.

"It's paid for." Kristen's even tone beat him up, more than if she'd raged at him the way he deserved. "Just like my condo and everything else I own. I don't do debt. I don't owe anyone anything. That way, when it's time to move on, I get to walk away clean."

Because of her parents. He knew enough about her past, and he'd felt enough emotional neglect himself, to understand the need not to depend on anyone but yourself. And he'd become one more person who'd let her down.

"I wanted to ask . . ." he said, and then he couldn't. If she said no, then they really would be through.

"Hey, Law," Webber Jackson called as he walked by. "It's good to see you."

The man waved and kept walking, glancing back before he headed inside with his wife and daughter. Webber's son was going to be the Strikers' first-string goalie. Which meant that at tomorrow night's first practice, if not before, gossip would be flying about Law and Kristen talking again. And Libby would hear. And . . .

And what?

You're already in hell, Law.

"You wanted to ask me something?" Kristen challenged him, pushing without demanding, strong and capable and confident.

She'd never once done anything but support him and want him to be a better man. How could he have convinced himself to give that up?

"Would you meet me for coffee sometime?" he asked. At her shocked silence, he blew out a breath. "I don't even know if you drink coffee."

She crossed her arms. "No, you don't."

"Well, obviously cocktails are a no-go for me." He laughed softly—at himself. He felt like a fool. Then he smiled. Because she was laughing a little, too, maybe forgiving him a little. Or at least not looking quite so much like she wanted to be anywhere but with him.

"I don't drink, either," she said, "because of my—"

"Mother. Yeah." Of course she wouldn't. "Ice cream, then? I know where to get the best milk shakes in every zip code between here and the Atlanta Zoo. But that sounds childish, right?" He was tripping all over himself, like an idiot. "Don't get me wrong. This is important to me—more important than you can know. But I've been an ass. I know that. I've messed up my chances with you. I've been trying to figure out what to say all the way over here from the bar. This is too important to screw up, and I'm screwing it up. But how do I ask you out on a first date, when I know I've probably already scared you away for good?"

"Date?" Kristen looked around. They were attracting more attention.

"Yes, there's frost on the ground in hell. I'm asking you out on a date."

"Important?"

"Yes, you're important to me."

"Important enough to kick to the curb as soon as things got rougher with your ex?"

He scratched behind his ear. "Yeah. I blew that. I should have at least called. But . . ." He exhaled. She didn't deserve excuses.

"I heard how bad things were with Libby over the holidays," she said, saving him. She shrugged, as if the concern on her face, despite everything, was nothing. "I tried not to listen, but I . . ."

"You couldn't help it?" Like she hadn't been able to stop looking at him in the park all these years, and he'd been unable to stop noticing her, and neither of them had managed to back off once they'd met face-to-face, until he'd asked her to. "Yeah, it's been ugly. But I made it rougher than it had to be by—"

"Refusing to let me help you through it? Because why would that be a good thing for either of us—growing closer while you pieced your life back together?"

He nodded. "It never occurred to me that that might work. I thought I was beating you to the punch, saving you from having to deal with changing your mind later. I still find it hard to understand how you wouldn't have."

"Well, I guess we'll never know, will we? You must not have a very high opinion of me. Not if you think I hadn't considered what I was getting myself into before I kissed you that morning in my office. I don't put myself out there like that, Law. I don't . . ."

"Trust that someone will be there for you, if you let them see how much you want them to be? I get that, Kristen. I'm sorry I hurt you that way."

She finally looked angry. "You could have at least called to say it was too much for you to even think about me anymore."

"I've thought about you every day."

"Is that supposed to make me feel better? It's been months. Now you show up here, rocking everyone's world while they walk by and see us together, making some kind of grand gesture in the YMCA parking lot, like you did at the Pockets opening. I wonder how many people have texted about it already. I wonder how long it's going to take for this to get back to your ex."

For the first time in his memory, Law didn't give a rat's ass what Libby heard or did.

"I like rock," he said, refusing to talk about his ex. Kristen had to understand how much she meant to him, even if this was the last time they spoke. Especially if it was the last time.

"What?"

"You've been *rocking my world* all this time, even when I wouldn't let myself call you. I hear rock songs in my head when I think of you. And jazz and blues and sappy ballads. And I think about you every day, Kristen. I mean that. I'm sorry it's taken me so long to get my head out of my ass, and to get my life into enough perspective to see how much I threw away with you. I have no idea what Libby's going to do when she hears about this, or how it's going to affect Chloe, or how it might back up on us. But I can promise you, if you give me another chance, I'll never up and disappear on you again. You're right. You don't deserve that."

She blinked several times, taking in everything he'd said. He tried to process it himself. He fought the impulse to sprint back to his truck.

"I'm usually the one doing the dumping," Kristen said. "When things feel too real, I break up with the guy in my life, before things get messy."

Law nodded. "It hurts less that way."

Her narrowed eyes stared through him, and into him, and, he suspected, back over the time they hadn't spent together since before Thanksgiving. He stayed put while she thought things through.

"Jazz . . ." she finally said.

"What?"

"And the blues. I hear more jazz and blues than rock, when I'm trying to sleep at night, and I can't because I'm thinking about you. I wonder what you'd sound like playing soul-bending songs that would break my heart."

"Or make it stronger." He'd kill to have that chance. "So, you know I'm a singer."

"I know a lot about you, at least I thought I did. You know a lot about me, too. And I think that's what really spooked you, more than the stuff with Libby."

The delicate necklace she wore—a tiny eternity symbol strung from a whisper-thin silver chain—captured his attention. He reached out to touch the pendant, nestled in the hollow of her throat just above her collarbone. Her heartbeat fluttered beneath his fingertip. Her eyes widened.

"What do I know about you?" he asked.

"You know what it's like to be completely alone inside, and to think that just might be the best you're ever going to feel—because *together* has never worked out. Not the kind of together that good families find. Good families aren't for me, Law, any more than they are for you. I told you that day in my office, I understand why you had to step away. I know how hard it is to go through what you are with Libby. I don't blame you."

His arms went numb.

His ears rang with a flash of recognition.

"Nothing in my life's been easy for a very long time," he admitted. "Except for those few days when it started to feel like you were going to be part of it. But being with me can't possibly be good for you. Look at what I've already put you through."

"Don't tell me I'm the one you've been protecting."

"No. I'm a selfish, closed-down son of a bitch. But I don't want to stay away from you any longer. Unless you tell me you need me to. And you probably should."

"Because you liking me is—"

"Me *wanting* you is dangerous. Because it's possible I'll hurt you anyway. And being careful to avoid people who can hurt you is something else we have in common, right?"

She looked down at the pavement. "Maybe careful isn't all it's cracked up to be. Or I wouldn't have been missing you so much."

"I really am sorry."

She looked up and smoothed a hand down his arm. She nodded, still unsure. "You're the most dangerous thing I've let myself need since I needed my mother to love me . . . and she never did. My dad either, not really."

Law took her hand. He kissed it, wanting to kiss away every bad memory, and then to keep kissing her until he'd replaced each one, loving her until she could only think about how amazing they were together.

"I won't rush you," he said. "Take your time deciding. But if it's not too late, I'd like to try this again. You're the music I hear,

Kristen Hemmings. The last two months, thinking of you late at night has kept me sane when nothing else could. I wanted you to know that. And from now on, when I think of you, I'll be hearing the sexiest jazz I know."

"Jazz can be pretty sad."

He shook his head. "Not when it's you. Your notes are deep and moody, and always looking for a way in, until one day they catch you off guard and you're lost in the music. And when jazz is that good, darlin' . . . one note, one perfect chord, can last forever. That's why I know, even if you can't give me another chance, I'm the luckiest man alive just for the few days you let me get to know you. And for the few minutes you're giving me now."

He laughed at himself.

He sounded ridiculous.

And yet, he hadn't felt this inspired since he was in college, to write down the music swirling through his mind.

"Coffee and ice cream?" Kristen asked again. "And jazz . . . That's going to be a funky first date."

"Whatever you want," he rushed to say. "Whenever you're ready. Call me. I'll wait to hear from you this time, Kristen. Forever, if I have to."

He kissed her softly, quickly. Stepping back was near to impossible, but he did it. *I need you*, he didn't let himself add, as she turned and disappeared into the gym. *Please come back to me . . .*

***

"I thought maybe you could think of a use for this again," Uncle Dan said to Chloe's dad, after they'd all gotten home from the park.

She was doing her homework at the kitchen table. Her dad was sitting in one of her aunt and uncle's fancy recliners, watching a hockey game on their humongous TV and scribbling something onto a notepad. Her aunt was cleaning up the kitchen the way she always was, even though everyone had eaten out tonight. Sally had disappeared upstairs with her dad, only Uncle Dan was back now. And he was holding a guitar.

Her dad looked up. He stared at the guitar, and then he looked back at the TV without answering Chloe's uncle. He tore the top sheet off the notepad and crumpled it with his fist.

"Is that yours?" she asked.

He never talked about his music, but she'd heard enough of her parents' fights to guess how good he'd been at it once, before he'd gone to prison—and how her mom always thought he should have been better. Chloe had always wondered what he'd been like before things had gotten so bad.

"Is that what you used to play in your band when you and Mom were dating?" She'd tried over and over to picture him up onstage in front of everybody, singing and happy. He spent most of his time alone now, when he wasn't at work or with her.

He looked at her and then at her uncle, but he still didn't say anything.

"He's a genius with this thing." Uncle Dan crossed the living room to where Chloe sat at the end of the kitchen table. He handed her the guitar. "You should get him to show you how to play. You take after him with soccer. Maybe you will with music, too."

Uncle Dan headed to where her aunt was doing something with one of her cookbooks, probably planning tomorrow night's dinner. Aunt Charlotte loved to cook. Chloe's mom hated it. He put his arm around Aunt Charlotte and hugged her. Her aunt leaned against him like it was the best thing in the world to rest her head on his chest—the way Chloe wished she had the memory of her parents hugging each other, like a real family, like everything was going to be okay.

She walked over to her dad, carrying the guitar.

She held it out to him.

"Is this part of what you miss?" She'd figured out a long time ago that her dad missed a lot of the things he didn't talk about from his life before her. "Don't you wish you still played?"

He sighed and turned off the hockey game. He took the guitar from her, but he didn't hold it the way people did on TV or in movies. He laid it across his lap. Instead of trying to play it, he reached for her. He took her hand and pulled her closer, until she was sitting on the recliner's arm and leaning against him a little in a kind of hug.

"I gave up my music," he said, his voice deep and real, like when he sang in the shower and didn't know she was sitting on the other side of the closed door, listening. "And I've always been grateful I did."

"Because you didn't like it anymore?" Every time she heard him sing, she couldn't get over how good he was at it. Uncle Dan was right. Dad was even better at music than he was at soccer.

"Because I loved you." He laid his head back against the recliner. He was staring at the TV again, even though there was nothing on now. "I couldn't have both you and music. And I'll never be sorry about the choice I made."

"I don't understand." But whatever he'd said, whatever it meant, she suddenly felt better than she had all day.

"There were things that came with being in a band like mine. Drinking, like your mom does. I used to do that a lot, too."

"A lot, like her? Is that what caused the accident when you got in trouble?"

Her dad looked so sad. "A lot more than her, honey. And yes, that's what caused the accident. I promised myself I wasn't going to do that anymore, and the rest of my band was into it heavy. And I'd have had to travel, to places I couldn't take you once I got out . . ."

"Of prison?" They never talked about it, but it came up almost every time her mom and dad fought.

"Yeah." He brushed his hand down her hair. And then he smiled, instead of looking sad. "And once I came home, I wanted you more than anything. I'd have done anything to stay with you."

Chloe thought of playing soccer earlier, with him and Fin, and how it should have felt good. But nothing today had, until just now. She wanted to ask her dad to say it again, to smile again. She wanted to tell him that this was the stuff she'd missed so much. Just talking with him, being with him, with nothing bad happening around them—without whatever her mom might do next ruining it all.

She reached for the guitar and rubbed her fingers over the parts on top of it that were a darker wood than the rest.

"You wanted me more than anything?" she asked.

Chloe believed him. A part of her had always known that was how he felt. Why couldn't her mom ever say things like that, feel them, the way Dad did? Why hadn't she wanted Chloe enough to help make their family better?

Uncle Dan was standing in the doorway between the kitchen and the den. Her dad looked up at him, and then covered her hand, pressing it against the top of the guitar.

"You'll always be my number one, Chloe," he said, his smile back. "No matter what it takes. I decided that before you were even born. There's nothing I wouldn't do to keep you safe and happy. I know you haven't been happy, and I promised you I'd fix that. And I will. Can you try to believe that, no matter how bad things still are?"

She nodded, loving this, hearing how much he loved her.

"I chose you," her dad said, somehow knowing she'd needed to hear that part again. She'd never, ever hear it enough. "I'll always choose you, Chloe, no matter what."

***

Law's little girl threw her arms around his neck and held on tight.

He held her with his free arm, and then he set his guitar aside and held on even tighter. It had been too long since she'd hugged him this way—since he'd gotten through to her and shown her how much she meant to him. Whatever else was still off-kilter in Chloe's world, tonight he'd found a way to say something, do something, *be* something that had made his little girl happy.

He committed to memory the scent of her shampoo and the perfumed powder Charlotte had helped her pick out at Nordstrom for Chloe's Christmas gift. He'd cherish this moment forever. The smell and feel of his daughter's happiness was . . . everything. He was going to find a way to be worthy of it.

He'd once wanted to do the same for her mother. For too many reasons, it was too late to salvage that for them. But he had a chance still with their child. Walter had helped him wake up and see that today. Law was going to keep Chloe close, keep her talking with him just like this. He was going to help her believe in all the good things she could have in life—the way he was trying to believe in what he and Kristen might still have.

"I love you, Daddy," she whispered, her head tucked against his neck.

She slid away in the next moment. But her words stayed etched inside him—deep, where he'd worried he was losing her.

"I can't wait for practice to start tomorrow," she said, even though he'd been able to tell earlier at the park that she wasn't enjoying their workout with Fin nearly as much as she should have.

Chloe scampered out of the den and up the stairs, leaving Law gazing across the room at Dan.

"She's going to hear about it tomorrow," his brother said.

"What?" Law pulled his guitar across his lap, his hand and fingers poised but not moving.

"You and Kristen."

The chord played itself—Kristen's sound, or at least one of the endless sounds she made in his mind. "Nothing's happened for Chloe to hear about."

"Something happened outside the gym before Sally's game." Dan lifted his root beer to his mouth and drank deeply. "The rest of the town has probably heard by now, if it was the same sort of something that was going on between you and Kristen at Pockets in the fall."

Law had been writing about Kristen while Chloe did her homework. Notes and snatches of lyrics that had all been Kristen had begun pouring out of him as soon as he'd picked up a pad of scratch paper and a pen from Dan's coffee table. His fingers brushed out another string of half-imagined notes. They made him think of long legs beneath a prim, pastel skirt, sparkling green eyes and golden hair and a smile that melted him the same as his daughter's hugs.

"I tried to stay away from her," he said.

"The way you've tried to bury your talent for music all these years, but it doesn't want to stay buried?" His brother stared pointedly at the guitar. "You look good holding that. Playing again."

"This isn't playing."

"It isn't ignoring the damn instrument that used to be your best friend, while it's sat in the corner of your bedroom upstairs since you moved in. It's a start."

Another chord sounded, Law's fingers finding it without him putting thought behind how they moved.

"You've been writing since you got home with Chloe," Dan said, "as if you couldn't stop whatever was coming out. I watched you do that when we were kids. I used to be so jealous of how easy music was for you. You were going to be so much better at it than I'd ever be at anything I did."

The melody flowing from Law's fingertips took a deeper turn.

"You've never even asked how I managed to have that thing here," Dan pointed out. "Were you just going to stare at it upstairs forever, if you hadn't seen Kristen today? Is it too much to ask for us to have a conversation about your damn guitar, at least, instead of what your lawyer thinks you should do, and how much it's going to cost, and how obsessed you are with paying me back for every dime I've spent helping you that I don't give a damn about being paid back for? Or are we gonna go on like this forever, back in each other's lives but not figuring out how to be brothers again?"

Law winced at the pain in Dan's voice. Twice in one day, he was facing someone he'd unintentionally hurt, because he'd been so hell-bent on white-knuckling through dealing with Libby on his own. "I figured you got the guitar from my ex-wife."

"It was the only thing I asked for."

"You mean when you started giving Libby the money that I told her not to take from our family, when I went into the system."

"Yeah. When I would have done anything to help you, even though you hated my ever-living guts, just because we have the misfortune of being born to the same parents. Libby was selling everything to raise cash, she said when she called me. She said you didn't want anything left from your time with your band when you got out of prison. I told her I'd send whatever money I could, but not to sell your guitar. It was too much a part of you. You shouldn't have to give that up, too."

Law stopped playing. He looked from the brother who'd been his first friend in this world, down at the instrument that had become his second. Only Dan could have known how much it had meant for Law to see his guitar again, when he'd moved to Mimosa Lane—or how hard it had been for him to hold it again today.

"I don't have anything from before my parole," he admitted, when he hardly ever let himself think about it. "I never wanted anything to remind me of how much I'd lost."

"I know." His brother seemed to be remembering, too. His voice sounded younger, and older. "I've watched you since you moved to Chandlerville. For so long, there was nothing familiar there. My brother was . . . gone. At least until a few months ago, when you and Kristen stopped circling each other and finally broke the ice. That's when I saw you start . . . needing something again. That's when I saw my kid brother in you—the one who needed Mom and Dad to be the kind of parents they were never going to be."

Law feathered his fingers over the too-loose strings. He caught Dan watching him play, his brother's frown softening.

"Why did you go see her today?" Dan asked.

"I don't know." Law kept playing softly, feeling the invisible vibrations of the music. Feeling his brother trying to understand, trying to help. Law couldn't tune him out the way he had so many times before. "That's not true. Walter Davis started throwing a bunch of stuff at me today at lunch. We were both pretty steamed by the time he was through. But it started me thinking . . . About Kristen and Chloe. About you. Was it ever hard for you?"

"What?"

Law made sure his sister-in-law was still busy in the kitchen. "Hooking up with Charlotte. Not running away from something that good, you know, after Mom and Dad?"

"It was terrifying. But I figured fighting for better was just as hard as settling for worse. I wasn't the easiest man to live with for a few years, until I got some things straightened out in my mind— mostly with Charlotte's help. Until I walked away from our parents, too, so I could have the life I wanted, instead of the 'better' one they would have always insisted I try for. By then Sally had come along, and we'd settled here. Somehow, we made it work."

Law studied his finger placement. More of the melody that had been rattling around his mind for weeks found its way out and into his brother's den. He could remember thinking he'd never want a speck of the moneyed life Dan had made for himself in Chandlerville. But his brother's family, the love he'd claimed for himself and Charlotte and Sally on Mimosa Lane . . .

Law found himself craving it like a starving man staring at a
banquet through a locked window.

"You always were an overachiever," he said.

"Damn it, Law. That's all I get?"

Dan's voice was furious, but so in control it commanded
Law's attention the same as if he'd shouted. His brother got quiet
when he was angry. Law had always been the scarier of the two
of them, intimidating and loud.

"I didn't achieve anything," Dan bit out, "but the chance to
start over with nothing, the same as you. I may have finished
college and grad school and been making money. But my parents were malignant, too. A couple of narcissists who took too
much from both of us. They had to have everything in their
world be all about them, or no one else could have anything at
all. They messed with my head and my life. They made my
brother my enemy, the same as they did you. I found a way to
get them out of my life for good. Maybe you should, too."

"I have."

"Then why haven't you played or sung a note since you went
to prison? Why are you still chained to the hip of a woman who's
been just as bad for you as our parents were? Why in God's name
has it taken you two months to stop pissing away the opening
Kristen gave you, and let yourself face wanting something for a
change? Why haven't you told Chloe, shown her before now, that
there's more to loving someone and family than the damage you
and Libby heap on each other, and the *zero* our relationship has
been since you moved to town?"

Law had no comeback. He had no defense. The absolute silence in his mind screamed that each word of Dan's accusations
was the truth.

He couldn't hear Kristen anymore. He could no longer re-member Walter's well-intentioned advice. He couldn't recall his daughter's priceless hug. All that remained was every unfair, loveless, hate-filled thing his parents and ex-wife had thought and said about him. And every time, as a kid, that he'd wondered what other boys' lives were like, the ones who had real families to take care of them.

There was a time, before Libby and drinking and torching as much as he could, as quickly as he could, that he'd promised to make that loving family for himself—the same as he'd been promising to do it for Chloe since she was conceived. How could he have silenced that part of him so completely for so long?

He laid his guitar on the coffee table. He couldn't bear to have it close. There was only darkness pouring out of him now.

"Walter thinks it's codependence," he finally said. "Some-thing about me being so mixed up, I'm more comfortable being miserable and seeing my daughter unhappy than I am risking trying for a different life that I don't believe I can have."

Dan frowned again, the way he had their first few meetings with the lawyer, while Law had described in detail what dealing with Libby's ups and downs had really been like.

"I think Walter's a very smart man," Dan said.

Law nodded, taking in his brother's empathy, accepting how much they had in common still, no matter how different their lives had turned out. He leaned forward in the recliner and rested his elbows on his knees. He dropped his head to his hands. Maybe he'd blown it for good with Kristen. He might not get his second chance with her. But his brother was there now. Dan had always been there, for years, waiting for Law to come to his senses.

Law pushed to his feet and reached into his pocket. He pulled out the business card Walter had left behind at McC's. He handed it to Dan.

"I don't think I can do this alone anymore," he said, parroting Walter's parting shot. "Would you go with me?"

Dan studied the Al-Anon card. He nodded without looking up. He pulled Law into a bracing hug that felt like brothers and family and . . . starting over.

"Thank you," Law said. "For everything. For all of this. I should have said it a long time ago. I'm sorry, Dan. Thank you for never giving up on me."

"Damn, Law," his brother said. "I've missed you so much."

Chapter Fourteen

Kristen slowed beside the Chandlerville soccer fields on Thursday afternoon. She parked on the street, near the corner of Baxter and Main. Only a handful of other vehicles were there so far. She'd arrived early, leaving work before she should have, hoping to catch Law before the bulk of his new team arrived for their first practice.

She cut her Mustang's engine and peered through the windshield like a scared girl. Why hadn't she just called him, like he'd said?

Because you wanted to see the man again, you twit.

Law's truck was there. Dan's Mercedes, and Marsha Dixon's van. And they were all standing together, not far from her, talking like old friends.

She was among friends.

Certainly she could make herself get out of her car and have the conversation she'd come there to have—in public, the same as Law had approached her yesterday. Except she couldn't get herself out of her car.

Come back to me, he'd said.

She continued to stare. She'd come to tell Law about the rumors she'd heard at school, and how much she'd been afraid it was disturbing Chloe—who'd seemed more isolated from her classmates than ever today, according to Daphne, even though Brooke and Summer had stuck close by her side. The best Daphne could tell, the other girls had been trying to gather details about what everyone else in town was talking about—Law and Kristen being seen together again.

Kristen needed Law to know all of that. She needed him to decide if she was what he really wanted, regardless. If he couldn't handle this, then he and Kristen even having coffee together in public was so *not* going to happen.

When he'd been so close yesterday and saying all the things she'd dreamed of him saying—that he wanted her still—she'd let herself hope. Of course, then she'd gone home to her condo and panicked most of the night. Which would have been fine, if she could be sure Law was going to stick this time. She'd come to the park to basically dare him to back away again. But she'd missed him all day, too, doubts and all.

He looked over from where he was leaning against his truck's grille, one leg lifted, the heel of his tennis shoe propped up on the bumper. And as she had every other time she'd seen him, she softened, wanting him, wanting to feel the unguarded way she did when she was with him.

Steady, girl.

He raised a hand to stall whatever Dan had been saying. Leaving his brother and Marsha to themselves, he walked toward Kristen, a smile on his lips, determination in his eyes. She got out of her car as he approached.

He looked as amazing as always, this time in his practice clothes: a ripped T-shirt that molded to his lean, muscular upper body, and midthigh shorts that spotlighted the ropes of muscle in his legs, plus the perfection that a sport like soccer sculpted from a man's backside. He didn't stop moving until he had her in his arms, crushing her mouth in a kiss, with his brother and Marsha looking on, not to mention that Fin and Chloe had to be somewhere close by.

She clung to his shoulders and his taste, letting herself hope that she wasn't setting herself up to be hurt all over again. When he eased away, she whimpered in protest.

"You're here," he said.

"No . . ." She couldn't catch her breath. "Yes, but not about us. Not exactly . . ." She cleared her throat. "I wanted to talk with you face-to-face."

He grinned. "Well, I'd say we've covered the face-to-face part. What did you want to talk about?"

He waited for her to speak. When she couldn't remember any of the things she'd rehearsed saying on her way over, his smile faded.

"Marsha's been telling Dan and me about the rumors spreading from yesterday," he said. "My guess is my ex is initiating the worst of them. I can't say Dan didn't warn me. Fin told Marsha that Chloe had it pretty rough at school—the boy's actually worried about her."

Kristen smiled. If nothing else happened, the two of them could be proud of helping Fin learn how to belong to other people.

"He and Chloe have become real friends," she said. "My staff is flabbergasted, but Fin's stopped trying to one-up the other boys he used to make trouble with. He hasn't skipped school again. And he and Chloe talk at recess and lunch more than either of them hang with anyone else. Fin's learning what being a friend is about, because you and Chloe took an interest in him."

"Because you hauled my butt out of the cave I'd been hiding in"—Law rubbed a strong hand down her arm—"and made me look at someone who had things a lot worse off than I do. You got me involved in this community, in my own life, doing something besides ducking and covering every time Libby turned up the heat."

"You've been a part of Chandlerville since you moved here." Kristen thought of the kids he'd coached, the lives he'd touched through McC's, especially the Davis family, and even her own happiness, getting to know Chloe as well as she had through all of this. Because Law had done everything possible to care for his daughter.

She looked over his shoulder to where his brother and Marsha were watching them. Law had looked so relaxed with them when she'd driven up. Something had changed. Something definitely for the better.

"You're learning to let the rest of us in," she said. "You're finally seeing what you could have had all along. I'm so glad."

He tipped her chin up with his finger, until she was gazing into his stormy eyes.

"Tell me you didn't come out here in that sexy yellow suit," he said, "just to talk about Chloe, and how I can now string a few more sentences together when I talk with a friend and my brother. I'm ready to deal with whatever I have to, to have you in my life. Tell me you're not going to let gossip and Libby's determination to be the center of attention scare you off. I want all the way in, Kristen. I want to know where this takes us. I want to feel what I feel with you for as long as it's good for you, no matter what happens next. Tell me you want that, too."

All the way in. . .

Kristen nodded her head, feeling her heart flower open, un-curling and reaching toward the light. She brushed his lips with hers again, accepting him, wanting him, needing all of him.

"But what about Chloe?" she asked.

Law braced his hands on his hips, staying close but looking worried. "I have to talk with her about us. She didn't say a word to me on the way over from school, but I could tell she was upset. I've got to try to explain, and then get us both through practice. Some of the other kids on the team are in her class, not just Fin. That might be rough. The only other time I've pushed her to talk with me was when she told me about Libby's drinking . . ."

Kristen cupped his cheek, rubbed her thumb along the shadow of his beard, bringing his attention back to her. "Talking with Chloe about Libby and me and the two of you, when she doesn't have to reveal some awful secret she's been keeping, sounds like a really good thing. Even if it makes things hard for a while, you'll be talking with her, helping her understand. It will be good for both of you. Have a little faith."

"You're good for both of us." He kissed her palm. "Be here when practice is over?"

Kristen thought of the mound of work waiting for her in her office. She thought of Law *and* Chloe walking toward her after practice. She wasn't certain which was making her stomach cramp more.

"I'll stay as long as I can" was all she could promise.

With his hand curling around her neck, Law leaned in for another kiss. This one lasted longer, a slow caress, until all she could feel or taste or breathe was him. "I'll come looking for you tonight, regardless. I've settled some things with myself and with Dan, and I'm going to settle them with Libby, too, the next chance I get. I've let myself off the hook for too long, not expecting more for my life. For Chloe's. She deserves better. Because of you, I'm beginning to see that we both deserve better."

He walked toward his truck to pick up a bag of practice balls from the bed. Then he struck off toward the bleachers on the other side of the field, where she could now see Chloe and Fin watching them. Law waved toward Dan and Marsha, not checking to see whether Kristen stayed. She could leave whenever she wanted. But he'd come looking for her tonight, regardless.

Kristen shivered.

She closed her car door and walked along the curb toward Dan and Marsha's cars.

***

"You wanna play?" Fin asked Chloe, while they both watched her dad head toward them. "We could just kick the ball around before everybody gets here."

No. Chloe didn't want to play. She didn't want to kick the ball around. She didn't want to talk, not even to Fin. She didn't want to be with anybody right now. And she *didn't* want to be around her dad.

School today had been the worst, after last night had been so good.

As soon as Chloe got to class, Brooke and Summer had started talking to her about her dad and Ms. Hemmings. Their moms had heard from Chloe's mom that her dad and Ms. Hemmings had been talking again last night, and holding hands, and she didn't know what else. She hadn't known anything, and she didn't know which of the rumors to believe.

Her dad had said he'd always choose her. So how could he have done this, when he knew that what she wanted most was for their stupid family stuff to go away? Mom would never let that happen now, if he didn't stop doing whatever he was doing again with Ms. Hemmings.

Chloe's friends had thought it was funny that she hadn't known. Then they'd told everyone they could, before school and at recess and lunch and after. They were probably still telling people, even though Chloe's cell phone hadn't rung once after school, and she hadn't gotten a text from anyone—except her mom, who'd wanted to know when practice started tonight.

Chloe hadn't answered. She didn't want her mom here, not now, even though she'd kinda been hoping before today that Mom might show up, and that her parents would talk about something else besides what they talked about with their lawyers. And that Dad would see what Chloe saw—that Mom was really trying again and probably not drinking at all anymore.

You'll always be my number one, Chloe, he'd said. But Ms. Hemmings had been the "something important" Aunt Charlotte said he'd had to take care of after school yesterday, instead of picking Chloe up.

"It's not so bad," Fin said. He was standing next to where she was sitting on the lowest bleacher—while they'd watched her dad and Ms. Hemmings talk and kiss and talk some more, like they would keep talking all night, the way Chloe had never seen her parents talk.

"What do you know about it?" She couldn't let any of the other boys see how upset she was. She couldn't look like she was going to cry by the time everyone else got there for practice.

"I know you don't want anyone to think this stuff bothers you. But it does."

"Go away." She wiped at her eyes.

She didn't really want him to go away. Fin was like the only kid she wanted around her most of the time now, because he was cool with her, however she was. He never made her feel like she had to be someone else. But her dad was coming. She didn't want Dad to see her crying, either, and Fin's talking to her was making it harder to stop.

"What do you care what anybody thinks about what your parents do?" Fin asked.

"I don't."

"Summer and Brooke dump on you every chance they get. Why do you still want them to like you?"

"I don't." She just wanted things to stop getting worse and worse.

"Don't be mad at your dad," Fin said. "It's not so bad. My mom . . ." Fin was the one who looked mad now, even though his voice didn't sound like it. He sounded sad, making Chloe remember that he didn't have any parents at all, even messed-up ones. "You've got the coolest dad in the world, even if your mom's a total zero, and people are talking about your dad and Ms. Hemmings again. Don't be stupid and not see that it doesn't matter, Chloe. As long as you have your dad and he takes care of you, the way the Dixons take care of me, who cares about anything else?"

***

Law heard more cars pulling up, announcing the arrival of his team. He checked his watch. Practice needed to start in about five minutes.

He had five minutes to say more of what he'd tried to say to his daughter last night—things he should have been trying to help Chloe understand for years.

"Hey, Thomas!" Fin yelled. He took off toward one of the cars, leaving Chloe sitting on the bleachers.

She stayed where she was, even though she'd known Thomas Kilpatrick for years—since they'd first started playing soccer on the same five-and-under team. She glared up at Law. She looked miserable.

"We're going to work this out," he said, believing it himself for the first time.

"Mom's mad." His daughter sounded terrified by that—exactly the way Libby seemed to like her, whenever Libby needed someone to feel worse than she did.

"Mom's going to have to be mad, then, if that's the way she wants to be every time one of us feels good."

Chloe glanced after Fin, and maybe even toward Kristen.

"My friends are being mean about it," she said, "about you and Ms. Hemmings. Fin says that means I shouldn't care what they think, or if they're even my friends anymore."

"Do you want them to be your friends?" Law had been proud of her lately. She wasn't trying to be so much like the mean girls who'd been giving her a hard time as far back as November. "Is that why you're so upset?"

Chloe shook her head. She sighed, like she was trying not to cry.

"Is Ms. Hemmings your friend?" she asked, honest and needing to know, the way she'd asked about his music last night. "Is that why you were kissing her?"

Suddenly, Law didn't think he could answer. He didn't know how he'd deal with Chloe telling him she didn't want him wanting Kristen in his life. But he was handling this and a whole lot more with his daughter from now on. His not handling things, not handling people, had damaged too much in their lives.

"Yeah," he said, as several of the boys laughed and headed across the field from the cars. "Even if it makes your mother mad, Ms. Hemmings and I want to be friends. I think Kristen will be good for both of us, darlin', if you'll give her a chance. What you think about all of this is important to me. I'm sorry I wasn't ready to talk with you about it last night. But I'd like to now."

There were tears in Chloe's eyes while Fin and Thomas ran past them onto the field, passing a ball Thomas must have brought with him. Another group of boys followed them, scrapping over the one ball. Law tossed the net bag onto the field, and the kids attacked it like piranha on a fresh kill, ripping open the ties and each of them claiming a practice ball.

"Warm up first," Law called out. "Stretch. Dribble two laps around the field, solo. Then another two passing with a partner. I'll be out there in a minute, and then we'll all be running for the next hour and a half until your folks get back. So hydrate, but don't drink too much. I don't want to have to answer for you puking all the way home."

Everyone laughed and took off to do their laps.

Everybody but Chloe.

Law knelt until they were eye-to-eye. "I want you to be happy, Chloe. I meant what I said last night. But we can't let Mom decide what makes us happy. She has to take care of herself for now, and we have to decide what we want. We have to make choices for us, for our family, based on what we all need—even if it upsets Mom. You keep telling me how nice Ms. Hemmings is to you at school. I think she's nice, too, and I'd like to get to know her better, even if it upsets your mother." He squeezed her hand. "Do you think that would be okay?"

"Hey, Chloe!" Fin called from the pack of kids rounding the far side of the field. "No laps, no play." It was something Law had said each time the three of them worked out. "Get out here!"

Chloe looked up at Law, unsure.

"I'm sorry the divorce has been so hard," he said. "I'm going to do everything I can to make things right from now on. No more not talking about stuff like this. No more hiding or avoiding it."

"Even stuff like you being friends with Ms. Hemmings?"

"Even stuff like that. You'll always have your mother, as long as she stays healthy. You'll always have me. But for all of us to get better, our family has to change. We have to start doing things differently, and . . . move on from where we've been for so long. Do you think you can be okay with that?"

Chloe looked at him for a long time without answering. He reached to hug her. She took off after her team before he could— leaving him to pull himself together so he could organize the scrimmage match he'd planned for tonight. The kids needed to get used to being teammates first, before they worked on improving their individual skills.

It was a principle he'd followed every season he'd coached— he introduced teamwork first, and only then did they focus on player performance. It was the philosophy that had kept him hooked on team sports his entire adult life. Fitting together and fighting together was what made his teams unbeatable. The whole of them were stronger than any one player on his roster. That was why his kids beat even more skilled opponents week after week.

It was the same with a family, he realized. A good family that the parents and kids could depend on even when things seemed at their worst.

He looked across the field to the parents' cars parked at the curb, either on Main or Baxter, depending on what part of town they'd come from. It was a good thing to see Kristen standing there now, too, talking with Dan and Marsha near Marsha's van. It was a good change.

He was going to fight for the family he'd talked with Chloe about—one that would help her feel safe and loved, not terrified of doing something wrong or making someone angry. A family he could imagine creating with a woman like Kristen. Assuming he could convince her to stick things out with him long enough, to see if she could want that kind of forever, too.

Chapter Fifteen

"Great game last night," Dan said to Kristen, toward the end of practice.

Law was still on the field, still running with the kids, an agile, breathtaking man who made the competitive athlete inside her drool—even if a more cowardly part of her had thought up an array of excuses for slipping away from Dan and Marsha before last night came up in conversation.

They'd already covered the weather and which kids on the team they knew and the growing community excitement for next week's Valentine's party at Pockets—where Julia and Walter Davis were renewing their vows, with their sons and everyone in town watching on. They'd talked their way around every topic they had in common except Law and Chloe and Libby. Evidently Marsha's stepping away to make a call on her cell had been the opening Dan had been waiting for.

"Sally's blocking out and rebounding like a demon," Kristen said. "She might be one of the smallest players on my team, but she's making up for it by asserting herself. She's rebuilt so much confidence since you signed her up after the shooting. Her defense is a big part of why we're still in the play-offs."

Dan smiled. Kristen saw him and Charlotte and Sally smiling more and more these days. "She keeps telling her mother and me she wants to grow up to be as tall as you, so she can play center in college 'just like Ms. Hemmings.'"

He laughed at that. Though he was almost as big as Law, Sally was taking after her petite mother. Not that Kristen had any intention of letting that dampen the girl's enthusiasm.

"Sally's got the makings of a fine guard," she said. "And she works hard. The extra practice time you're spending with her on the weekends is paying off, in more ways than just on the basketball court. She loves you very much, Dan. You're . . ."

The words tugged at Kristen's voice and her heart, refusing to come out.

"I'm a lucky man," he said. "And so is my brother. You got him and Chloe out here with Fin. I suspect you're the reason, at least part of it, that Law's taking a stand with Libby. And—"

"He did this for Chloe." Kristen glanced over to see Marsha still on the phone, standing several yards away.

"He did. But he came to find you last night for himself." Dan's expression hardened. "And even though I suspect Libby's already retaliating, spreading the gossip that's upsetting Chloe, I'm glad my brother's stepping out of the shell he's been determined to live in—thinking he has to, to keep his daughter happy."

"I . . ." Kristen shook her head. Dan made it sound as if Law were choosing her over Chloe. "I'm not . . ."

"You're not as in love with my brother as he is with you? Of course you are. Anyone can see that, especially Libby."

Kristen opened her mouth to deny it. She couldn't say a word.

Oh, my God.

She couldn't be. Not this soon. Not with so much still confused and unsettled and threatening not to work between them.

"What do you think Libby's going to do?" she asked.

"I think she's going to do whatever gets her the most attention. I don't know much more about my brother and ex-sister-in-law than most people in town do. Law has never let me close enough before now to really understand what happened between them when they first got married, around the time they were in the accident that sent him away. I think she tried to be a good mother to Chloe at first. But some people just shouldn't be parents. Libby's always wanted everything, all of Law, for herself. I don't think there'd ever have been enough for her. He moved here for her, when he didn't want to. He's spent nearly a decade in a joyless marriage, trying to make it work. He put up with a contentious divorce that didn't have to be, because he'd already agreed to give up everything Libby wanted except for his time with Chloe. He's done his best to atone for the mistakes he made before his daughter was born. But still, Libby couldn't manage to keep herself sober."

"That's the saddest thing I've ever heard," Kristen said. "And the most amazing."

"When I think of the kind of father I want to be for Sally," Dan said, "I hope I can be half as selfless as my brother has been."

Kristen turned back to the scrimmage match as a whoop went up on the field from the direction of one of the goals. She watched Fin and Chloe high-five—they'd scored on Thomas Kilpatrick's team. They took off running in a mad victory lap, with all the kids, including Thomas, giving chase and celebrating with them. Many of the parents on the sidelines joined in, clapping and shouting. Chloe and Fin looked transformed by their love for the game that Law was sharing with them, just as Kristen felt transformed each time he touched her.

Ex-con, rebel, bad-boy Law Beaumont was that . . . magical. And he'd been shutting huge parts of himself away for years—to be the kind of father any daughter would dream of having. What couldn't a selfless, powerful man like that do? What wouldn't Kristen do to stay part of his life for as long as he'd let her?

"Law needs someone who's as strong and responsible and sensitive as he is by his side while he finishes this," Dan said.

"Finishes it?"

"I think things are going to get worse with Libby. I don't think she's through self-destructing." Dan stared over Kristen's shoulder, in the direction of Baxter Street. Kristen could hear another parent's car approaching to pick up their sweaty, grass-covered player. "I don't think she's capable of letting Law go without completely imploding. Tell me you're in this for the long haul, Kristen, and my money's on my brother. I don't care how low Libby's determined to sink."

At the anger creeping into Dan's expression, the hair rose on the back of Kristen's neck. She turned to see who he was watching approach from behind her.

***

"I'll call when we head home," Marsha said to Joe.

She closed her phone and said a silent prayer.

This wasn't going to be pretty.

She glanced worriedly toward the kids still running around on the field, and then watched Libby walk up to Kristen, where Chandler's AP had been talking with Dan.

"Isn't this a cozy family scene," Libby said, as lavender twilight deepened around them, even though it was barely five thirty. "I bet you like this model a hell of a lot better than you ever did me, Dan. She's got some kind of fancy pedigree, from what I hear, even if she slums it here in Chandlerville with the rest of us. Too bad that means she'll get her fill of my husband before spring shows its face." When Kristen's only response was to stare at Libby with as much loathing as Dan was showing, Libby's smile grew sickeningly sweet. "Law might be a lot to look at, honey, but he's hell on his women. You're flirting with trouble. Stay away from my family, if you know what's good for you."

"You gave up your family"—Law had made it to Kristen's side in a flash, when he'd been running down the field with the team moments ago—"because you wanted to kick me around more than you wanted to grow up and help me keep us together. And now you've lost your daughter because you want to drink and feel sorry for yourself more than you wanted Chloe with you. You said we were done with this, Libby."

"We're not done with a damn thing, buddy." Libby didn't sound or look drunk, but she was definitely losing control. "I don't care how much money you wheedle out of your brother to pay off his shark of a lawyer. You don't intimidate me. Is this why you refused to talk about letting me have my little girl back, no matter how much I've done to prove myself? So you can get your groove on again with Ms. Perfect here, and start a whole new, ready-made family with *my* daughter?"

Marsha watched Dan step closer to Kristen, flanking her other side. The Beaumont brothers were a united wall of menace, glaring down at Libby.

"I'd sell my house and everything I own," Dan said, "before I'd let you take my niece back until we're certain you're sober. Law's not fighting you alone anymore. That's what's got you scared. Not Kristen. You know you're beat. And you don't want to do what you have to, to make the best of what you have left."

Chloe and Fin and the other kids made their way over, along with several sets of parents. Chloe walked up to Law and Kristen and her uncle. Fin went with her, instead of coming to stand next to Marsha.

Law's entire team grouped around his daughter—Thomas Kilpatrick included, whom Marsha had heard hadn't exactly been the best of friends the last few months to either Fin or Chloe. They all stood there, silently staring at Libby. No one was snickering or making jokes, nothing that would make this harder than it already was for Law or his daughter.

"You sure do know how to draw a crowd, Ms. Hemmings." Libby's smile trembled. "Are you gonna kiss my husband again, like you did last night? Is that what gets you off, when you're not prancing around, pretending to be our perfect paragon of academic excellence?"

"I should go." Kristen looked furious, but worried. She cupped the back of Chloe's head and smiled sadly down at the little girl.

Law took Kristen's elbow. "Stay, please. Libby's beef is with me, not you. Not Chloe."

"You betcha it's with you. And don't think I'm going to stand by while you embarrass our daughter by—"

"Leave Daddy alone!" Chloe cried, leaning back against her father. Kristen patted her shoulder. "Just leave him and Ms. Hemmings alone. You're the one who's embarrassing. You always are. Go home, Mom. Why can't you just go home and stop being so . . ."

"So what?" Libby's demeanor shifted into a parody of a loving mother: sweet and caring, but empty. "I'm the fun one, honey.

You and me, we have a blast together with all your friends and their mothers. You can't tell me you really want to be with your dad out here. Not like you want to be with me. Just tell him. Tell your uncle and all of your friends that you want to come home with me now. Tell the judge, and we'll have fun again soon, I promise."

Chloe looked around at the crowd of friends and parents that had gathered, at the support Law had pulled around the two of them. Everyone, even the kids, looked angry at the way Libby was trying to manipulate her. For an instant, Chloe looked ready to run. Then Fin shoved her arm with his elbow. It was the same gesture of support Marsha had seen Chloe use at school in November, the morning after Fin had gotten himself into so much trouble.

"Please go home, Mom." Chloe sounded sad, but she also sounded sure. "Until you get better enough to be part of our family again, we can't have fun together. And I . . ." She looked up to her dad, two tiny tears rolling down her cheek. "I don't want to, not the way you are. You ruin everything for us like this, while Dad's trying to make us better. I want my real mom back."

Libby's expression grew absolutely ashen. For the first time since she'd arrived, she seemed to be experiencing honest-to-God emotion.

"I'm still your mom, honey." She looked to where Law was holding Kristen's arm. Kristen's hand still rested on Chloe's shoulder. "I'll always be your mommy."

"Not when you're sick." Chloe crossed her arms, more brave, more mad than she was sad now. "And you've been sick a long time. You have to get better. That's all Dad and me want. Right, Dad?"

Law nodded.

To his ex, he said, "And you're not spending another unsupervised moment with Chloe until you've proven to the court that you're ready—no matter how many times you call and beg, or how much of a spectacle you make of yourself. Look around. No one's buying your act anymore. Not when you're like this. You're just making yourself look desperate."

Libby rocked on her heels as if she'd been slapped.

No one said a word. No one rushed to comfort her. She edged away, her eyes glassy with fury, and hopefully *not* from the effects of drinking anything before she'd come to the park. She drove away in anticlimactic silence, looking as if she were crying behind the wheel.

The February moon and a sky full of stars seemed to shine brighter in her wake. After an overly warm day, things were cooling down fast. Marsha watched parents motion quietly to their kids, handing them jackets and sweatpants to put on over their dirty shorts and T-shirts.

Families waved at Law and Chloe. One or two of the dads patted Law's and then Dan's shoulders in silent support until, with the sound of more cars starting and heading out, it was finally just Marsha and Fin and Kristen and the Beaumonts standing there looking a little shell-shocked.

"You okay?" Law knelt in front of Chloe. "I'm so sorry, darlin'."

Chloe gazed around at the people still there—her uncle and her friend and one of the staff at her school. Marsha could almost see her figuring out that everyone already knew the worst, so why keep pretending that things weren't as bad as they really were?

"Is Mom ever going to get better?" Chloe asked. "Is she ever going to really stop drinking?"

"If she wants to, she will." Law's gaze connected with Dan's. "I got better. I'm happier than I've been in a long time."

"For me . . ." Chloe looked up, her gaze stalling on Kristen, as if she wanted to be sure Kristen knew most of all. "You got better for me, right? You're happy because of me?"

Law crushed her in a hug so beautiful, even Dan wiped at his eyes.

"It's all for you, Chloe," he said. "Everything's always been for you."

Kristen reached for Law's hand while he still held his daughter. Fin kicked the dirt at his feet and rolled his eyes at Marsha. Because what else was a nine-year-old boy to do when things were getting entirely too serious?

"I'm hungry," he said.

"Me, too." Chloe pushed away from Law.

Her dad let her go, though it looked as if it just about killed him to.

"Milk shakes?" he asked with a watery smile. The fingers of his left hand were still tangled with Kristen's. "How does that sound?"

Chloe looked up at how close Law and Kristen were standing, then at their intertwined fingers, and nodded.

"Yeah!" Fin chimed in.

"Would you mind if Kristen joined us?" Law asked his daughter.

Slowly, she shook her head. "I guess not."

"The Dream Whip's got the best burgers and fries in town," Marsha suggested. "It's my treat." When Law inhaled to argue, she rushed on. "It's the least I can do, after the personal time you've given Fin. I won't take no for an answer. Chloe, why don't you ride over with us? Maybe your dad can give Ms. Hemmings a ride, since we're going in the opposite direction of her place?"

"Dad?"

"I can—" was all Kristen got out.

"We'll be right behind you, darlin'," Law said. "As long as you're feeling okay enough to ride with Fin. I'd like a few minutes to talk with Kristen alone."

Chloe hugged her dad's waist, standing between him and Kristen for another moment before she let him go.

"Beat you to the van," she said to Fin, both of them taking off for Marsha's ancient, always-in-the-shop Chevy.

"We'll meet you there," Marsha said.

"I can give Chloe a ride home after," Dan added, "if you two need a little more time."

Law nodded, sharing a silent moment with his brother. "Thanks."

"I'll get the kids started," Marsha said. "We'll keep Chloe occupied until you join us. Do what you need to do, and don't worry. We'll make sure she has a good time."

Chapter Sixteen

Law turned to Kristen. She couldn't let go of his hand. It felt as if they'd faced down an unconquerable foe. And they were still standing, together, neither of them with a clue what to do next.

She supposed Libby's appearance had been predictable. Kristen should have expected it and avoided the scene. Or *had* she expected it, subconsciously, and come anyway? Had she needed to know what Law would do?

Law tucked a lock of her hair behind her ear.

"How amazing does it feel," she asked, reveling in his touch, "to have your daughter, her entire team, your brother, and all those parents who were here tonight stand with you, on your side against Libby?"

His thumb brushed the underside of her jaw. The feel of it was electric, lighting her up. It was everything she'd dreamed it would be, as the evening breeze swirled around them. It was every reason she'd been so afraid of this man.

I want you, she couldn't say.

I want this to be real.

I want you to be the someone who never goes away, no matter what happens next or who tries to take this away from us.

"You're forgetting someone," he said.

"Who?"

"You. You were here, too, Kristen. You stayed."

"I was worried about Chloe. She had a pretty bad day at school."

"You're amazing at your job." He shook his head. "But you have my cell number. You could have called me later and checked on her."

Kristen nodded into his touch, sinking into his cool blue gaze. "I was worried..." She'd been downright panicked. "I was worried what my life would be like if I let you disappear from it again, without at least trying to make this work."

Her confidence in them was still shaky. She almost wished Libby would come back and give her another excuse to give up. She didn't say that to Law. How did she tell him that maybe *she* was the one who was too weak and afraid to see this through?

Love, Dan had said.

Could she really trust someone to love her as deeply and as unconditionally and as forever as she wanted to love this man and his little girl? Law studied her, as if he could tell how troubled she still was.

"Maybe you just wanted one of Chloe's chocolate milk shakes," he said, smiling. "And this was a way to get your fix and have someone else pay for it."

"Strawberry," she corrected.

"Strawberry?" He winced. He stepped away, but he kept his hand on her arm. "Do grown women—fearless, all-star athletes and kick-ass APs who order teachers and kids around all day— really drink strawberry milk shakes?"

She shrugged, charmed by his teasing.

"I guess you're going to have to find out for yourself," she said, agreeing to join his family and the Dixons.

He led her to the passenger side of his truck. It was getting cold out—even though it was the South, and February could sometimes feel like spring everywhere else. She shivered and felt his arms wrap around her, trapping her between his body and the passenger door.

"I'm going to want more than milk shakes tonight, Kristen."

He kissed her, and she let him, losing herself in his taste until they were both shaking. They inched apart.

"If Chloe goes home with Dan," he said, "I'm going to want a lot more."

It was past time.

Technically they hadn't spent more than a few minutes alone together since that first morning at school. But they would be so perfect for each other. Kristen knew it. She'd wanted it so badly, for so long—the rightness she knew she'd feel with Law tonight, in his arms, in her bed.

She'd let every other man go long before she'd had the chance to discover this kind of closeness with them. As if she'd been waiting her entire life for the connection she'd found only with Law. He challenged her, terrified her, amazed her with everything he could make her want.

"I'm ready if you are," she said, giving him her heart, and trusting him not to break it.

***

Law had never wanted a woman more.

It seemed like forever since he'd been with Libby. And since the divorce, her escalating demands for attention had pretty much obliterated whatever desire he might have had to want someone new.

A handful of Chandlerville women had shown an interest, looking for either a bad boy or a man with too many commitments to want anything long-term. Two of them had been married, to men Law knew personally—husbands who stopped by McC's several nights a week looking for some no-strings-attached distractions of their own. But in all his time in Chandlerville, no other woman had come close to tempting him the way Kristen did just by sitting in the truck with him.

Before her, there'd been no music in his mind. No melodies. No strings of words and emotions and dreams for him to fiddle with. Now those long-ago dreams returned every time he thought of her.

She was curled up next to him as he drove down Main Street to the Dream Whip. She was still in her suit from work, as if her effortless elegance had always belonged beside him in his run-down Ford. She was glowing and full of life and always giving so much of herself away, while she'd kept the best parts hidden deep, waiting for him to discover them.

"This town is magical." She inhaled, stretching the silk blouse covering her breasts—and Law's patience with the fact that they were minutes away from joining Marsha and Dan and two kids.

He focused on the picturesque scenery rolling slowly by beyond the windshield.

"It's a pretty town." He pulled into the parking lot next to the burger joint. It was teeming with customers. It had been built to model a 1930s ice-cream parlor, and folks around Chandlerville couldn't get enough of its vintage charm and handmade greasy mainstays. "Everything here is prettier than anywhere I've ever lived since leaving home."

"You sound almost like you resent it for being so quaint."

He'd parked and killed the ignition. Kristen caught him staring at her. She laughed at him. Maybe at both of them.

"*Pretty* has a way about her," he said, "that makes you want her too much."

A neon sign, an ice-cream cone, hung above the door to the building, lit up and dazzling. It cast fantastical colors across Kristen's smile.

"You don't trust pretty?" she asked.

"I don't trust myself around pretty. Not someone as pretty as you. It's too easy to forget the damage that I could do, wanting too much of it."

He was sweaty and covered in grass and dirt from the soccer field. All he'd done when he'd gotten to the truck was throw on a sweatshirt. Libby would have had a seizure at the thought of going anywhere in town with him looking like this. But not Kristen. She just kept gazing at him as if she wanted to gobble him up.

"I've always wanted to be pretty." She looked at the restaurant. "You know, the easy kind of pretty that you don't have to take a second look at to find something you like."

She wrinkled her nose. She unstrapped her seat belt and opened her door. Its screech reminded him he needed to oil its hinges—*and* that he needed to be getting out himself, instead of sitting there, dumbstruck by what she'd said.

She was leaning against her door staring at the ground when he reached her side.

"I say too much sometimes," she explained, "when I'm not being careful. I wasn't fishing for a compliment, Law, I swear."

He took one of her hands and kissed her palm. "I don't want you to ever be careful with me again. I want you in my life, just the way you are. All that you are, you and your ridiculous self-esteem issues. And anytime you want to hear how beautiful you are, just come back to me, Kristen. It'll be the first thing I tell you every time I see you, because it's the God's honest truth."

"I . . . I didn't have nurturing parents, any more than you did."

"I know. But that doesn't make you any less pretty, just because you didn't have people in your life when you were Chloe's age to show you how to feel good about yourself."

She glanced past him into the Dream Whip. When she looked back, there was doubt in her eyes. He felt her confusion, down to his soul.

"Are you?" she asked.

"Am I what, darlin'?" He'd be absolutely anything she needed him to be.

"Are you in my life?" She smiled then, the way she'd smiled as he'd driven them through town. "I want you to be. I want *us* to be. I've wanted this kind of thing, what I feel with you, for so long, I don't remember *not* wanting it. But I've never let myself try. It seemed better that way, than to be wrong again about what love and family seem to mean for everyone else, and—"

Her breath caught when he leaned in and kissed her.

He kept his hands to himself. But listening to her saying how much she'd wanted him, how long she'd waited for him, how could he not kiss her? Her lips softened beneath his. Her kiss back was seeking and finding and giving and asking, sweet and fierce. Perfect.

It was his doing when they slipped apart. He either let her go now, or he opened her door, bundled her back into the truck, and drove away without going inside.

"I . . ." She brushed the back of her hand across the sexy blush on her cheek. "I didn't mean to keep you from Chloe for so long. I tend to ramble when I'm nervous."

"I make you nervous?"

She nodded.

"And you make me want to sing," he admitted.

"I do?" She sounded as if he'd given her the finest of diamonds. Did she understand how rare she was?

"From the first Sunday you jogged that pretty ass of yours past me at the park—even if I wouldn't let myself hear it then. Now, more notes and words and melodies come back every day. I can't stop it, Kristen. You're inside me. You keep spilling out in the way I'm talking with Chloe now, and Dan, and dealing with myself and Libby. I'm singing in my head all the time."

"Thank you. I think that's the nicest thing anyone's ever said about me."

"You're welcome. We're both scared of this, Kristen. But we're going to make it work."

"What . . . what happens when Libby gets worse again?" Kristen asked. "Dan thinks she's going to. What if she's drinking again, and it's because you've decided to be with me?"

"Then we protect Chloe, the way we have been." They would protect the family he could see them one day becoming, if they kept fighting and didn't give in to the fear they both had of love never working out. "We protect each other . . ."

"I like the sound of that." There were still shadows in her eyes.

He'd protect Kristen, too. He'd do whatever he had to do, now that he'd found a woman who would fight for him just as fiercely as he would for her.

"Let's go." He tugged her toward the door, not letting go until the last possible second, just before they stepped inside.

Chapter Seventeen

"There's nothing wrong with strawberry milk shakes," Kristen said, because Chloe's dad and Uncle Dan wouldn't stop teasing her about ordering one.

Ms. Hemmings had just asked Chloe to call her Kristen when they weren't in school. She lifted her glass and held it out to Chloe. Chloe thought for a second, wondering what Kristen wanted. And then she lifted *her* strawberry shake, the one she'd ordered instead of chocolate after she'd heard Kristen order hers, and clinked glasses, the way the adults did on TV and in movies.

"Don't tell me you like them better than chocolate now," Chloe's dad said, "after all these years not drinking anything else."

He was teasing her, too. And he was smiling, the way he had last night when Chloe had told him she loved him. The way he had after soccer, when he'd hugged her so close again.

And everyone was smelly and sweaty still—at least, she and Dad and Fin were—the way her mom would never have let Chloe go out smelling. And . . . Chloe loved it. All of it. She suddenly never wanted today to end, no matter how bad some parts of it had been, even the part where Mom had shown up tonight.

This felt good, like last night had. Being at the Dream Whip with Dad and Kristen and Uncle Dan and Fin and Mrs. Dixon felt better and better the longer they were there.

"Strawberry milk shakes are the best," she said, and her dad winked at her this time.

"Girls are so weird," Fin said.

"But wonderful," Mrs. Dixon said, teasing him, too. She smiled at Chloe, and then at Fin. "I'd make it a point never to forget that, if you know what's good for you."

"Some of us like being weird," Kristen said.

Chloe and Fin stared at her.

"You?" Chloe asked, liking the assistant principal even more than before, even if she wasn't sure yet how much she liked Kristen and her dad being together.

"Sure," Kristen said.

"But you're the assistant principal," Fin said.

"And I've been the tallest girl in every class, at every job, and on most every ball team I've ever been on. I got picked on about it plenty as a kid, and about a lot of other things." She looked sad for a minute, but then she smiled and looked right at Chloe. "You can learn to live with standing out, and with all the other things about your life that don't seem so good at first. I did. What choice did I have?"

"You fly your freak flag proudly . . ." Dad held up his chocolate shake for Kristen to clink. They were looking at each other now, like they couldn't stop. "My kinda girl."

Uncle Dan grunted, but he didn't say anything. He hadn't said much the whole time they'd been at the Dream Whip.

"You mean . . ." Chloe thought of all the times that her mom's crazy behavior had made Chloe wonder if she'd ever feel good again, for real, instead of just acting like she did. "You like being different?"

"I'm me," Kristen said. "The only me there's ever going to be. I could let other people make me feel bad about it, or I could get over it. And I deserve better than to feel bad about myself the rest of my life."

Chloe glanced at her dad, to see what he thought. The way he was looking at Kristen made Chloe look harder. He seemed so happy, like he'd said back at the park that they both deserved to be happy, no matter what Mom did.

Only if her mom got even worse after today, then what? It made Chloe afraid to think about it, but it also made her mad, the way she'd been mad at the park when she'd told her mom to go home.

She looked at Kristen and tried to imagine the pretty assistant principal who practically ran the school being afraid of anything, like Chloe was of her mom sometimes. Or of her dad finally deciding that her mom couldn't be part of their family at all. Kristen had gotten over being afraid, she'd said. Chloe *really* wanted to, too.

"I guess being different can be kinda cool." Chloe glared at Fin before he could say something stupid about it. "As long as you're not so different you almost get kicked out of school."

"Hey!" He wiped his mouth with the back of his hand. Yuck. "That was months ago."

"Three of the calmest months of this school year," Kristen said, smiling at Fin now, instead of Chloe's dad. She raised her glass again. "Here's to you, Fin. Now if we can just get you to focus on your schoolwork as well as you've focused on staying with the Dixons, we'll be golden."

"Which reminds me," Mrs. Dixon said. "You've got homework and chores waiting at home."

"Man . . ." Fin slid down in the booth and drank more of his shake.

"Do your homework, or no soccer," Chloe's dad reminded him. "You keep your grades up and do your work, you stay in school and do what the Dixons need you to, and you'll have more soccer than you can handle. That's our deal, right?"

"Right." Fin pushed back up in the booth.

"He's brought all of his grades up to A's and B's." Mrs. Dixon sounded proud, making Fin smile.

"You're capable of all A's," Kristen said.

"All A's are boring." Fin rolled his eyes. "Who cares?"

"I do," Chloe admitted. She wouldn't have said it if her mom had been there.

Mom thought friends and doing things with them and what Chloe wore to school and what everyone thought about Chloe and how she looked were more important than what she learned.

"I've always made straight A's on everything," she bragged, "and I like it. I don't care what anyone thinks, or if all of my friends think I'm a geek or whatever. I like school as much as I like soccer."

She waited for Fin to make fun of her. But he just looked at her weird, like he wished he could make all A's, too.

"I could show you how," she said. It would be fun, like they had fun together at the park. "It's not like *you* care what anyone at school thinks about you."

He shrugged, drinking some more.

"You're an amazing kid," her dad said, hugging her against him. "You know that?"

Chloe could hardly swallow her next sip of strawberries and milk. It felt so good to hear him say things like that, and to be at the Dream Whip like this, not worrying about anything and having fun.

"Mrs. Dixon's right," Uncle Dan said. Chloe had almost forgotten he was there, at the end of the booth next to Fin. "I need to be getting home to Sally and Charlotte. Chloe, why don't you ride with me, so we can get you into the bath before some of that dirt becomes permanent? Your dad's got to return Ms. Hemmings to that racy car of hers."

Chloe looked up at her dad. He was waiting for her answer. She finished her milk shake, slurping it and remembering all the times Kristen had been nice to her at school, after things had gotten so bad at home. And now she was being nice to her dad the same way. Why had Chloe ever thought that was a bad thing?

Her mom divorcing her dad had been bad. Really bad. Her parents still fighting and her mom still drinking were bad, too. But that wasn't what tonight felt like. Tonight felt like . . . getting better, the way her dad had promised they could.

"Okay." She slid out of the booth and stood next to her uncle, not letting herself care what her mom would think if she found out about milk shakes with Kristen, or even Chloe calling Ms. Hemmings *Kristen*, or Dad driving the assistant principal back to her car.

You're an amazing kid, Dad had said. Chloe hugged him around the neck, feeling amazing and loving him for making tonight happen.

"I love you, Daddy."

***

Kristen walked into her condo's living room to find Law deep in thought on her couch. She'd offered to make coffee while he took a quick shower and changed into the spare workout gear he kept in the truck. She'd sensed he needed a little space before they had the conversation they'd both known was coming.

They'd ridden back to the park in virtual silence, the cab of his truck warm—from the heater he'd turned on for her, from Chloe's tentative acceptance of the closeness growing between them, and from their anticipation of what lay ahead.

Are you sure about this? he'd asked Kristen, after he'd walked her to her Mustang. *I won't be able to stay the night. I don't want to rush you. And . . .*

She'd silenced him, putting her finger to his lips, and then she'd kissed him there. *I'm a big girl, Law. I know how to say no, if no is what I want. I'm still nervous about a lot of things between us. But not about tonight.*

She set their mugs on her coffee table. She'd changed, too, into jeans and a light sweater.

"Black?" she asked.

He'd been watching her, in an absent way, from the moment she'd stepped through the door from the kitchen. His expression shifted from disconnected to devilish now. His grin followed.

"My thoughts?" he asked.

"Your coffee. I guessed black was how you liked it." She shook her head. "You were right. We don't even know how the other one likes their coffee."

"But I know you like strawberry milk shakes." He tugged her down beside him. "And I can't wait to see what else makes you fly your freak flag."

She settled into him and tucked her head against his shoulder. Neither of them reached for their drinks. She suspected their mugs would still be sitting there, cold, when he left hours from now.

And Law's having to leave was okay with her, as long as he came back—just as she'd be happy to stay right where they were the whole time, doing just this, if that was what felt good to him for now.

Something was troubling him.

"You have a piano," he said.

She inhaled and accepted the distraction for what it was. No use overthinking it. If Law needed more time, he needed more time. She looked across her living room at the baby grand she'd found in an antique store in Athens. Shiny and black and majestic, it dominated the curtainless bay window that framed her landscaped backyard.

"Yes," she said. "Isn't she beautiful?"

"I didn't know you played."

"I don't. Not a note. I always wanted to. I thought I'd take lessons sooner or later. But it's never happened. I don't regret bringing it home, though. I've always loved music so much. It's . . . comforting to have it here."

He chuckled. The sound rumbled from inside him to her, where her back was pressed to his chest. "Maybe it's been waiting for me."

She thought that maybe it had. "You'll play it for me?"

"One day. Who else have you had entertain you with it?"

That was an interesting segue.

"No one has," she told him.

Law ran his hand up her arm. "You've never dated a musician before?"

"I've never brought a date to my home before. This is my private world. No other man's been here but you."

His hand kept up its soothing glide, down her arm to her elbow and wrist, and then his fingers found hers.

After a while, he said, "I have a confession to make, too."

She nodded. She'd been expecting as much.

"It's about me and Libby."

That she hadn't expected. But she'd opened up the ex-files, so she waited. When he didn't go on, she asked, "Can you tell me why you've stuck by her for so long, even the last year after your divorce, when she's done so much to hurt you and Chloe?"

He had to have loved his ex-wife very much once upon a time.

"I guess . . ." he said. "I guess I was just too young when we met to know what real love was. And once we had Chloe, I wanted to make sure my daughter had the best family we could give her. I didn't trust myself to give her that on my own. I wanted her to have her mother."

"Trust is important. It's everything. I've never done it very well, either."

He caressed her cheek. The palm of his free hand smoothed down her other arm, brushing the side of her breast and beguiling her into wanting this—them—even more.

"You've trusted this place," he said. "Chandlerville. You had the shooting at school dropped in your lap. That would have scared most folks off. And if Roy Griffin had had his way, he'd have had everyone believing it was all your fault. But you fought back. You fought to stay. And here you are. The community can't get enough of you now."

"I've learned a lot about myself over the last year." Once or twice, she'd almost let herself leave, no matter what the school board decided about how well she had or hadn't done her job. "In the end, I couldn't go. Maybe I should have. It's been hard ever since to—"

"Keep your distance? I'm glad you didn't. You reached out to me last year, you let me get closer, and look at all the good that's come into my life. You, Fin, the Dixons, Dan, and how much better Chloe and I will be doing from now on."

"Yeah. But if you need space now, that's fine. I totally understand. We don't have to do this tonight. If you need to slow things down again . . ." She forced herself to go on. "If there's still more for you to figure out with Libby before you can be with me and not regret it later, let me know now. I'm falling . . . I'm falling for you, and I'm not going to be able to stop if we go any further. So don't let me, if you can still put on the brakes. This is a lot for me. I haven't let myself be intimate with many men. And when I have, it's never felt . . . this important."

He lifted her face for a tender kiss. "That's what I'm trying to tell you. This is new for me, too. I've never . . . Except for Libby, I've never . . ."

Kristen sat up, pushing herself around until she was facing him. She needed to be certain she'd heard him right.

He looked so sexy, his hair wet and curling from his shower, his beard growing in and making him look rough-and-tumble in his wrinkled gym clothes. And his eyes were storm clouds piercing into her, promising her the dangerous, unbridled connection she craved.

"Libby was your first?" How could someone like Law, who in his teens and twenties must have looked and behaved as bad as a bad boy could, *not* have had every woman he'd wanted, every chance he'd gotten?

"She's been my only," said her reformed rebel. "I met her practically my first day in college. And before that . . . Living at home with my parents didn't exactly make me want to get close to anyone else."

Kristen shook her head. "And even since . . ."

"Even since my divorce? There's been no one. Libby had my heart once, a long time ago. I've never trusted anyone else with it. Until you."

Kristen shook her head again.

His heart. He was giving her his heart? Suddenly she was in his lap again, facing him, kissing him and settling her body against Law's, needing to get closer until there was only the needing of him, wanting him, both of them open and vulnerable and no longer thinking, no worrying, just feeling.

"Be with me, Kristen," he said.

He wasn't promising her forever, she warned herself. He might back away again tomorrow. But he was giving her his heart tonight.

"Let me love you," he said. "Let me show you how good we can be."

***

Law curled Kristen into his arms and carried her to her bedroom, feeling stronger than he had in his whole life. And weaker. He wanted her. He wanted her to want him. But more than that, he wanted *them*. This moment, this closeness, he wanted it to stretch and stretch into a symphony that they'd never stop playing.

He settled her onto the softness of her comforter, pressing her body into the mattress and covering her with his. Somewhere along the way, their clothes had disappeared and there was nothing but skin against skin, smooth and rough, tender and hard, her and him. They didn't know each other, not well enough for sinking into her, becoming one with her, to feel so right. But there was nowhere on earth he'd rather be.

"You're perfect." He kissed her, loved her, deeper and longer. When she shuddered and arched into him, all desire and desperation, he sent his body deeper still. "I never thought . . . All these years, I never dreamed you'd want me like this."

"I . . ." Her long, endless legs slid up his thighs, her knees hugged his hips, and she found his rhythm, found him, as if they'd been this close countless times. "I didn't know how to stop wanting you. I couldn't make it stop. Please . . ." She gasped, her bottom filling his hands, her sweet center opening, accepting more. "Please don't ever let it stop."

"Never," Law whispered into her ear.

She was a promise. She was forever. This was a healing forever, for both of them. They may have only just met, but he had to have her now, tomorrow, always.

"I'm never going to stop, love," he whispered. He felt her passion become demanding, overwhelming, calling to his. "I'm never going to stop. I . . ."

She trembled. Her lips clung, and then they slid to his neck, her teeth nipping at his skin, marking him, her body clenching his until he couldn't hold back another second. Driving them both toward completion, feeling her arms tighten around him, holding him, taking him, he pressed Kristen to his heart and held her there . . .

Until they both fell.

"I love you," he said, as they came undone, knowing she wasn't ready to say it back, but trusting that she felt it just the same. Because being in Kristen's arms, he knew now, was the home he'd been searching for his entire life. "God, I love you . . ."

Chapter Eighteen

"Congratulations," Law said to Walter and Julia a week later.

He and Chloe were working their way through the couple's receiving line at Pockets. The Davises had just renewed their vows. They were about to kick off the community Valentine's party that they were hosting. There was a dance floor and a DJ and tons of food and decorations and couples and families eager for a night of fun. It was going to be another unforgettable Chandlerville event.

"You're so pretty." His daughter patted the sleeve of Julia's soft, white-and-red casual dress. Julia had insisted she'd chosen it for a party, not a wedding. Walter had worn a suit, rather than a tux. But Julia was glowing like a bride, regardless. "Thank you for the flowers," Chloe said.

"Well, thank you for being one of our flower girls," Julia responded. She and Walter had decided last-minute to buy three of the girls from Mimosa Lane—Chloe included, now that she and Law were at Dan's—a bouquet of tiny pink rosebuds to hold during the ceremony. The delicate flowers complemented the larger red ones Walter had presented to Julia, before they'd walked toward the front of the room, through the crowd of friends who'd come to help celebrate. "You and Polly and Sally are so special to us. We thought it would be a nice surprise."

The Davises had written their own vows, and they'd taken only a few moments of everyone's time for the renewal cere- mony—not wanting to monopolize the party, Walter had in- sisted. But Law had watched as their boys and the entire community smiled and held back emotion, while Walter and Julia reminded themselves of why they wanted another twenty- five years together—to learn and grow and fail and succeed and never give up on the love they'd found. Not a single person there had minded the delay in getting to the night's festivities.

He'd watched Kristen, too. She'd stood beside him, her hand in his for all the world to see. She'd struggled to keep her silent tears to herself. And even though she hadn't yet returned his vow of love, he'd found himself wanting the same thing he had that first night they'd made love, and every other moment they'd spent together.

Forever.

When he looked at Kristen—when his daughter did, and he saw Chloe thriving again, in part because of how she'd accepted Kristen into their lives—he knew he'd made the right decision, no matter how increasingly agitated Libby had become.

After Libby had backed down from the scene she'd caused at soccer practice, she'd been careful to keep her litany of com- plaints about his new relationship limited to his lawyer and to Law in private. She seemed to have rededicated herself to being on her best behavior in the community. There'd been no more public displays, at least as far as he'd heard. Chloe hadn't said anything, either, and she was opening up to Law more each day. But Libby wasn't happy, and a day didn't go by that she didn't give him an earful about just how selfishly he was ruining her and Chloe's lives.

Regardless, he had to believe they were going to work through this. And he was going to convince Kristen to believe in their relationship.

Since those first few hours at her condo, they'd stolen as much private time as they could. It was never long enough. But every second in each other's arms had been more perfect than the last. She'd find her way to trusting him, the way she'd said she'd wanted him.

"You ready for your surprise performance?" Walter shook Law's hand and clapped him on the back. "The mic's all yours whenever you want it."

"Are you going to do it now, Dad?" Chloe asked. "I want my friends to hear."

Law gazed through the crowd still milling about the Pockets café where Walter and Julia had staged their ceremony. Julia had decorated every wall and booth and counter with enough glittery hearts and Cupid cutouts and carnations and crepe paper to tempt even the most jaded of souls to overdose on romance. Kristen had wandered away with Mallory a few minutes ago. Her friend looked as if she might deliver her baby at any moment.

He didn't see them nearby or beyond the café, where activities for the kids and family bowling were being set up by Walter and Julia's staff. But he knew Kristen would be there—close enough to hear him when he started to sing. And he hoped, with her love for music, that her song—the one he'd been tinkering with for more than a week—would tell her everything he hadn't yet been able to say.

"I'm going to do it soon," he told his daughter.

Chloe had stayed up late with him the last few nights, even though there'd been school the next morning, helping him get ready for this.

Kristen's going to love it, she'd said. *Don't be so worried.*

Law saw Dan coming their way—his brother, who'd taken Law into his home and back into his life, and even gone with Law to his first Al-Anon meeting over the weekend. He was bringing Law's guitar to him now, the way he'd brought back so many of the good memories of their early childhood together.

"I'll be ready soon," Law said.

"No, you won't." Walter squeezed Law's shoulder. "But Kristen's worth taking the risk for. She'll love whatever you've come up with."

"I'm supposed to be singing a song for the two of you." Law glanced suspiciously between Walter and Julia, wondering just how much of what he was about to do had actually been their idea, when they'd approached him with the request to perform a song for their renewal ceremony.

"We appreciate it so much." Julia's smile was bright and far too smug. "But you've got more inside you than just one song, Law Beaumont. We're thrilled you're going to be sharing your talent with us, and with Kristen. Let her know how much she means to you. It's the perfect way to kick off the Valentine's party."

"Can I tell everyone about your surprise now?" Chloe begged him as Dan handed over Law's guitar. "Can I at least tell Fin?"

Law nodded, only half listening. Her happiness was a fragile thing still. He couldn't stop worrying about saying or doing the wrong thing, and setting her back. Or that Libby would find a way to shatter the good he was finally doing for their daughter.

"Fin!" Chloe ran toward her friend. Fin was standing beside Thomas and a few of the guys from their soccer team. "Guess what . . ."

"She's getting better," his brother said, watching Chloe race away. "You're making sure of that."

"Yeah."

Law shook Dan's hand. He'd never felt more proud of anything he'd done, or more humbled by how lucky he was. He wouldn't have accomplished any of this without his brother's help.

"Thank you," he said again.

"You're welcome." Dan gave him a one-shoulder hug before heading back toward Charlotte and Sally.

Law looked for Kristen again, suddenly as eager to get started as his daughter. It was crazy, what he had planned, after not doing this sort of thing since he'd been a kid himself. But music had a way of wanting what it wanted, and his music was back. The song playing over and over in his mind needed to be heard, by one special lady in particular.

He headed for the mic near where the DJ had set up in the café, picking up a stool and carrying it with him, so he could sit for the most important—and the most terrifying—performance of his life.

***

"You're looking—" Kristen started to say.

"Huge?" Mallory interjected. "Yeah, I think I've gotten bigger since you saw me at school today. It feels like he's putting on a pound an hour now, and every single one of them is pressing on my bladder."

"*He?*" Kristen grabbed her friend's arm. She pulled her into an excited hug. "Mallory, it's a boy?"

Mallory nodded against Kristen's shoulder. She wiped at her eyes as she pulled away.

"We finally told the doctor we wanted to know," she said. "Pete and Polly are over the moon. I'm already picking out blue things for the nursery. Online, of course. It was enough of a challenge just to get me here tonight. Long shopping sprees at the mall are definitely out until I can find my ankles again. But it's impossible not to obsess about it. I want to make everything perfect for him . . ."

Kristen smiled down at one of the most beautiful pregnant women she'd seen. "It will be perfect, because you and Pete love each other. You've created a great home for Polly. That's one lucky baby brother you've got growing in there."

Mallory knew even more than Kristen did about how it felt for a child to be unloved and unnoticed—she'd grown up homeless with a mentally ill mother who hadn't loved Mallory enough to get well and to make a safe home for her. That would never happen to Mallory and Pete's baby. Just as Law had refused to let it happen to Chloe. And if he and Kristen were to have a baby of their own . . .

Kristen put her hand over her mouth to stop the thought, as if she'd said the words out loud.

She and Law were closer than ever since he'd said he loved her. It had been an incredible week. But they were just finding their way, their start. Babies? Family? There was no way either one of them was ready for something that long-term. She couldn't even get herself to say she loved him.

"What's wrong?" Mallory asked, her voice filtering through the buzzing in Kristen's ear.

"Nothing." Kristen shook her head. She focused on the happy activity around them. Law understood that she needed more time. She wasn't going to ruin a beautiful, fun evening by worrying that their time might be running out.

The song the DJ played next made her smile. "I love this ballad."

"Jim Croce?" Mallory asked.

"'I Got a Name' is one of my favorites."

"I remember you saying that once. Someone was playing it on the radio in the school office, and I thought you were going to melt into a puddle and we'd have to shampoo the carpet."

"I love all his music."

As a writer and a performer, Croce reminded Kristen a little of what she thought Law might sound like, if he'd ever let her listen to him play. She'd told him that the other night, when they'd had dinner at Dan and Charlotte's. But he'd refused to perform for them even though his guitar had been sitting in the corner of the living room, no matter how much she'd tried to wheedle something out of him.

"I especially like his songs that talk about time and change and learning to grow and looking back at how far you've come so you can move forward a little more. A lot of Croce's work is about time. 'I Got a Name' is one of his best."

The ballad swung into its final stanza. Croce was learning how to dream about tomorrow when the DJ cut the recording and Walter took over the mic, asking for everyone's attention again. Kristen and Mallory turned toward him, along with the rest of the crowd. Law was standing there, too, beside a stool, holding his guitar and two long-stemmed red roses.

Mallory surprised Kristen by handing over a wad of fresh, folded tissues.

"What's this for?" Kristen asked.

"You. A little bird's told me what's about to happen. And if watching Walter and Julia renew their vows got to you, you're going to be bawling your eyes out for sure in a few minutes."

Chapter Nineteen

"We have a little surprise for you all," Walter said, while Law set aside the roses he'd ordered from Hearts in Bloom florists, to be delivered along with Julia's bouquets.

He tuned up his guitar and told himself to calm down. He'd done this hundreds of times before. He could do it at least once more—for his daughter and Kristen.

"Julia and I wanted to have a dance," Walter continued. "And Julia always gets what she wants. My only job was to pick the music. So I asked someone I hear is one of the finest musicians any of us will ever know for his advice, and he up and volunteered to play for us. Well, my wife kinda talked him into it, but he seems to be warming up to the idea. So, ladies and gentlemen, help us make Law Beaumont feel good about kicking off tonight's Valentine's fun."

Applause started slowly.

No big surprise there.

Law figured most everyone knew he'd played something at some point, just like they knew he'd been convicted of something. But telling his own story about his past—about who he'd really been and who he'd once wanted to become—had never been all that important to him. Not enough to share with neighbors he'd thought of as strangers.

When he'd first moved here with Libby, he hadn't let himself feel connected to Chandlerville or Dan or the people who'd tried to befriend him. But because this was Kristen's community, his daughter's community, it was now becoming his. It was past time that he gave something back to this place and the people who'd welcomed him long before he'd appreciated it.

He started playing the opening chords of the song he'd selected for Julia and Walter, thinking of what he wanted it to mean to them . . . and to Chloe. He hoped, once he was through, that his daughter would understand a little better how much he'd loved her every moment of her life—even the ones he hadn't been there to share.

He nodded as Walter placed the microphone in its stand in front of Law. He made himself more comfortable on the stool. Thanks to the DJ's amps, his music was being projected throughout the bowling center.

But for Law, this was about more than the crowd eagerly pushing closer now. It was about connecting. Music had always been his way to do that. It was about everything he wanted to say but too often couldn't, until a song pulled the truth from him.

"This is for Walter and Julia," he told his audience. "And I understand it's a favorite of a friend of mine."

He caught Kristen's eye, finally, and winked. Mallory nudged Kristen's arm with her elbow. Chloe had found them. His daughter was standing in front of Kristen. Kristen's hands settled on her tiny shoulders, and Chloe relaxed into her.

"This one's been on my personal playlist for a long time, too," he said. "When I suggested it to Walter, he said it would be perfect.

And tonight, I wanted to dedicate it to my daughter, Chloe, as well as the Davises. You're every wish I've ever had come true, darlin'. Never forget that."

His hands stilled as he finished the instrumental for the song's chorus.

A murmur began moving through the crowd, picking up speed and intensity. Heads were nodding as people guessed what he was about to sing. Smiles popped up—none bigger nor more excited than his little girl's and Kristen's. Law's stomach knotted. Sweat broke out everywhere a man could sweat. He closed his eyes regardless, listened to the music still filling his thoughts, and then began to play.

Jim Croce's "Time in a Bottle" came to life as his fingers moved over his guitar strings and his voice filled the bowling center. The melody and lyrics were so simple, timeless, deep. Their message was bottomless, what it meant to him every time he heard it: dreams, wishes, yesterday, forever. The songwriter introduced his themes, and then he stripped them bare. He showed the listener the heart of each truth he'd magically set to verse. It was a ballad. It was an endless love song. It was the beating soul of what every couple, every parent and child, every friendship, and every community could be.

Law gave himself to singing it, feeling the connection deeper than ever before, washing over him, through his voice and the instrument in his hands . . . and between him and the audience listening to him, silent and transported. When he opened his eyes at the end of the song, he found everyone's attention riveted to what he'd done.

Julia was crying, like most of the other female faces in the crowd. She kissed Walter, thrilled. She rushed to Law's side and kissed his cheek, too. But Law couldn't look away from the two beautiful faces he needed to see most as he played his next song.

"I'm going to be a little selfish here," he said into the mic as Walter drew Julia away, "and snatch the limelight from the DJ for another minute or two. It's been a long time since something's inspired me to want to arrange something new. But Kristen, I've been hearing pieces of this for close to three months now. And in the last few weeks, it's let me know exactly who it was for, and what it needed to say, so I finally wrote it down. This is my heart, Kristen, and it belongs to you, whenever you come back to me . . ."

He'd decided on "Come Back to Me" as the title, thinking of how she'd accepted his apology that afternoon at the Y, no matter how angry she'd been, and then she'd shown up at soccer practice the next day. She was still nervous. Maybe she didn't know how to completely believe in them yet. But she'd come back to him and given him another chance. He'd never let her down again.

And as he sang, he was picturing them running in the park, or him and Chloe teaching Kristen to play soccer, or her teaching Chloe basketball, or them playing on her piano, all three of them sitting together in front of her sparkling bay window, or eating together, or living together as the family he knew they could become. Or maybe Kristen and him even bringing a new life into the world.

A new family. New love. He and Kristen making their way, and no matter the challenge, Kristen always coming to find him.

When he finished for the second time, the crowd applauded again, and it was his daughter he looked to first. She and Kristen had begun to become friends, but was this too much for Chloe, too soon?

She ran to him and gave him her biggest hug, and said, "I love you, Daddy."

He handed her one of the roses. "I love you, too, darlin'."

Only then did he lift his gaze to the woman he'd just announced to all of Chandlerville that he wanted to love forever. Kristen joined him more slowly, took her flower more hesitantly. A tear slipped from her eye as she smelled the fragile bloom. But her smile was radiant.

"That was beautiful, Law," she said. "I—"

"I'm going to puke," a sarcastic voice cut in, flashing Law back to another night at Pockets, and another confrontation in nearly the same spot.

Kristen and Chloe turned toward the rest of the bowling center—and toward an obviously drunk Libby. Law stood up, setting aside his guitar. The place had grown freakishly quiet after his ex-wife's scathing comment.

Libby crossed her arms, missing the gesture the first time, her limbs slipping away from each other until she tried again and managed a pose that she probably thought looked intimidating. In her current state—hair a mess and no makeup, when she usually took such pains with her appearance, and her clothes so wrinkled she'd likely been sleeping in them for days—she looked pathetic.

"What a pretty little family." She zeroed in on Kristen. "Too bad it's not yours, Ms. Assistant Principal."

"Dad?" Chloe said.

"It's okay," Law said.

Of course her mother had found the most self-destructive way possible to implode again.

By publicly blowing her sobriety, Libby had to know she was torching her chances to win back even partial custody of Chloe.

Law's lawyer had a petition ready to send to the court that Law had told him to hold off on, asking that a stint in rehab be added to the judge's final ruling, plus mandatory regular drug and alcohol screening once Libby was out, before she was allowed unsupervised access to their daughter. Law had let himself hope his ex was finally seeing reason, and that he wouldn't have to take things that far.

"It's *okay*," she mimicked. "What's okay? That my life is over, and you get to start a new one? Is that what you've been waiting for all along? You get me back for all the years you've hated me, by finding someone else? Singing to everyone that you love her, right under my nose?" She glanced at Kristen and then back. "Did you tell her? Have you told everyone now, that this is all because it should have been me, not you, and even before that you didn't want me?" She was babbling and not making sense— to anyone but Law . . . "Does your new muse know that you're the kind of man who marries a woman you don't love and goes to prison for her when—"

"That's enough." Law stepped in front of Chloe and Kristen, blocking their view of his ex-wife. Never in a million years had he thought she'd ever bring up his conviction. There was no reason to. Not this way, in front of Chloe, making her hear about it along with the entire town. "Stop it, Libby. Why are you doing this?"

"Why not? You never loved me. You never wanted me. Why not tell everybody just how much you've hated me from the start, and why?"

"Dad?" Chloe was crying. A minute ago she'd been over the moon. She was pulling on his pants leg, trying to pull him away from her mother.

"Outside," he said to Libby while he cupped Chloe's head. "You're drawing a crowd. Come talk with me outside."

He glanced an apology to Kristen. She seemed as afraid as his daughter. There was something broken about the way she was looking back at him, something he refused to accept. He could still hear her asking him to be sure, before they'd made love their first time—to be free of all the mess he'd thought he'd left behind. She'd been skittish ever since. But he'd been okay with giving her time, trusting her to trust him. With this latest outburst from Libby, what if Kristen had decided she couldn't?

"I'm sorry," he said to her. "I'll be back as soon as I can. I'll explain everything. But—"

"You need to deal with your wife first?"

"*Ex*-wife." He bit the words out and grabbed Libby's arm. This was supposed to be his and Kristen's night, the night he showed her how committed he was to the life he wanted them to have. "Please wait here for me. Keep an eye on Chloe, and try to help her calm down." He looked down at his daughter, hugging her close, letting her go. "I'll be right back, darlin'. Wait with Kristen."

Without pausing for either of them to respond, not wanting to give Libby a chance to start ranting again, he dragged his inebriated ex toward the side door, to the alley where they'd had their last fight—the night Kristen had stuck by his side, instead of looking like she wanted to run from him as much as his daughter did.

***

Chloe watched Kristen stare after her dad and mom. She watched her parents walk out of Pockets. She threw down her rose and slipped away before Kristen could notice, not that Kristen seemed to be looking at anything but Chloe's dad walking away from them both, after singing the most beautiful song Chloe had ever heard.

Not that Chloe cared. All she cared about was getting out of there before her mom started yelling at her dad again.

"Where are you going?" Fin asked, stopping her from running toward the front door.

"I don't care," Chloe said. "Anywhere but here, with my parents. My mom's—"

"A train wreck," Brooke said from behind Fin, with Summer standing right there next to her. "I can't wait to hear whatever crazy, drunk thing she's going to say next."

"Leave her alone," Fin said. Thomas and Jake from their soccer team were there now, too.

"Yeah," Thomas said. "It's not Chloe's fault her mom's the way she is. It's not like your parents are normal or anything."

Brooke pouted at Thomas, the way she did at school a lot now, whenever Thomas hung out with Fin and Jake and Chloe, instead of Sam and Brooke and Summer. Brooke and Summer turned their backs and left. It should have made Chloe feel better. The DJ started playing again, and the adults started dancing or doing stuff with their kids, forgetting what had happened this time instead of following her parents and trying to listen in.

Only Chloe couldn't forget.

She couldn't get what her mom had said out of her head. What had Mom meant, that it should have been her, and that Dad had hated her all along? What did any of that have to do with Dad going to prison, or him singing to Kristen now?

Chloe looked at Fin. "Where did my dad and mom go?"

Fin pointed toward the side entrance on the other side of the bowling alleys. Chloe took off through the Valentine's party, with him running behind her. She hated the party now. It had felt perfect for a while, her dad singing for her and Kristen, while everything was so sparkly and pretty around them. Now she had to get out of there. But first she had to know what was going on with her family, once and for all.

"Wait." Fin grabbed her arm by the side door.

"I can't," she said, crying again. "I have to know. I have to know what my mom meant."

"Are you sure?" Fin asked. "Your dad said he'd be right back."

"My dad says a lot of things, but he never tells me anything. Not really. Not the important stuff."

"What if it's something you don't want to know?" Fin asked over the sound of the party and people laughing all around them. "Maybe that's why he didn't tell you."

"He made me talk about my mom. He said we have to be honest with each other to be happy." Except she felt like she knew even less about her parents now than she ever had. "I have to do this."

Fin shook his head. But he let her go, and then he followed her. Chloe checked behind them to make sure no one was watching as they left through the door, cracking it open just enough for them to slip through. As soon as they were outside, Fin dragged her behind one of the Dumpsters, where a lot of the boxes and wrapping for the Valentine's decorations had been tossed.

"You're going to stop this," her dad was saying halfway down the alley and away from the door, by the corner of the building that led to the parking lot. "You're going to stop right now, and give me time to tell Chloe myself, the right way. I can't believe you want to do this after all this time. It doesn't matter."

"Of course it matters!"

Her mom sounded like she did at night sometimes, just before she fell asleep on the couch after she'd been drinking so much that nothing Chloe did would wake her up again until morning. She was crying and sad, but she was so quiet, not yelling like she had been inside.

"It's the reason for everything, right?" her mom said. "All the things you've hated me for, all the reasons you never loved me. It's all about that night and what I let you talk me into doing. You blame me—"

"I've never hated you," Dad said. "I don't blame you. It could have been either of us. I was just as drunk as you were. I let you drive, Libby. It was my fault as much as yours. I'd make the same choice now that I did then, after the accident."

"Of course you would." Mom was crying even harder. "Because you're perfect, and I'm the bad one. Ever since I got pregnant and you married me, even though I knew you didn't love me, you've gotten to be the one who always did everything right. And then you went to prison, for me, when I was the one who was driving. You told the police and the court it was you, so there was no chance I'd get sentenced while I was pregnant. I never thought you wouldn't do whatever your dad wanted. No matter how you felt about your family, I thought for sure you'd let them help you. But you wouldn't even do that. Not you. What did you do? You went to prison for a year and a half for something you didn't do, so you could spend the rest of our marriage making sure I knew you'd always be better than me."

"That wasn't it, Libby." Dad reached for her, but she jerked away from him. "I loved—"

"Chloe," Mom sobbed. "It's always been about her, not me. I tried to make it up to you. I tried to make you love me when you got out, but I couldn't, so I drank. And then we moved here, and

I thought for sure you'd see how your brother lived, you'd see his perfect family and want the same thing. But no, you didn't love me here, either. Coming here, everything you've done here, it's all been for Chloe. I bet your new girlfriend is about Chloe, too, now that I'm out of our daughter's life and you need someone to mother her."

"You're our daughter's mother. You'll always be Chloe's mother."

"Then why were you singing to that woman in front of our child and everyone else? Why haven't you ever sung to me, not once, since Chloe was born? You win, Law. You're the ex-con, but you're the good guy. I'm Chloe's mother, but I'm always going to be the bad parent, your awful, drunk ex-wife that you don't want. No matter what I do, you've made sure she'll always love you more. And now she's going to love that woman in there. And before long, I won't have any family at all . . ."

"You're drunk, Libby," Dad said. "You're not making any sense. Give me your keys and I'll take you home. Sleep this off. We'll talk tomorrow. And then we'll tell Chloe together."

"No!" Mom backed away from him, whispering in a yelling kind of way. "Now! You're not going back in there to that woman, not until we've told our daughter why she's getting a new mommy, because you never loved the one you married the first time around."

"Stop it." Dad followed her mom around the front of the building.

Chloe and Fin didn't follow them.

Because Chloe didn't want to hear any more.

"My dad . . ." she swallowed. She couldn't believe it. But Fin looked just as weirded out as she did. "He went to prison for my mom." But that wasn't the worst. "He went to prison for *me*, when he didn't do anything wrong. And he hates my mom. My dad's never loved her. How could he? That's why Mom drinks so much. My family . . . that's why we're so messed up. My mom's never going to get any better. Why didn't he just tell me?"

Chloe looked at Fin, wanting him to say that she was wrong. But he was staring back, not saying anything at all. And then she was running away. She didn't care to where—anywhere but there, where her parents were still fighting, inside now, probably, where everyone would hear them and know the truth.

Her dad had never loved her mom. It had all been a lie. Chloe had never really had a family at all.

***

"Stay," Mallory said to Kristen near Pockets' front doors.

"I . . ."

Kristen looked down at Law's rose and then at the families having fun around her. She thought about the scene Libby had made, even worse than the one she'd made in November, and Chloe's tears, and Law's panic to get Libby out of there again. And even though Kristen should be staying put and trying to keep Chloe calm until her father came back, she couldn't do this again.

"I know I'm being a . . ." she started to say, but couldn't finish.

"A coward?" her friend asked. "You're not, Kristen. You're upset, and you have every right to be. That was bad. You're not imagining it. But let Law handle his ex-wife. Let him explain. Everyone can see how much he loves you. Libby's out of her mind. He had to get her out of here. Don't leave without trying to understand the rest."

"I do understand." And she loved Law, too. She'd wanted to tell him after his song—her song. She'd wanted to say it in front of everyone, the way he had. But now . . . ? "I don't see how this can work."

The Valentine's party was in full swing around them. It was a beautiful night, exactly the kind of night that lovers and happy families shared and remembered and reminded each other about forever. But that wouldn't happen for her and Law. He was going to regret this. He was going to regret her and how much being with her was hurting his daughter . . . his family.

Libby wasn't better. She was worse than she'd been last fall. She'd driven herself over here so drunk she wasn't even making sense. But the one thing she had made clear was that Kristen was the reason she hadn't stayed sober. She would always be the reason Libby never let go, never stopped hurting Law and Chloe like this.

"How could I have thought this was going to work?" Kristen was going to be physically ill, watching everyone dance and laugh and eat and enjoy themselves.

I don't know how to stop wanting you, Law had said. And she'd always want him, too. But Law was probably outside now, thinking of how he was going to tell her this had all been a mistake.

She'd listened to his beautiful song and let herself imagine what the rest of their lives could be like together, her and Law and Chloe.

"I'm so scared of losing him," she finally said.

"I know." Her friend pressed both hands over her belly. "We're all a little scared of the ones we love. It's just that you're not as used to it as the rest of us mere mortals." Mallory smiled at Kristen, understanding, but she'd also put her pregnant body between Kristen and the front door. "Tell him how you feel,

Kristen. Trust him. Maybe you're right. Maybe this can't work. But you two need to figure out together what happens next."

Mallory nodded over Kristen's shoulder. Kristen turned as Law approached alone from the side of the building where he'd left with Libby. He reached her in three long strides.

She wanted to throw herself into his arms, but he looked so furious and worried. He looked around her instead of taking her hand or kissing her. His gaze never quite made contact with hers.

"I got Libby into her car," he said, "and I've taken her keys. I need to drive her home and . . . try to get her calm. And then . . ." Resignation ruled his expression. Ten years of it. He scanned the party. "I need to talk with my daughter. Where's Chloe?"

"I . . ." Kristen looked around then, too, realizing she hadn't seen the little girl in several minutes. She looked back to where they'd all been standing beside the DJ. Chloe's rose was abandoned, crumpled on the ground. "I don't know. I . . ."

He glanced back from studying the crowded party. "What do you mean, you don't know?"

Marsha Dixon approached them, looking apologetic for intruding. She also looked concerned.

"I hate to bother you two," she said. "I know you have your hands full. But have you seen Fin? I've been looking for him all over the place. But he's gone."

"No." Law shook his head. "I'm trying to find Chloe, too."

Kristen's heart clenched. "They wouldn't have . . ."

"They wouldn't have what?" Law's attention snapped back to her.

Kristen swallowed. "I'm so sorry, Law. I don't know how I could have let her slip away."

"Slip away?" He took her arm, finally touching her. His grip was so fierce, it hurt. "You think she's run away?"

"I . . . I don't know. I don't think so. I hope not. I'm so sorry, Law. I . . ."

Kristen reached for him, suddenly desperate not to let go, but she touched only air. He'd backed away. His expression was hard, distant now, like it had been during their first discussion about Fin.

"I asked you to wait for me with her," he said. "Just a few minutes. I needed you to trust me, trust us, for just a few more minutes, and watch out for Chloe while I couldn't. And you couldn't even do that. Of course she's run away." He looked behind Kristen, toward the front door. "Why wouldn't my daughter run from me and her mother, when that's exactly what you were doing, right?"

Chapter Twenty

Chloe had thought about running before.

She'd been jealous of Fin, because he'd run from school and made it look so easy. And sometimes she'd wanted it to be easy for her, too—leaving everyone behind and never thinking about them again. He'd show her how now, she'd thought when they'd left Pockets—how to really not care about her family and how they'd never been right, no matter how much her dad had promised they could be.

Only Fin hadn't wanted to go this time. He'd stayed with her all night. He'd said he wasn't going home until she did, and he wasn't going to tell anyone what they'd heard if she didn't want him to. But he'd been trying to get her to go back, too, and he'd said he wasn't going to let her leave Chandlerville. Not the way he'd left so many places before he'd moved in with the Dixons.

"You have to go home, Chloe," he said. "It's morning. We both have to go."

"If you want to go, go. Why are you here anyway, if you won't help me?"

"Because . . . you're my friend. I'm not going to leave you. You don't know anything about being by yourself. You'd just get hurt."

He made her want to see her dad again when he said things like that. Her dad had said he'd always be there, and that he'd make everything all right and that they had to stop letting what Mom did, when she did bad things, hurt them. But why hadn't he told her? Why had he told Chloe it would all be okay, when he'd known all along it was a lie?

"It's not so bad," Fin said, for like the hundredth time.

"You saw my mom. You heard her. My dad went to prison when it should have been her. He stayed with her when he never loved her. She's never going to forgive him, or give him up, or stop drinking. My family's . . ."

"The worst, yeah. I know." He'd said that a lot, too, like he didn't really believe it but he wanted to be nice.

They'd been sitting inside the Y rec center all night, in the dark. At least they hadn't been outside, where it was colder. He'd known which window one of the staff people always kept cracked, and he'd known how to get it all the way open so they could sneak inside. He'd done it once before when he'd run away, he said.

"My mom was the worst, too," he said. "She never got better, either. Until she was . . ."

"Dead." Chloe looked at him, crying again, because Fin looked so sad. He'd looked sad all night, no matter how much he'd told her things weren't so bad.

"Your mom could still get better," he said.

"She doesn't want to. She's never wanted to, not when my dad . . ."

"Yeah . . ." Fin wiped at his own eyes. "But your dad is great, though. Look at what he did for you."

Chloe shook her head. She didn't want to think about that, about how much he'd done, and how it had all been for her, and how it had somehow still meant she'd never had a family. It was too confusing. It made her too scared. It made her want to run again.

"I wish my dad . . ." Fin looked away, out the window across the room. "I wish I'd had a dad to at least try to make my mom be better. Even if it didn't work, at least I'd know . . ."

"What?" Chloe felt even worse.

"At least I'd have known," he said, "that someone loved me like that once."

"You have the Dixons." Chloe scooted closer to where Fin was sitting next to the wall. "You have that now."

"Yeah. Maybe." He didn't sound like he believed it. He sounded scared.

"What do you mean?"

"I'm going to get into trouble."

"For running away again?"

He nodded.

With her. Because she'd been so freaked out about her family, and he'd been her friend.

"Then don't stay with me!" she said again.

She was crying harder, thinking about being alone. But she wasn't ready to face her dad yet, or her mom. She *really* wasn't ready to face her mom. But Fin had to go. She didn't want him to get into trouble because of her.

"Don't do something stupid," she said, "just because I'm too scared to . . ."

"Have a family?" Fin asked. "Your family may be totally messed up, Chloe. But at least you have one."

"So do you." It was starting to get light in the rec room. She could see that Fin was more mad now than sad.

"All I got is foster families, from now on," he said. "*That's* the worst. Don't you see . . . ?"

"What?"

"Messed up is okay. As long as it's yours, and you get to keep it, and no one can ever take it away. And no matter how bad your mom acts or if she never gets better, no one can take your dad away from you, not like people can take the Dixons from me."

Chloe shook her head.

"They wouldn't do that," she said. "The Dixons and Kristen will talk to the people who decide. You've been better since the last time, at school and at home. Even my dad will tell them how great you've been with soccer."

Her dad, she realized, would never let anyone take Fin away now, just like he'd made sure Chloe hadn't gone back to her mom's until he'd known if Mom was better for real.

Fin shrugged. "I've run away a lot."

"But this time you did it for me."

He nodded. "But I won't tell them why, Chloe. I mean it. Not if you don't want me to."

She believed him. He was her friend. He wouldn't do what Summer or Brooke would do—blab to everyone who'd listen, if they'd heard what he had last night. He wasn't going to say he was her friend but act like he wasn't as soon as Chloe turned her back. Fin wasn't like them. He wasn't like her mom, who Chloe didn't think she could ever trust again. He was like . . . her dad. Messed up and all, her dad had always been there for her, no matter how much it had hurt him.

She moved closer to Fin, sitting next to him on the carpet.

"Go home," she said, "before you make things even worse."

"Where are you going to go without me? You can't stay here. The Y will be open soon. You don't know how to stay out of sight. I do. I'm not—"

"You're going to get in trouble."

He shrugged again. He was scared of what would happen when he went home, just like she was.

"You've got to go," she insisted.

"So do you."

Chloe looked out the window they'd crawled in through. She thought of trying to run away from him, and of staying out of sight on her own and hiding from everything forever.

Then she thought of what Fin had said, about her still having people who'd never be taken away from her. Her dad. Her mom again, maybe, one day, if she wanted Chloe enough to get better. And even Kristen. Chloe's dad really liked her. Last night, while Chloe had listened to him sing to her, and he'd given both of them roses, Chloe had figured out that he more than liked Kristen. He loved her, and that had felt . . . okay, she remembered now. More than okay. It had felt great, until her mom ruined everything.

Chloe felt herself start crying again. She loved her dad so much. She loved her mom still, too. Maybe she even loved Kristen. How could that have made her so scared she didn't want to go home and face anybody?

Except, if she didn't go back, Fin wouldn't go back. And then he wouldn't get to keep the Dixons. And she couldn't let him do that. She had to help him—the way Fin had helped her, and her dad had helped her, and Kristen had, too—no matter how hard going back would be.

***

"I have to get her back," Law said to the police officer who'd come to Dan's to take Law's statement for a missing persons report. He and Marsha had jointly filed one for both Chloe and Fin.

"You will," Dan said, standing beside Law the way he had been all night. Neither one of them had slept. "You'll get them both back."

They shared a long look.

Dan had seen Libby's meltdown inside Pockets, along with the rest of the Valentine's partygoers. He'd been close enough once Law had come back inside to witness the awful moment by the door with Kristen and Mallory and Marsha, when they'd realized the kids had run off together. And when Law had lost what was left of his sanity and blamed Kristen, because *he* hadn't taken better care of his daughter.

He'd had no idea all these years that Libby had been so out-of-her mind fixated on the accident—her obsession feeding her insecurities about them, even after the divorce.

"Do you have a recent picture?" the officer asked.

Law stared at the man hard. Because if he didn't keep staring, he was going to break down. All his pictures of Chloe were packed with his things in storage. He'd been so caught up in everything else since November, he didn't have anything current. What kind of father didn't have a recent picture of his daughter to help the police find her?

"Maybe at my ex-wife's house . . ." Where Libby was drying out, probably out cold, even though Chloe was still missing. "I can go check."

He'd rather spend another eighteen months in minimum security than face Libby right now. He felt sorry for her. He even understood her a little better. But he couldn't deal with his ex again yet.

"Will this work?" Dan pulled his smart phone from his pocket and accessed his camera roll. He selected a shot and held it up for Law and the officer to see. Chloe was smiling, beaming, hugging Fin's neck, both of them a sweaty mess. "It's from soccer practice."

The officer pulled out a business card, handed it to Dan. "E-mail it to this address, and I'll get it to dispatch. Do you have any idea where she might have gone?"

The officer was speaking to Dan now.

Law couldn't blame him.

Law had been useless since he and Dan had rushed out of Pockets, leaving Kristen behind when she'd been so worried, too. They'd driven all over town, looking for the kids. Marsha had kept in touch with Dan ever since, not that she or Joe had heard from Fin, either. But Kristen was with them, at least.

Law wanted to talk to her so badly, to explain the way he'd promised he would, to apologize for being so rough with her at Pockets and then running out. He wanted, he needed her to understand and still give them a chance, once they had Chloe back.

She obviously still cared. She'd been worried sick as soon as she'd realized the kids were gone. But after Libby's latest meltdown, he wouldn't blame Kristen if she decided that caring about him and Chloe was something she just couldn't keep doing.

This is a lot for me . . .

"We don't know where my niece is," Dan responded to the officer. "No one's been able to find her or Fin anywhere. The park might be somewhere they'd show up eventually. But we've checked there. And if they don't want to be found . . ."

"We already have an officer at the soccer field. He'll patrol the area through the morning, trying to stay out of sight as best he can. The foster mother says the boy's run off before?"

"Yes," Law responded. "But not recently. Not since November."

"We've pulled his file from Family Services. He's definitely trouble."

"He's a good kid," Dan corrected. "They're both good kids. It was a bad scene last night, and I think Fin might have been looking out for Chloe, leaving with her the way he did."

"I'd hate for this to ruin his chances with the Dixons," Law agreed.

What a mess.

"That's for the boy's caseworker to decide." The officer closed the pad he'd been scribbling in. "Let's just get them both home, and then you can worry about the rest. We'll be in touch if there are any developments."

If . . .

Law had been terrified of losing his daughter for so long, and now he had.

Dan stepped closer, once they were alone in his den. He knew it all now. Law had told him about the fight in the alley, about what he'd done for his family so long ago. He'd made Dan swear to never document any of it—that Libby had been driving that night instead of Law. What difference would it make now? Law didn't need his record cleared. He just needed his daughter back, and the chance to finally make all of this right.

"We'll find her," Dan said.

"Yeah." Law had never needed his brother more. But he was going to need even more help once they got Chloe home and he tried to explain what he'd never thought he'd have to.

"It all happened so long ago," he said. "How could that one night still be messing everything up for my child?"

"Because no matter what you did for Libby to show her you'd be there for her," Dan said, "she was never going to believe you loved her. That's not your fault. It's not because of the accident or you taking the rap. It's just how Libby is. Stop beating yourself up about any of it. Stop giving her the same kind of control over your future."

His future, hopefully with Kristen and Chloe.

Kristen had conquered so much in her own life. She'd recognized the survivor in him, and she'd believed in him—bad rep and bad attitude and all. She genuinely cared about his daughter. Kristen was the strongest, most loving woman he'd ever met. But had her own past left her too fragile to come back to him one last time? Could she trust him to love her, the way Libby never had?

Dan was right. He had to be right. Law would get Chloe home. He would explain everything about last night, and he and his daughter would be okay again. But what about Kristen?

The thought of losing her, of not having captured her whole heart in the first place, nearly dropped Law to the floor.

Chapter Twenty-One

"Yes, Mrs. Sewel," Marsha said into the phone. "I understand. Either Joe or I will be there at noon, and I'm hoping we'll have Fin back with us by then."

Kristen, sitting on the Dixons' couch, wanted to step to the other woman's side and give her a hug. But she couldn't move. She was so tired and frazzled and worried for Chloe and Fin and Law and even Libby. She simply couldn't move.

"It's hell being part of a family sometimes, isn't it?" Marsha asked.

Kristen blinked up at her from Law's rose. The other woman had hung up with Family Services. She crossed the room to the couch.

"Don't get me wrong," Marsha said. "Family can be wonderful. But it can also cut you off at the knees when you're worrying about someone. And you've become a part of Law's family. You know how I know? You look like I feel at times like this. Like I want to run and hide from the people I'm thinking I might lose. And I'm guessing you've been thinking just that, pretty much since Libby showed up at the Valentine's party."

She sat next to Kristen and took her hand, squeezing it.

Kristen thought of Marsha and Joe and Fin and the rest of their kids, fighting to belong to one another, no matter their differences. Was this how family felt to them, too? Terrifying? Not that Kristen was even sure Law wanted her to be part of his life anymore, after the way she'd behaved last night.

"How do you do it?" she asked.

"You love. The kind of love that doesn't go away. The kind of love that's so good when things are at their best, and their worst, that you're a little afraid sometimes to believe in it."

"The kind of love Law sang about last night."

Kristen set her rose on Marsha's coffee table. It had been the best moment of Kristen's life, hearing the man she adored tell her and everyone how he'd always be there for her, whenever she came back to him, caring about her, wanting her, and never letting her go.

"And"—Marsha squeezed again—"the kind you both are still feeling for each other, even with Libby doing her worst to destroy it. It's all love. Good and bad, you can't run away from something that deep. Whether it lasts for a few months or years or a lifetime, even if it breaks your heart, there's no getting away from love when you care as deeply as people like you and Law do." She released Kristen's hand. "That's why he's stuck by Libby and maybe done too much for her and let her get away with more than he should have. Their marriage didn't last, but he'll never stop trying to make things work for Chloe. He'll love you the same. Give him the chance to show you how much, even if it's not going to be easy for a while."

"Give *him* a chance? I'm the one who freaked out, when he needed me to be there for his daughter. I don't know how I'll face him again."

She'd refused to go to Dan's last night, though Mallory had insisted she should. Kristen had come to Marsha's instead and kept up there with the search for the kids, trying to help any way she could—including, on her way over, checking all the places in town she could think of that Chloe and Fin might have run to. She wanted to be with Law now more than anything, but she'd just be a distraction.

It was too important that he stay focused on Chloe now, rather than figuring out things between him and Kristen. Or to hear her say she loved him—which she was going to tell him the second she saw him next, even if the very next thing *he* said was that they were through.

"Law will understand how scared you were last night," Marsha said. "Once he has Chloe back, once both kids are back, the two of you will work things out, learn from this, and you'll go on from there. If . . . that's what you want."

Kristen didn't know what to say. She'd once told him that she didn't believe in lost causes, but now she wasn't so sure. Beyond apologizing to Law, she hadn't figured the rest of it out. There was still Libby to deal with, and whatever Law and his ex had argued about. There was Kristen, still not knowing for sure if she could really handle any of it, no matter how much she loved him.

She glanced at the phone on its table across the room. Joe and several of the older kids were out, looking up and down Chandlerville for Fin and Chloe and reporting in from their cells. The younger of the Dixons' foster children were still asleep, their Sunday morning not yet on the horizon. And Fin's bed was empty, his place in this accepting, hardworking, loving-through-anything family on the line when the Dixons met with Family Services at noon.

"Is Fin going to be able to stay?" Kristen asked.

Marsha's smile was strong, but sad. "The county is seeing us as kind of his endgame with group homes. He's run too many times before us. He's not attaching. Maybe a residential placement isn't right for him, they're thinking, and he needs more structure and supervision than he can get with a family."

"He's attached." Kristen's heart sank. "I've been watching him, Marsha, at school and at soccer and with Chloe and his friends. I've heard it from other teachers, from parents. He's learned how to *be* somewhere, how to be part of something, how to love something and believe it will be there to love him back—because of you and Joe. I don't know what happened with him last night. But if he's not back in time, I'll talk to Mrs. Sewel with you. I'll tell her how much better Fin's doing, and why it's so important that he stay here. They can't take away his family, now that he finally believes he has one."

The words rattled around in Kristen's already turbulent thoughts.

Fin wasn't the only one who'd had to learn what family meant, or how lucky he was to have people in his life who cared about him, for who and what he was. Hadn't she stumbled across the same thing on that November morning that had turned Fin's life around? And maybe she was about to lose it all now, too. Because she'd panicked last night, the way she eventually had with every other relationship she'd been in.

"I'd appreciate you talking with Family Services," Marsha said. "But Joe and I have already said all of that to them, more than once. I'm afraid Mrs. Sewel is going to have to hear it from Fin this time. I don't see anything else convincing her. And I don't know what happens"—Marsha's voice caught, her worry and fear bubbling to the surface for the first time since the kids had disappeared—"if we don't have him back before noon, when we meet with her."

Kristen pulled Marsha into a hug, returning the support and comfort and encouragement that the other woman had showered on Kristen throughout the night.

"He'll be back," she insisted. "And he'll speak with Mrs. Sewel. And—"

The front door burst open, interrupting them. Marsha and Kristen both sprang to their feet, hopeful. Joe walked in, dragging, exhausted from being up all night. He smiled when he saw them.

"Guess who I found walking up the drive just now, when I turned in off the street?"

He pushed the door open wider, and Chloe and Fin trudged into the Dixons' foyer. Marsha hurried to Fin and Kristen hurried to Chloe, pulling the kids into desperate hugs.

"You're here," Chloe said, clinging to Kristen, needing her, making Kristen need right back. "I'm so scared. I'm scared of going home."

"I know you are, sweetie." Kristen knelt in front of Law's daughter. "But you don't have to be scared. You'll see that as soon as you talk with your dad. Everything will be fine."

"She came back for me," Fin told Marsha. For the first time since Kristen had met him, he was openly crying. "She was worried that I'd get in trouble, so she came back for me."

"Well . . ." Joe joined Fin and Marsha. "That's what good friends do. Everyone we know has been worried about the two of you. Half the town's been out looking for you all night. Where did you go?"

Chloe and Fin shared a long look. Neither one of them spoke up. They'd grown even closer, Kristen realized. They weren't going to say anything that might get the other one in more hot water.

"Am I in trouble?" Fin asked Marsha.

"We have an appointment in a few hours to talk with Mrs. Sewel. She wants to see you alone, today, instead of waiting until next week. You're going to have to try to do something more this time than just staring at her and refusing to say anything. I know you don't like Family Services. I know it'll make you mad to be there. But you need to tell her what's going on. All of it. Everything since last fall, when you were having so much trouble here. Right up to last night, after you'd been doing so well but you ran away again anyway. She's going to want to know why."

Chloe and Fin looked at each other again, a world of silent communication passing between them. Fin shook his head, not answering. He looked positively defeated.

"Come on." Joe steered him toward the kitchen. He hugged Marsha close as she joined them. "Let's give Kristen and Chloe a few minutes alone, while we go call the police and Law and try to talk this through a little bit."

"Will you take me home?" Chloe said, before the others had gotten too far. The Dixons and Fin turned back to see her throw herself into Kristen's arms. "Please come with me to talk with my dad. I don't want to, not alone. I can't."

Kristen's gaze connected with Marsha's.

Law will understand how scared you were . . . the two of you will work things out, learn from this, and you'll go on from there. If . . . that's what you want.

Kristen closed her eyes as Joe and Marsha led Fin away, praying that Marsha had been right.

"Kristen?" Chloe asked.

"I'll drive you home, sweetie. But I don't know if my being there when you talk with your dad is such a good idea."

"But I can't. Not by myself. Not now that I know."

Kristen shook her head. "Now that you know what?"

Chloe hugged Kristen again, clinging even longer. "My mom ... she was the one who did it."

Kristen smoothed her hand down Chloe's back and led her to the couch. They sat, and Kristen hugged the little girl close, worried about saying the wrong thing. At least this, she would do right for Law.

"What did your mom do, honey?" she asked while Chloe cried softly, silently against her shoulder.

"The accident. The reason my dad went to prison. My mom was the one. I heard them arguing about it, and her saying that was why my dad had never loved her and they never should have gotten married and he'd done it all for me, not her . . . and I couldn't stay. I just couldn't. What's going to happen now? My family's never going to get any better. My mom and dad . . . they never should have been together at all!"

My mom was the one . . .

Kristen sorted through the possible meanings for what Chloe had said. Her thoughts screeched to a halt when she finally understood.

Law hadn't been driving the night of the accident that had sent him to prison—Libby had.

"He didn't want me to know," Chloe said. "He wanted me to have my mom, so he . . ."

"He went away, so your mom wouldn't have to."

He'd loved Chloe and his family so much, he'd given up his freedom to keep them together. He'd still loved them and tried to make things work, after paying for Libby's mistake. He'd put up with Libby all these years, for Chloe's sake, after all his ex had done since their divorce.

He could have punched out so many times: when Libby relapsed back to her alcoholism the first time, when they'd moved to Chandlerville and she still hadn't settled in, or even last year, when she'd relapsed again. But he'd stayed, for his daughter.

. . . there's no getting away from love, when you care as deeply as people like you and Law do.

Law, the man Kristen had been so worried she couldn't let herself trust, loved to the bottom of his heart. He loved forever, completely, unconditionally. Exactly the way Kristen had dreamed her entire life of being loved . . . and of learning how to love in return.

***

Law opened Dan's front door the second he glimpsed Kristen's Mustang pulling into the driveway. She'd texted ten minutes ago that she had Chloe with her, and that they were on their way over from the Dixons'.

Chloe opened her door and shot out of the car before Kristen had completely stopped. His daughter ran across the lawn and the crystal-clear Mimosa Lane morning, meeting Law halfway because he was running, too. He dropped to his knees and scooped her close and prayed that he could do or say or be whatever she needed him to be, so she'd never think she had to run from him again.

"I'm so sorry, Daddy," she said.

"I'm sorry, too, darlin'. Tell me what I can do. Tell me I can still make this right for you."

"You already did it. You already did everything, but Mom . . . Did you never love her, like she said? Did you really do it all for me?"

"Do what?"

Law wanted to drive over to Libby's, drag her out of bed, and force her to face the fresh pain she'd caused their daughter. Instead, he watched Kristen walk up to him and Chloe. She was carrying her rose. He saw the worry and love in her eyes, and he felt a flicker of peace come back to him, after the darkest night of his life.

"Chloe heard you two arguing in the alley," she said.

"She heard . . ." Law leaned back until he could see his daughter's tear-streaked face. "You heard what, darlin'?"

"Mom . . ." Chloe hiccupped the word, and then the rest came gushing out. ". . . saying that you hated her and you always had, you'd never loved her, and you'd done it all for me, marrying her and staying with her all these years and . . . going to prison, even."

Law looked again to Kristen, who nodded. She knelt beside Chloe and rubbed a gentle hand down his daughter's back.

"I don't think your dad knows how to hate, sweetie," Kristen said.

Law wasn't so sure about that, no matter how much it touched him to hear Kristen say it. He thought of his parents, whom he'd be content never to speak to again. And his impossible situation with Libby all these years. But then there was Dan, the brother Law had thought he hadn't wanted in his life either, and everything Dan had come to mean to him again.

"Did you?" Chloe asked Law. "Did you always hate Mom, and only try to have a family because of me?"

Law swallowed, trying to find the right words, wanting to be honest when he'd hidden the truth from his daughter for too long. "I've never hated your mother, Chloe, but the things she's done to hurt you . . ."

"Like sending you to prison?"

"No. That wasn't your mother's fault. I don't think that, and I never want you to."

Law thought of the chance he'd had to plead to a lesser charge and stay out of the system. He remembered the rage he'd let consume him, because his father had still been trying to control his life, even then. If Law had just swallowed his pride and done whatever his father had asked, he'd have never been taken away from Libby or Chloe. He'd have been there for his daughter's birth, her first year, and who knew how much of the damage between him and his ex-wife could have been avoided.

"I was just as drunk as your mother that night. The accident could have been my fault as much as it was hers. I don't want you to blame her, Chloe. We both made mistakes when we were young, before you were even born, and you're still having to pay for them. *That's* what I hate. That's why I'm so angry with Mom now, that she's still so reckless after everything we've already put you through. She's never made the changes she needed to, for you."

"Like you have?" Chloe turned her head toward Kristen. She looked back at Law. "Like you're trying to give us a better family, now that you've found someone you really love, like Mom said?"

Law cupped Kristen's cheek. "Yes, that part of what Mom said was true. That's exactly what I'm hoping we can have, if it's still what Kristen wants."

Chloe shook her head, breaking Law's heart with the confusion clouding her already sad expression. She looked at Kristen again, but only for a second.

"So you really don't want Mom in our family anymore?"

Law pulled Chloe into another hug. "Of course I want your mother in our family. I've always wanted your mother for you. I always will. That's why—" He cut himself off, not wanting to talk about the accident again until Chloe understood what was most important. "All I've ever wanted is for your mom to be the best mom she can be for you. As long as she can do that and stop hurting you the way she is, as long as she gets better and stops hurting herself, I'll always want her to be part of your life."

"But if Kristen . . ." Chloe trembled. "If you love her like you've never loved Mom . . ."

Kristen took Chloe's hand and waited for her to ease away from Law and look at her. "That just means more love in your family, Chloe. Not less of your mom. I'd never try to take her place. I'd never do that to you or your dad. And I hope she gets better, too, for you both. I just want the chance . . ."

Law brought Kristen's other hand to his lips and kissed her fingers, hoping she could see in his smile how much he still needed her, how he'd love her forever.

"What do you want?" He gave her lips a gentle kiss.

"I just want to be part of it," she said to him, and then she looked at Chloe. "I want the chance to love you, both you and your dad, the best I can, the way your dad's always given you his best. I want to know what that's like, Chloe. Do you have any idea how lucky you are to have someone in your life who loves you that much? I want to learn how to love the same way, to love you any way you'll let me, and to . . ." Kristen smiled up at him. "I love you, Law. I love you so much."

Law pulled Kristen into his arms, bringing Chloe with her, encircling them both.

"Thank God," he said. "I don't know what I'd do if you hadn't come back to me. If you hadn't brought Chloe back . . ."

He held on tighter, never wanting to let go, kissing Kristen again, and then the top of his daughter's head until Chloe started squirming to be free.

"But what about Fin?" she asked.

Law brushed her damp bangs from her eyes. "What about him? I thought he came back home when you did."

"Yeah. But he doesn't have anybody like I do. Not really. And now he's in trouble. Who's going to love him when the foster people find out he ran away again, and they take him away from the Dixons—because he took care of me last night?"

Chapter Twenty-Two

Now

"You don't have to tell me exactly what made you and Chloe run away together," Mrs. Sewel says, after I finish telling her about how cool soccer has been since November, and how much better school has been, and how I even liked last night's Valentine's party, and even a little about running away with Chloe.

"You said I have to tell you everything."

We're still sitting in the chairs in front of her desk. We've been there forever, while I finished saying how it had hurt Chloe to have her mom show up at the party the way she did. I've told Mrs. Sewel a lot. But I'm not telling what we heard outside, or what made Chloe run.

"I said I needed to understand what happened," Mrs. Sewel says. "And I think I do now. You've helped me understand enough to guess that it was Chloe who ran first. From what you've told me about how important your friendship has become, it's not hard for me to believe that you were worried about her. Is that how you got mixed up in this?"

I want to say yes. But isn't that the kind of question adults always ask you when they want you to agree with them, so they can catch you doing something you're not supposed to, so they can be mad? What if I say yes, and Mrs. Sewel says I still can't stay with the Dixons, because I should have done something else?

"Why didn't you come home last night?" Mrs. Sewel asks. "You have every other time you've run away."

I can't stop myself from staring at her.

She's not supposed to know I've run from the Dixons before now.

"Your foster mother told me over the phone this morning about the other times. She wanted me to know how long it's been since you've disappeared. She swears you like where you are now. But if that's true, why didn't you come home last night, when you knew your foster parents would have to call the police if you didn't? Why not just help Chloe get wherever she went, and then take care of yourself?"

"Because . . ." What does Mrs. Sewel want me to say? She has my file open again, even though she's still sitting next to me. She's writing things down. Who's she writing it all down for?

"Because?"

"Because she's my friend, okay? Because I don't care what you do to me, or who's going to read about what I say. Chloe wasn't going to come home, so I didn't come home!"

I'm expecting Mrs. Sewel to write some more. I'm expecting her to be mad, because I'm mad, and adults get mad when kids do. Instead, she looks up at me and smiles. She closes the file again and puts it back on her desk.

"Was that so hard?" she asks.

"Is what so hard?" I'm still mad. Or maybe I'm scared now. I don't know. All I know is she shouldn't be smiling, but she is.

"Telling me what I've been trying to get you to say all this time."

"What?" What did I say?

"That you've learned how to care for your friend, Fin. You came home to your family, but only after you made sure Chloe was okay—that she was going home to her father to talk to him about what she needs to. You have made things work with the Dixons. Marsha and Joe are right outside, waiting for you to go home with them, and they've made it clear they'll fight to keep you. They'll fight my supervisor and her supervisor and whoever's boss above him that they have to fight."

"They will?"

"They already are. They want you, Fin. They've made you part of their family, and you didn't run from that. You ran to take care of someone else." Mrs. Sewel smiles again. "And then you came back, even when you knew you were in trouble. In my book, in my report, I'd call that a success. As far as I'm concerned, this is the last meeting Family Services will need to have with you, unless some event in the future shows us that we need another face-to-face. Otherwise, your foster parents can file quarterly paperwork from now on, just like they do for all their other kids. If that's what you want. Is it?"

"I . . ." All their other kids. My family. My foster parents. "I get to stay in Chandlerville?"

"You get to—"

There's a noise outside, a lot of voices, and then Mrs. Sewel's office door flies open—and Chloe runs in.

"Stop!" she says.

Behind Chloe, in the hallway, I see Mr. and Mrs. Dixon. And next to them, Coach Beaumont is standing with his arm around Ms. Hemmings, both of them smiling at me like they're there for me, too.

"Stop," Chloe says again. "Don't take Fin away from his family. He was only helping me, because of what my mom said. And *he promised not to tell. But I will. I'll tell you everything. Just let him stay. He ran away because of me and was gone all night because of me and wouldn't come home until I said I wanted to. And now everything's going to be okay for me, because he helped me to go back to my family." She looks out into the hallway, too, at her dad and Ms. Hemmings. "Please let Fin stay with the Dixons."*

"Well, Fin?" Mrs. Sewel asks. "What do you think? Are you ready to go home?"

I don't understand. It's too hard to think about anything, with Chloe there when she shouldn't be, and her dad and Ms. Hemmings, too. And then it's too hard to think about anything else. Everyone being there for me. Chloe willing to tell Mrs. Sewel about her mom and dad, to help me. Remembering Mrs. Dixon hugging me this morning when I came home, the way Coach Beaumont is hugging Ms. Hemmings now. Like forever.

"Fin?" Mrs. Sewel asks again.

"Fin?" Chloe says.

But I can't answer them. All I can do is run—to Mr. and Mrs. Dixon, who're hugging me now, like they'll never let me go.

Epilogue

"Play it again, Dad," Chloe said, sitting between Kristen and Law, the three of them crowded onto the bench in front of Kristen's baby grand piano.

Their baby grand, Kristen corrected herself with a smile. Since she'd asked Law and Chloe to move in a month ago—the night he'd first asked for Chloe's approval, and then asked Kristen to marry him—Kristen had said she wanted them to think of her things as their things. She couldn't imagine anything better than sharing her home with the family who had fallen in love with her.

"Why don't we give Kristen another try?" Law asked.

"Me?" She sounded freaked out. Because she *was* freaked— by how bad she'd turned out to be at learning to play. She'd never been so bad at anything in her life. Not to the point where it felt like it was hopeless, which her learning music definitely appeared to be.

Law kissed her. And then he insisted, "You."

"I have no rhythm."

"Me either," Chloe said.

"*Neither*," Kristen corrected. "It's 'me neither.'"

"Whatever." Chloe rolled her eyes. "I'm just sayin', I'm as bad as you."

"You're nine," Kristen pointed out.

Chloe had celebrated her April birthday last week. The three of them had climbed into Kristen's Mustang and escaped for a long weekend at Disney World—a shared, unrealized dream of Chloe's *and* Kristen's, since when Kristen was little her father had disapproved of well-bred children wasting time at amusement parks.

"And you're better than me," Kristen added. "You're absolutely brilliant. Why can't I just enjoy listening to you learn how to play?"

"You're not supposed to quit things," Chloe reminded her. "That's what you said to me about my mom. I didn't, and you were right. She's getting better. She even sent me a birthday card, and I get to see her again next weekend."

Law caught Kristen's attention over the top of Chloe's head. After the Valentine's party, once they had the kids back safely, Dan had agreed to finance Libby's three-month stint in a top-rated rehab center.

"That's right, darlin'," Law said, his tone light, the mischief in his eyes dimming ever so slightly. "Don't let Kristen off the hook just because she's pouting that we've found the one thing she's not good at."

Kristen jabbed him in the arm as Chloe started fiddling with the keys again, striking random notes but instinctively making sweet music with them, by ear alone. That she had all the makings of a natural musician had thrilled Law. It was fun to watch. But it was worrisome to hear Chloe getting excited about seeing Libby. It had taken most of the last two months for her to recover from how upset she'd been after the Valentine's party. Kristen knew anxiety about next weekend's reunion had been keeping Law up nights.

He had plans to rent his ex-wife a two-bedroom apartment near their old house—which he'd let the lease go on. He and Libby's doctors had agreed that less responsibility would be better at first, while she eased back into her life. Law now had primary custody of Chloe. He was planning for their future, dealing with the last of the past, and he was creating a new life that Kristen would be sharing with them.

"I'm not pouting because I can't learn how to play as well as a child prodigy," Kristen teased Chloe. "It's because you and your dad will be playing duets together in no time, while I'm still stuck figuring out 'Chopsticks' by myself."

Law and Chloe laughed. The moment where they'd all been thinking about Libby passed.

Chloe noodled with the latest melody she'd discovered. Kristen and Law shared a moment of silent understanding. They'd handle whatever came next—as long as they dealt with things together. They'd already faced so much and were thriving. He was enrolled in a local community college's summer minimester, in the music program. When the summer soccer season started up, Law and the Strikers, winter city champions, would be back. He and Dan were closer than ever, on the same bowling team now, in the Tuesday-night men's league at Pockets.

And Law and Kristen . . . She fingered one of the red blooms of the beautiful roses Law had brought home from his day shift at McC's. A dozen—half for Chloe, he'd said, and half for Kristen, the two women who owned his heart. Kristen would never look at another rose without thinking about the first one he'd given her and the song he'd composed to go with it. The afternoon light from her bay window caressed the velvety petals of his most recent bouquet, washing them in gold and making Kristen think of the crimson flowers and gold ribbons she and Law had chosen for the Christmas wedding they were planning.

He reached for her hand and brought it to his lips. "You're going to make a beautiful bride," he said, as if he'd known where her thoughts had veered.

She nodded, visions of their beautiful day and every new day they'd spend together misting her eyes.

The music stopped. "Are you okay?" Chloe asked.

Kristen nodded down at her soon-to-be stepdaughter. "I'm just so happy. Sometimes it's a little hard to believe still, that you're both here. That everyone's so . . ."

"Happy?" Chloe asked.

Kristen nodded again.

"Because of my mom?" the little girl asked.

"No, sweetie." Kristen hugged her close. Law's arm wrapped around his daughter, too, until she was cuddled between them.

"We all want your mother to get better, and to get happy, too," he said. "Your mom will always be a part of us."

Chloe nodded, even though she still struggled with all that had happened on those difficult days at the heart of her mother's relapse.

"Mom's going to stay sober this time," she insisted.

"That's what we all want," Law agreed. "I know it's what she wants. But whatever happens, I'll be here for you, darlin'. Kristen, too, and the rest of our family and your friends. You won't have to deal with anything alone, not anymore."

Chloe nodded again. "I'm hungry."

"Someone promised me a milk shake," Kristen agreed, relieved at the lighter topic, though she'd have sat there into the evening if Chloe had needed to discuss things more.

They'd talked through a lot of long nights since February,

Law and Kristen and Chloe, helping Chloe understand what had happened, including Law sharing experiences from his Al-Anon meetings and encouraging Chloe to go with him—which she had, several times. Chloe was finally dealing with the divorce and her mother's disease—and healing from both. She'd never again have to lie or run or try to change who she was because she was afraid of her life. She was learning to face everyone and everything, all the good and the bad things, knowing that she could be herself, because she was supported and loved.

So were Kristen and Law. Now that they'd found each other, as long as they fought together for the things they needed, *whatever* they needed, they'd always have the loving family each of them had dreamed of for so long.

Law checked the display on his phone.

"Dan texted," he said. "He and Charlotte and Sally will meet us and the Dixons and Fin at the Dream Whip in half an hour." He kissed Chloe's forehead. "Wash up so we can go."

Chloe scampered away.

She'd been excited since she'd gotten home from school about hanging with Fin and Sally tonight. She'd been just as excited to visit Ben yesterday, Mallory and Pete's new baby boy. Chandlerville was full of friends and people she loved spending time with now—more people to help take care of her and make her part of their lives and show her that she'd always have a place to belong. People were taking the time to do the same for Fin, who was thriving just like Chloe, both at school and in the community.

Kristen reached for Law. He pulled her into a hug and a kiss that she wanted to last all afternoon.

"Chloe's going to be okay," she said, when he allowed her to breathe again. "We're both going to be here for her, whatever happens with Libby."

"We will." He kissed the tip of her nose.

She tinkered with a few keys, making a mess of one of the simple melodies Chloe had mastered her first try. She banged her hand down on the keys. Chuckling, Law smoothed his fingers over hers, charming her into relaxing against him.

"You're enjoying this," she said. "Admit it."

"Spending all afternoon with you, touching you? Always."

"Seeing me bungle something that's so simple for you and your daughter."

"*Our* daughter," he reminded her.

In bed last night, curled around each other and clinging and falling in love all over again, the same as every night since Kristen had helped Chloe come back to him, Law had said the same thing: that however Libby recovered, whether her and Chloe's relationship improved again or deteriorated, Chloe would always have parents to love her. Kristen and Law would make certain they all had the good family they deserved.

Honest.

Caring.

Forever.

"I love you." She wrapped her arms around Law, trusting him and them and the dangerous dreams they'd made each other dream. "I love you so much."

She'd never get tired of saying it.

"I love you, too, darlin'." He reached around her to the piano, to play the first notes of her Valentine's song.

And then he began singing "Come Back to Me," the promise she'd waited her whole life for him to fill her heart with, until she couldn't imagine being anywhere else but in his arms, listening to his voice, and believing in the tomorrows they would build together.

Acknowledgments

I want to acknowledge my friends and fellow authors Dorie Graham and Catherine Mann, who first taught me the power of offering family to kids who weren't their own, but who needed to know the power and beauty and unconditional acceptance of belonging.

Though neither of these amazing women have formally fostered a child, they've both opened their homes and lives and hearts to teens with no easy choices and the bottomless need to know that they are wanted, just the way they are. Dorie and Catherine are mothers to everyone they meet, in that honest and ruthlessly caring way all mothers should be. They are my inspiration.

Ladies, the Dixons are a complete fabrication. But they were lovingly crafted in hopes of capturing the drive to help that I know fills your hearts, and the hearts of all heroes who step into a lost child's lonely world, determined to help.

I admire you more than I can say.

About the Author

ANNA DESTEFANO

Anna DeStefano is the award-winning, nationally best-selling author of more than twenty novels, including *Christmas on Mimosa Lane*, *Three Days on Mimosa Lane*, *Secret Legacy*, and the Atlanta Heroes series. Born in Charleston, South Carolina, she has lived in the South her entire life. Her background as a care provider and adult educator in the world of crisis and grief recovery lends itself to the deeper psychological themes of every story she writes.

With a rich blend of realism and fantasy, DeStefano invites readers to see each of life's moments with emotional honesty and clarity. The past president of Georgia Romance Writers, she has garnered numerous awards, including twice winning the Romantic Times Reviewers' Choice Award, the Holt Medallion, the National Excellence in Romance Fiction Award, the Golden Heart, and the Maggie Award for Excellence. She has also been a Golden Quill finalist and finalist in the National Readers' Choice and Booksellers' Best awards.

Join Anna each week on her blog: www.annawrites.com/blog.